Published in
the United Kingdom
by Pulse Records Ltd
info@pulse-records.co.uk

Copyright © 2012
Rob Fennah and Helen A Jones

Authors' website
www.juliasbanjo.com

Rob Fennah and Helen A Jones have
asserted their rights under the Copyright,
Designs and Patents Act 1988 to be
identified as the authors of this work.

ISBN-13 978-14793-9298-8
ISBN-10 1-47-939298-7

Also available as Kindle and epub ebooks

A CIP catalogue record
for this title is available
from the British Library.

Cover illustration
Alan Fennah

Pre-press production
www.ebookversions.com

All rights reserved.
No part of this publication may be
reproduced, stored in or
introduced into a retrieval system
or transmitted in any form
or by any means electronic,
photomechanical, photocopying,
recording or otherwise without
the prior written permission
of the publisher. Any person who
does any unauthorised act in
relation to this publication may be
liable to criminal prosecution.

ABOUT THE AUTHORS

Born in Liverpool, 1958, **Rob Fennah** began his career in the music industry on leaving school, signing a major recording contract with RCA records in 1976. He has had numerous hit records in Europe and Japan, receiving his first gold album at the age of 19. Rob has performed at some of the most prestigious venues in the world including The Sydney Opera House, Australia and The Budokan in Tokyo.

Rob has composed music for television and film and was responsible for writing and producing the hugely successful theatre show, Twopence to Cross the Mersey, based on the best selling book by Helen Forrester.

Rob is currently working on both a screenplay and theatrical adaptation of *Julia's Banjo*.

Born 1965, **Helen A Jones** attended school in Liverpool prior to enrolling at nursing college, graduating in 1988. She has worked as a senior nurse in the field of Neuroscience Critical Care for over twenty years, achieving academic success at MSC level and in published work relating to Critical Care.

Helen worked with co-writer Rob Fennah on the critically acclaimed Twopence to Cross the Mersey and will continue to collaborate with him on current and future projects.

ROB FENNAH & HELEN A JONES

Julia's Banjo

PULSE

For Alan and Sam

*With sincere thanks to
Gerry White and Lynn McDermott*

"The very first tune I ever
learned to play was 'That'll Be The Day'.
My mother Julia taught it to me on
the banjo, sitting there with endless patience
until I managed to work out all the chords."

JOHN LENNON

PROLOGUE

Since John Lennon died, anything connected with him has soared in value. In 2000, a piano he once owned sold at auction for 1.5 million pounds so it doesn't take a genius to figure out that the very first instrument he learned to play has got to be worth millions more.

It was John's mother, Julia, who taught him to play her banjo and turned him on to Rock 'n' Roll. And that's what makes Julia's banjo so important; without it, The Beatles would never have existed and, without *them*, everything we know today would be different.

So where is the holy grail of pop memorabilia; the catalyst that changed the world? Well that's what this is all about. Shortly after Julia Lennon died it went missing and no one has set eyes on it for over 50 years.

CHAPTER ONE

The five imposing buildings of Liverpool's Albert Dock had seen many changes since its construction in the early 1800s. Once a hub of the Victorian maritime world, its parade of vaulted red brick arches no longer echoed to the sound of pulleys, creaking ropes and the shouts of dockers unloading cargoes. Now it handled a trade of a different kind – tourists. There were countless reasons why someone may wish to visit this thriving town and businesses made a tidy profit pandering to the needs of the many that pounded the cobbles in search of the ultimate Liverpool experience.

A brightly coloured Magical Mystery Tour bus pulled up outside the dock and its doors hissed open. "Bye! See you again next time," cackled an oversized American woman as she lumbered her colossal backside down the aisle of the bus.

Sid, the driver, glanced at her as he discreetly rolled up a cigarette on his knee. "Not if I see you first love," he muttered under his breath.

Barry dutifully held out his hand to steady the woman as she got off, her cheery face bringing a smile to his lips.

Another satisfied customer. He felt warm inside.

Barry Seddon had worked as a Beatles tour guide for the last three years and loved every second of it. While Sid drove the bus around the city, he would entertain the tourists with fascinating Beatles tales; point out their old haunts and explain in infinite detail how each venue played a pivotal role in the group's rise to fame. People from all around the world flocked to take a ride on the iconic Beatle bus and, with only a couple of days to go before the annual Beatles Convention, business was booming. Barry bade farewell to the last of the passengers and felt the familiar pangs of disappointment washing over him as his usefulness was terminated for another day. To make matters worse, he now had to endure a ride home with the most cynical man he had ever met. Ever the optimist, Barry tried to keep the conversation positive.

"Good crowd wasn't it Sid?"

The middle-aged driver sneered and ran a jaundiced hand through his greasy dyed black hair. "I'll tell you what, I've seen some sad bastards on this bus over the years but that fella with the big nose and the sunglasses took some beating didn't he eh?" Sid held the loaded cigarette paper to his mouth while his protruding wet tongue slithered along its edge. "You know," he continued, spitting a rogue strand of tobacco from his bottom lip, "the one who thought he looked like Ringo Starr?"

Here we go. Barry shifted uncomfortably. "I thought he looked great."

As far as he was concerned, anyone who could mimic the Beatle drummer with such well observed precision deserved respect.

"Well you would say that wouldn't you?" scoffed Sid, regarding his colleague's Beatle attire with the contempt it rightly deserved. The drainpipe trousers, Cuban heeled boots and round rimmed spectacles conveyed only one thing to the disgruntled driver; the bumbling nerd staring back at him was just another sad bastard trying to look like someone famous – in Barry's case, John Lennon. But the peaked Lennon style cap perched on top of his pumpkin round head looked more like a sprig of holly on a Christmas pudding than the famous Beatle and it only served to fuel Sid's resentment of everything 'Fab'. Unlike Barry, he had no interest in The Beatles and trundled the tourists around the city for one reason only; the pay cheque at the end of every month.

Sid pushed the lid back on his tobacco tin and slid the freshly made cigarette behind his ear. "Alright ," he sighed, "let's get you home."

With expert hands, he swung the colourful hulk onto The Strand and then up towards the Anglican Cathedral, its Benedicite windows reflecting the amber tones of a late summer afternoon. The Magical Mystery bus then laboured up the hill of Parliament Street before taking a right turn towards Sefton Park. The Palm House at its centre was the jewel in its crown. In the haze, the shards of light bouncing from its myriad of glass panes made it shimmer as if having been freshly turned out from a giant Victorian jelly mould.

The mansion houses surrounding the park had long been converted into small affordable dwellings and were now occupied by students, young professionals... and Barry. Bought outright with inheritance money after his mother's death four years ago, he had somehow managed to transform his once smart piece of real estate into a place even a pig would turn its nose up at.

The bus lurched to a stop at the end of Barry's street and he moved to get off. "See you tomorrow Sid," he said, not expecting a reply.

"Wait a minute soft lad. Haven't you forgotten something?" Sid strained to reach a spot behind his seat and wrenched out a polythene bag. "Your dirty books."

"They're old Beatles Monthly magazines if you must know," Barry huffed. "I bought them in a car boot sale this morning."

"Bloody hell mate, aren't you sick of The Beatles after working on this bus all day?" Sid dangled the bag in front of his nose. "Don't you think it's about time you were taking a woman home instead of these? People will start talking you know."

Barry's pendulum eyes kept time with the taunting swing. Then, with a leap, he snatched the precious bag from the bus driver and clutched it to his chest. "I don't follow Sid. What are you on about?"

"You, mate, I'm talking about you. A bloke in his forties should have had at least one girlfriend by now. I mean, what is it with you? You're single; you own your own place?" Sid rubbed his chin; his corrugated brow hinting at the possibility of genuine concern. "What about Brenda from the pub? She seems to like you."

Barry's eyes widened. "What, Brenda? She's never said anything to me."

A sigh escaped from Sid's lips. "Well she wouldn't would she? You're the man; you're supposed to do all the running."

The tour guide paused for a moment to consider the prospect of him and Brenda becoming an item. *Yeah, I could live with that.*

But Sid's mischievous sneer shattered the illusion and Barry shoved him in the arm. "Ah, you're just winding me up like you always do."

"Alright have it your way," the driver replied, holding up his hands. "But if I were in your shoes I'd be taking a different woman home every night."

"You don't get it do you? I want someone who has the same interests as me; that likes what I like."

"But you only like one thing! And there's more to life than the bloody Beatles you know. Women aren't interested in what colour socks John Lennon was wearing when he wrote Please Please Me."

Twisting the plastic carrier bag awkwardly between his fingers, he looked up from beneath the peak of his cap like a chastised puppy. "They might be."

"No Barry, they won't. You'll bore 'em to bleedin' death!"

Sid extricated his wiry frame from the grip of the driver's seat and put a friendly hand on his shoulder. "Look mate, a woman needs a man who can talk about a whole range of subjects; cars, football, that type of thing. You mark my words; treat a woman right and you'll have a companion for life *plus*…you'll get your leg over every night."

Barry had heard enough. "Is that right? Then tell me this; if you know so much about women, how come your missus ran off with another bloke?"

Ouch. The lovable buffoon had unwittingly delivered words to match his workmate's sarcastic snipes and the expression on Sid's face was one to behold. Never the hurtful type, he immediately regretted opening his mouth. "I'm sorry Sid. I didn't mean…"

"Well thanks for bringing that up," Sid interrupted, realising he had Barry on the back foot. "Kick a fella when he's down, is that it? Christ, I try and give you a bit of friendly advice and you throw it back in my bloody face." Sid shot a disdainful look at the shoddy bag within the tour guide's protective clutches. "Just take those books of yours and piss off."

The doors of the bus swung open and Barry made his escape.

"And don't expect a lift from me in the morning!" Sid shouted after him. "You can make your own way in!"

* * *

Steve Benson stood in front of a full length mirror in the poky stock room of The Beatles Store and admired the cut of his trendy new shirt. He unscrewed the top from a tube of hair gel and squirted a liberal dollop onto the palm of his hand before rubbing it roughly through his neatly styled brown hair. "Put another CD on will you, we've been listening to this one all week!" he shouted to his older brother through a haze of Homme D'Amour body spray.

Joe sat behind the counter and casually flicked through the sports pages of the Liverpool Echo. "No! The customers like it," he shouted back, too engrossed to look up. "And when you've finished poncing yourself up in there, do you mind coming out here to help me get that display up!"

An elderly lady approached the till and placed a Yellow

Submarine key ring and two postcards on the glass counter top. She coughed politely to gain Joe's attention.

"What are you worrying about the customers for?" ranted Steve, unaware of the transaction about to take place. "They only come in here to keep out the rain. And when they do buy something it's only the cheap shit; tight-fisted arseholes!"

Joe ran a hand over his receding, cropped silver hair and laughed in an attempt to pass off his brother's tirade as a joke but the outraged woman turned on her heels and stormed out empty-handed.

"You haven't got a bloody clue have you?" he cursed, barging into the stock room. "That big gob of yours has just lost us another customer. I don't know why you bother coming in!"

"No, neither do I. Look, I never wanted to buy this store in the first place. I'm only here because you talked me into it. If I'd have had my way we'd have stayed working on the docks."

"What? Don't make me laugh. We were out on strike, remember? If we hadn't taken the redundancy money and put it into this place we'd have ended up with nothing. Look what happened to the lads that did try to stick it out; poor buggers."

Joe had hit a raw nerve. "Yeah," said Steve, "and that's what we should have done; stuck it out; all of us; together! Things might have been different if we had."

"Well what stopped you?" his brother challenged. "I didn't force you to take the money?"

"I wanted to help you didn't I?" Steve shot back.

Joe folded his arms and looked at him with an

incredulous glare. "Help me? How do you work that out?"

"Don't play games," Steve rebutted through a sarcastic laugh. "You thought if you got working again and had some steady cash coming in Carole would come back to you. Admit it. That's the only reason we ended up buying this place."

"Yeah, so, what if I did?" Joe squared up to him. "The other lads on the picket line would have done exactly the same if they'd been put in my position. Loyalty starts with the family or have you forgotten that?"

"No I haven't. That's why I'm here isn't it?"

"We're making a living aren't we?"

"Call this living? How many years of our lives have we wasted in this dump and what have we got to show for it eh?"

The transition from dock worker to shop owner had not been easy for Steve. He wasn't cut out to work behind a counter and he missed the camaraderie and banter of his workmates.

It was in 1997, after a bitter twenty-eight month dispute over overtime pay that the Liverpool Dockers' strike ended in humiliation and defeat. Joe and Steve Benson were amongst the three hundred strikers who eventually accepted a payoff from the Mersey Docks and Harbour Company but eighty of their workmates, considered by their employers to be the instigators of the dispute, were excluded from the settlement and ended up penniless. Steve's sense of honour took a severe pummelling after the strike and, despite Joe's protestations about them having no option but to cut and run, he couldn't come to terms with the fact they accepted their thirty pieces of silver while some of their fellow workmates were thrown to the wolves.

He knew his brother was right of course, he just couldn't find it in his heart to admit it. From the moment he and Joe pooled their redundancy money and bought The Beatles Store, Steve viewed it as nothing more than a symbol of their betrayal; and he wanted out.

"Listen," Steve sighed, attempting to defuse the situation, "all I'm saying is isn't it time we moved on? What about opening that bar in Tenerife we always talked about?"

Joe's voice quavered with frustration. "How? What with? This place is mortgaged to the hilt. We can't even afford to buy new stock. It's a nice dream mate," he said, resting a consolatory hand on his younger brother's shoulder, "but that's all it is. Now come and help me get this display up."

* * *

Barry meandered down the tree-lined avenue which curved gently around the open spaces of Sefton Park until he reached a large Gothic mansion. Its ornate white painted veranda spoke of tea on the lawn, croquet, and ladies in long white taffeta dresses shading under lacy parasols. The communal door was located at the side of the property; a plain affair with eight scruffy intercoms and a large brass letterbox.

Hauling himself up the flight of worn stone steps, he fumbled for his key and let himself in. It wasn't perfect, but it was home.

Inside his dingy living room, the greying woodchip walls were plastered with frayed posters heralding long forgotten Beatles gigs together with tatty newspaper clippings which

Barry had cut and pasted into messy collages. Under the window, a stack of old vinyl records leaned against a mountain of magazines, books and CDs. A microwave oven sat alongside them, once white but now pebble-dashed with the remnants of reheated ready meals. The empty can of cola and a half-eaten pizza lying on the unmade bed complemented the haphazard arrangement of dirty washing scattered around the floor. Perched on the mantelpiece over a two bar electric fire stood framed photographs of the three most important people in Barry's life; his late mother, Paul McCartney and John Lennon.

He dumped his jacket onto the mess and arranged himself somewhere in the middle of it all. A quick sniff of the pizza confirmed it was still edible and after cramming a whole slice into his mouth he wiped his hands on the bed and liberated The Beatles Monthly's from the sweaty polythene bag. They were to be consumed page by fascinating page until every photograph had been analysed and each word read.

A fully intact edition was a rare find and his palms tingled with every measured turn of the page. Missing inserts alluded to on a front cover were always a disappointment, as was the promise of a poster in the next issue, and these were put to one side for a later date.

It was nearly four o'clock by the time he had worked his way through three copies and he was beginning to feel the strain. Slumping back onto the bed he fluffed up a pillow, pulled the covers over and closed his eyes to take a nap. But with the magazines sitting like a pile of unopened presents on Christmas morning and Barry the big kid with a goofy smile who still believed in Santa, it wasn't long before curiosity got the better of him and he sat back up and peeled open another copy. It was going to be a long night.

The front cover of this issue was cup stained, the colour quality somewhat disappointing and there was no prospect of an interview with one of the Fab Four. He threw it aside in favour of a more promising edition but, as the discarded magazine fluttered across the room, something fell from between its pages and landed softly on the crumb-laden rug. *A bonus poster after all,* he thought. *No, too small for that.* Barry lifted the piece of paper to his myopic eyes and scrutinised it.

A letter?

His focus sharpened on the postmark. *April - 1962.*

But it was the recipient's name scrawled on the pale blue Air Mail envelope that caused his heart to race. He flipped it open. The letter was still inside. He quickly scanned down the messy handwriting and cartoon doodles until he reached the signature. Barry did a double-take as his brain refused to believe what his eyes were telling him and he raced over to the sideboard. Scattering the contents of one of the drawers out onto the floor, he plucked a magnifying glass from a tangle of elastic bands and computer cables. With trembling hands he examined the signature again. There was no doubt about it. Barry had just made the discovery of a lifetime.

CHAPTER TWO

TEXAS, USA – FOUR WEEKS AGO

"C'mon move it for Christ's sake!" Travis smashed his fist down on the horn and gripped the steering wheel as if his life depended on it. His beautiful wife Cheryl sat calmly in the passenger seat and dabbed her nose with a soft makeup sponge. She pouted at her reflection in the car visor and waited for an even stretch of road before deploying the killer red lipstick to her puckered lips. Satisfied with the result, she flicked up the visor mirror and glanced at her irate husband. "Rocking backwards and forwards like that ain't gonna make the car go any faster," she sniped. "You look like a freakin' retard."

Travis shrugged off her comment and peered through the bug-streaked windscreen at the rusty pickup jangling along in front. The 120 mile trip to Coopersville should only have taken a couple of hours but Interstate 20 out of Dallas had been gridlocked when they set off that morning and they were impossibly late. Taking a shortcut across country may have seemed like a good idea at the time but it soon became clear that a monkey knew more about quantum mechanics than Cheryl did about the workings of a Sat Nav. Strange really; for a woman who could find her way blindfold around the glitzy malls and boutiques of Dallas, Travis could not begin to understand how she could get them so hopelessly lost. And today of all days; this was the day that was supposed to send his career soaring into the stratosphere and leave his rivals quivering in his wake.

Travis observed his wife through the corner of his eye as she pulled the visor mirror back down and carefully load her long lashes with even more mascara. He cursed under his breath for being so stupid. What was he doing charging her with such an important responsibility? But the damage was done and here he was; stuck on a dirt track somewhere in the middle of Parker County with his dream in serious danger of being scuppered by the dip-shit hillbilly blocking the road ahead. Ten torturous miles further down the road saw him craning his neck out of the window to get a clearer view of the person he felt was now deliberately trying to ruin his life. This was getting personal. Cheryl noticed her husband's left eyelid twitching; a tell-tale sign he was about to blow a gasket and succumb to another bout of road rage. She flopped back into her seat, closed her eyes and waited for the inevitable.

"Jesus Christ!" Travis wailed; his outburst punctuated with a fist pounding down on his seat. "If he don't get that heap o' shit out of my way I swear to God I'll follow him back to his tin shack and stick my foot so far up his hillbilly ass he'll be trimmin' my toenails with his teeth!"

"You're gonna give yourself a heart attack if you don't calm down," his wife snapped, her eyes still screwed shut.

"And whose fault would that be huh?" he retorted

bitterly. "If you hadn't spent all morning prettying yourself up we wouldn't be running this late."

Cheryl turned to face her husband square on. "You know I won't go out unless I look my best."

Travis rolled his eyes. "Damn it Cheryl, we're going to a town out in the boonies not the freakin' White House. You're gonna stick out like a peacock in a field of crows."

"At least I won't look like no crow," she muttered, rearranging her blonde tresses into a neat pony tail. She winced as she pulled it tight.

A sudden break in the oncoming traffic gave Travis the opportunity he had been waiting for. He slammed his foot to the metal and Cheryl was flung like a crash test dummy into the back of her seat as the G force kicked in. "Are you crazy," she squealed, "you're gonna get us both killed!"

Travis screeched up alongside the pickup and thrust up a middle finger at the bemused driver. "Eat my dust you interbred son of a bitch!"

Glaring in the rear view mirror, Travis let out a slow measured breath as the truck faded to a distant dot and eventually disappeared beyond the horizon. He relaxed back into his sticky seat and checked the time. With a little luck he could still make it.

For the next fifty miles Cheryl kept herself occupied manicuring her nails and watching the scenery speed past. Acres of cotton eventually gave way to vast oil fields. "They look like dinosaurs don't they?" she remarked sweetly, a cute grin spreading across her face.

"What do?" her husband replied, a confused look spreading across his.

"The pumping jacks bobbing up and down over there.

They look like herds of grazing dinosaurs."

"Sure honey," Travis sighed, "whatever you say."

Sensing his irritation, she huffed and began rummaging inside the glove compartment for a fresh packet of cigarettes. The outer cellophane wrapper clung to Cheryl's fingers as she peeled it off and Travis bit his lip when her attempt to discard it out of the window backfired and it blew back inside the car. Fluttering up and down the dashboard like a dying daddy longlegs he swatted it flat, squashed it into a tiny ball and buried it in the ashtray.

"Where is Coopersville anyway?" she asked, cascades of blue smoke curling from her lips.

Travis felt the tension flooding back into his veins as his blood began to boil. "How the hell am I supposed to know? You're the one with the Sat Nav!"

Travis threw a condescending glare in his wife's direction and knew in an instant he had made a mistake. She flicked the air conditioner up to twister strength and the sudden rush of air sent his bolo tie slapping into his contorted face like an eel wriggling on the end of a fishing pole.

"Alright, alright," he coughed, wafting away the choking dust. "No need to get your panties in a wad."

Cheryl slapped him across the shoulder. "Don't you *ever* look at me like something you just scraped off your god damn boot so help me I'll...?"

"Okay, calm down will you, you've made your point. Jeez."

A few miles of uneasy calm passed before Travis blurted out, "I just don't think you understand what's at stake here that's all."

Cheryl's head did a sharp left. "'Course I understand. The part I don't get is why you had to borrow all that money from some psychopathic loan shark who's spent most of his adult life behind bars. Why couldn't you go to a bank like a normal person?"

"A bank?" He yanked at the gear stick and it crunched in protest. "Are you being serious? Banks won't lend jackshit to anybody these days. Don't you ever watch the news?"

Cheryl's refusal to answer confirmed he had made a valid point.

"Besides," Travis continued, "I only got the tip-off yesterday and needed to move fast."

"You could have at least tried," she argued.

"What for? I didn't have time for all that bullshit paperwork they make you fill out. I needed the money now, not next Christmas. No honey, believe me; Danny Bakula was the only guy prepared to lend me that kind of money at such short notice."

He flicked a lock of dark wavy hair from his piercing green eyes and stared confidently at the road ahead. "Hell I can't wait to see the look on DeVito's face when I snatch this little beauty from under his nose. Almost makes life worth living don't it?"

Cheryl glimpsed Travis's cash-laden briefcase peeping out from under his seat and a shiver ran up her spine. She knew her husband was prone to making snap decisions but the consequences of this particular venture going belly up did not bear thinking about. Seven years had passed since she first set eyes on the handsome cowboy but in recent months it seemed more like an eternity.

Maurice Zukerman, a high flying senior executive with

The Lanaco Oil Company, had invited Travis Lawson to the annual Christmas party shortly after meeting him on a wild hog hunting expedition in Centerville, Texas. It was there that Travis met Cheryl, Zukerman's underpaid secretary. At that time she was still carrying the stigma of having being raised on a trailer park and was desperate to make a better life for herself. As a teenager, she had made the fatal mistake of trying to marry her way out of poverty but, before the ink was dry on the wedding certificate, she and her young estranged husband found themselves leering at one another from the opposite ends of a divorce court. In the aftermath of her marriage break-up she went back to college, studied hard and secured employment with the oil company. Although her salary left a lot to be desired, it did enable her to rent a cosy one bedroom apartment in Austin; a big step up from the trailer park life she had left behind, but miles below where she wanted to be.

Enter Travis, a dashing, smooth-talking charmer with a successful business under his belt and a big house to prove it, or so he told Cheryl. Pressing all the right buttons, Travis promised her a much larger salary if she tendered her resignation and came to work for him. How could she refuse?

Cheryl was mortified when she discovered the 'successful business' Travis had bragged about at the Christmas party was little more than an online sales room, run from a converted woodshed nestling in the garden of his modest home on the outskirts of Dallas. Potential buyers would key in a desired item and Travis would set about acquiring it for them. It did make money, but not enough to pay Cheryl the salary he had promised her and within a few short weeks her bank balance had run dry forcing her to quit her apartment in Austin. This left her with a difficult choice to make; either head back to the trailer park she thought she had left behind or move in with her new employer. She chose the latter.

Despite Travis's later admission he had wangled it that way, they fell in love and together turned the business around. Whilst he looked after the wheeling and dealing, she kept the Internal Revenue Service off his back ensuring his book-keeping and accounts were all up to date. Now, with Cheryl's cautious work ethic firmly embedded, the business thrived enabling them to open a small antiques showroom in Dallas. They eventually bought the big house they had spent their lives dreaming about and moved in the day after returning from honeymoon. But as the business flourished, so too did Travis's burning ambition.

His ability to sniff out a bargain and turn it into a fast buck developed at an early age; skipping high school to help out in a local pawnbrokers shop. Impressed by his keen eye and eagerness to learn, Jack Wilson, the elderly proprietor, offered him a full time job the day Travis officially left school. He spent the first couple of years working in the stock room and as his knowledge of the antiquities and oddities passing through his hands accumulated, so did his desire to repay the old man he had grown to respect and admire. With Jack's guidance, the young entrepreneur quickly worked his way through the ranks until, at the age of twenty-four, he had risen to the heady position of Chief Buyer. Jack could now look forward to his retirement safe in the knowledge that, with Travis running the business for him, his old-age pension would be in good hands.

But all was not well. As Jack's health deteriorated, a critical oversight on his part was to ruin his well-laid plans. He had forgotten to renew his lease on the property gifting his main competitor with an opportunity to buy it behind his back and force him out of business.

Travis's last day at the pawn shop would haunt him for the rest of his life; the new owner Michael DeVito, together with his fat son Tony, heartlessly discussing the changes they were going to make while the old man sat hunched at his desk sobbing over the letter to quit; Tony DeVito's smug grin as he watched Travis helping Jack up from his chair.

"How could you do this to him?" Travis's voice trembled, as he escorted the distraught old man to the door for the last time.

DeVito junior's reply was short and to the point. "Because we can."

Within six months Michael DeVito was dead and the property sold to a supermarket chain by the new man at the helm. Tony DeVito had no interest in running a back street pawn shop; he had his sights set on far greater things.

* * *

The sign for Coopersville eventually loomed into view and Travis swerved his red Shelby Mustang towards the slip road. "Just a couple more miles now sweetheart."

His wife did not respond. She just stared into her lap and fidgeted with her wedding ring.

Travis rested a hand on her knee and squeezed it

reassuringly. "Trust me honey; I know what I'm doing."

Cheryl raised her eyes to the screech of locking brakes. "Travis! Look out!"

CHAPTER THREE

The white clapboard church standing at the head of Coopersville's main street had been decked out for a special occasion. Red, white and blue bunting fluttered along its guttering and swooped web-like towards the patriotic flagpole. A selection of farming vehicles cluttered the parking lot and men wearing baseball caps and Stetsons kicked tyres and tinkered under hoods. Today was auction day and the town folk were out in search of a bargain. Inside the church hall, proceedings were in full swing.

"Alright, I'm selling at five hundred and fifty dollars. You all done? 'Cause I sure have been." The hammer descended and let out a nutty clack as another deal was closed. The elderly auctioneer peered over his half moon spectacles and gave a friendly wink to a spotty youth sitting in the front row. "You got yourself a fine vehicle there Luke." He cleared his throat. "Movin' on then; most of you folks will remember old Ma Dillon who passed away in the fall." The respectful mutterings around the hall confirmed that this was indeed the case. "Now, as you know, her ranch was sold last month and today we have the very sad duty of selling off its contents. There are six lots in all; forty to forty-five. I'm starting with lot forty then; a fine collection of porcelain and bone china. Do I hear one hundred dollars?"

Outside in the church hall parking lot, Carl swaggered over to an old tractor and bounced his boot off a withered tyre. He wiped a spy hole in the dirt of the cab window and peered inside. The dusty grey cobwebs spanning the dashboard told him it had not seen a field in years. He pushed back his hat and scratched the knobbly stump on the side of his head; the other half of his ear having been bitten off in a bar room brawl.

"Look at all this shit Wayne. The boss must be crazy if he's fixin' to buy any of it."

Twenty paces ahead, Tony DeVito's ears pricked up and his feet crunched to a halt on the gravel. Spinning around so fast his white Stetson didn't quite make the one hundred and eighty degree turn, the short rotund antiques dealer marched towards his employees with a face that could curdle milk. "Did I ask for your opinion?"

Carl chewed out his defence. "Er…hell, I didn't mean nuthin' by it. I just thought . . ."

"What?" spat DeVito, "that I'd drag us all the way out here to buy me some hand-me-down shit spreader? Is that what you thought?"

Carl dotted his prominent brow ridge with a red neckerchief in anticipation of his boss's wrath.

"Now I'm only gonna say this once Carl so you'd better point that good ear of yours in my direction." Carl stooped down and did as instructed. "If you ever question my integrity again you're gonna wind up back at that stinkin' roach infested hostel you called home and you'll be shovellin' shit for the rest of your life. Do I make myself clear?"

"Yes sir," Carl muttered, swallowing his embarrassment having just been belittled in front of his buddy.

Tony DeVito then turned his attention to the dumber of the two men. "And as for you Wayne; the only thing *you* need to think about is remembering to open your fly before takin' a piss. You got that?"

Wayne checked his flies. "Sure thing Mr DeVito."

Suitably appeased, DeVito straightened his hat and brushed the creases from his white double-breasted jacket with chubby porcine fingers. "Now then, unless either of you have got any other bright ideas on how I should be runnin' my business I'd like to proceed inside."

Bulk, brawn and precious little brain pretty much summed up DeVito's associates. But he employed them for their fear factor, not intellectual prowess, so he tolerated their obtuse commentary most days. Today, however, was different. There was far too much at stake. If everything went according to plan, Tony DeVito's business rivals would be blown clean out of the water and his arts and antiquities organisation would be reaffirmed as the number one dealership in Dallas. He would be untouchable.

Travis's lame red Mustang limped up the main street and pulled into the church parking lot with steam cascading from the hood. Cheryl kicked open the crumpled passenger door and escaped the clutches of the hot leather interior. Other than the post-traumatic frustration of Travis not heeding her pleas to slow down, the only scar she bore from their collision with the rear end of a cattle truck was a streak of red lipstick smeared across her cheek. "My God, I didn't believe places like this still existed," she griped, glancing at the only other two buildings in sight; a liquor store and gas station. "I reckon a trip out to Walmart must be the only fun people get around here."

"I'd keep those thoughts to yourself if I were you. Folks 'round here are touchy about things like that." Travis grabbed his briefcase and ran for the door of the church hall. He knew his wife would not consider entering such a public arena without fixing her makeup first but there was no time to lose. "See you inside honey!" he shouted, leaving her with mirror in hand and mascara wand at the ready.

Just inside the main door, spread across three long trestle tables, was a selection of cherry, apple and pecan pies together with a variety of odd-shaped preserve jars crammed with misshapen pieces of home-made peppermint and fudge. Chattering behind the expanse of tables a group of grey-haired women busied themselves putting the finishing touches to a brightly painted 'Bake Sale' sign. Travis wondered if he was in the right place. "This is where the auction is being held ain't it mam?" he asked one of the softly rounded women.

"I'll tell you if you buy one of my pies," she teased, prompting a stifled cackle from her friends.

Travis held up the palm of his sweaty hand. "Thank you mam, maybe later. I'm in kind of a hurry." He ventured further inside and searched for someone who wasn't covered in flour and looked a little more official. Pushing through a maze of stalls he eventually stumbled upon the auctioneer seated at a table enjoying a well-earned break. "Lot forty-five sir," said Travis urgently, "I'd like to view it." The old man gave no response and continued to nibble on a barbecued chicken leg.

Perhaps the old-timer is hard of hearing?

Travis lowered his mouth to the auctioneer's leathery ear and shouted. "Lot forty-five sir, I'd like to view it!"

Startled, the auctioneer jumped up from his seat. "I ain't deaf god damn it, I heard you the first time! What is with you city folk huh? Always rushin' around like there's no tomorrow."

Travis doffed his Stetson politely. "Sorry sir, I didn't mean to…"

"See that big crate over there?" the auctioneer interrupted, a spray of barbeque sauce cascading from his twisted mouth.

Travis recoiled and flicked a stray blob from his jacket. "Yeah sir, I see it."

The old man wiped his lips with a nicotine-stained finger. "That's lot forty-five." Another quick doff of his Stetson and Travis was off, pushing his way through the busy crowd with the crate firmly in his sights.

Cheryl entered the hall and scanned the room for her husband. But it was Carl who spotted Travis first and a broad grin stretched his mouth to reveal a row of uneven gold-filled teeth. He threw an elbow into Wayne's ribs.

"Go and find DeVito. I wanna see the look on his fat face when I tell him who just showed up."

Cheryl found Travis delving inside the large dirty crate. Stacked against it were torn canvasses, some dusty and sun bleached, some framed and some not. Each sorry painting bore the scrutiny of a chancer's desperate eyes. She arched an eyebrow and tapped Travis on the shoulder. "Are you serious? They wouldn't fetch ten bucks in a yard sale."

Travis continued rummaging. "You're wrong sweetheart. Somewhere in here is a painting by a guy called Pissaro."

Cheryl popped a cigarette between her strawberry lips and flicked at a Zippo. "Pissaro huh?" she said, savouring the first drag. "And who's he when he's at home?"

"Oh, no one special," Travis sighed, "just one of the most famous impressionist artists that's ever walked the planet."

"Is that right," Cheryl scoffed. "Then tell me something mister art expert; if this guy's so famous, what the hell is his painting doin' in some hillbilly auction?"

"Don't you ever listen to a word I say? My contact told me the painting belonged to an old woman from this town but she died recently and left all her belongings to her grandson. Thing is, this grandson of hers lives in Europe and he has instructed everything be sold in his absence." Travis looked up and met Cheryl's bemused face staring back at him.

"Well don't you get it?" he said, moving in closer. "He obviously don't know nuthin' about the Pissaro otherwise he'd have been over here faster than a speeding bullet to claim it for himself."

Cheryl remained unconvinced. "That's as maybe. But I still can't believe one of those things could be worth millions of dollars!"

"Sshh! Keep your voice down for Christ's sake," Travis hissed, his eyes darting around the hall. "I paid a lot of money for that information and here you are giving it away free of charge."

Cheryl noticed the veins blowing out in his neck and thought it best not to question him any further. Instead, she lent her support with an occasional sigh of regret each time another painting was pulled out, scrutinised and discarded with the others.

Travis hauled one more dust-laden canvas from the crate and his eyes roamed the scene. "My God," he gasped.

"What is it?"

"Look honey, a lone tree, thick with late summer foliage. Rich golden light dappled on children at play. And there, in the distance, ripe corn and a rash of poppies bent under the scythes of harvesters."

"You're so full of shit Travis. Just listen to yourself. 'Rich golden light…a rash of freakin' poppies.' You know jackshit about art!"

"Is that so? Then cast your pretty little eyes over the god damn signature." He held up the painting to show her.

"My God you're right," Cheryl gasped.

Camille Pissaro had indeed bore witness to this idyllic rustic afternoon in the year 1878. His child-like signature, dashed across the bottom left of the canvas, could not be mistaken.

"Honey," Travis gloated, hardly able to contain his excitement, "I think we just hit pay dirt."

A familiar but unwelcome voice suddenly boomed from the other side of the canvas. "Seen anything you like?" Travis froze momentarily before casually sliding the painting back inside the crate. Tony DeVito and his boys faced him from across the hall.

"Nope," said Travis calmly. He grabbed Cheryl by the hand. "Come on honey, let's go find a seat."

DeVito snapped his fingers and his employees dutifully moved in to block their exit. "Okay Travis, let's cut the bullshit. How the hell did you find out about this?"

Cheryl sensed trouble was looming and coiled her arm tightly around Travis's. "I got my sources Tony," he answered nonchalantly.

DeVito took a step closer and eyeballed him. "It wouldn't be the same source that's caused me to lose my last three deals to you now would it?"

"Maybe you're just losin' your touch?" Travis replied, a sneer evolving on his lips.

Wayne cracked his knuckles and waited for DeVito's instruction to let him off the leash but his boss remained silent. Instead, he did something which took them all completely by surprise. Reaching inside his jacket pocket, DeVito produced a bulging manila envelope and thrust it at Travis. "Here; ten thousand dollars; take it. All you got to do is turn around and go on home."

Travis's rebuttal was swift and to the point. "Don't insult my intelligence Tony. I know what that painting's worth."

DeVito turned his attention to Cheryl. "Darlin', can't you talk some sense into this husband of yours? He ain't got the balls to go the distance; he's all hat and no cattle. All he's gonna do is push up the price and it'll end up costing me more money." DeVito turned back to Travis. "C'mon now, you've had your fun but this is way out of your league. Now take the money and leave this to the experts. Besides, you don't really want to lock horns with me over this do you?"

Wayne took this as his cue. "What Mr DeVito's trying to say is that you're about as welcome here as a turd floatin' in a punchbowl so if you know what's good for you you'll accept his offer and drag your sorry ass back into town."

With his nose pressed up against Wayne's chequered chest, Travis grimaced as the smell of beef jerky infused with body odour wafted up his nostrils. Travis shoved him aside. "Back off boulder head."

Quick as lightening, Wayne grabbed him by the lapels of his jacket and hauled Travis up for a face-to-face audience. "You watch that mouth of yours city boy or I'll break you in half." His southern drawl was laced with menace and onions.

"Hey, take your hands off him!" Cheryl shrieked, beating her fists on Wayne's shoulder. Carl swiftly intervened, scooping her up by the waist and dangling her under his arm like a rag doll. "Put me down you moron!" Cheryl protested; kicking out with her stiletto heeled boots.

"Alright Carl, let the lady go," DeVito ordered. "Wayne, put Travis down." His henchmen did as instructed and Cheryl ran into the arms of her husband.

"You'll pay for that DeVito," Travis spat, through gritted teeth.

The fat man remained composed and smiled. "Hell you got guts Travis, I'll give you that. You remind me of me in my younger days, full of confidence, fire in your belly, always chasing that big deal. Come to think of it; I could use a guy like you in my organisation."

This was DeVito's second surprise of the day and it was followed by stunned silence.

"Are you offering Travis... a job?" asked Cheryl, unable to hold her tongue any longer.

"Sure, why not," came DeVito's upbeat reply. "He'd be working for the largest art and antiques dealership in Dallas. Think about it, nice steady income; security? I'm sure that's what you're really looking for ain't it darlin'?"

Cheryl turned to her husband but he refused to meet her gaze. Travis knew it would have *maybe DeVito's got a point* written all over it. She was growing tired of all the game playing and gambling on deals and was looking forward to a quieter, less stressful life. Sure, things had come good for them but there had been plenty of rough times too. A reliable, steady income would be very appealing to a woman like Cheryl. After all, she had her needs; Gucci, Prada, Chanel…

DeVito held out his hand. "You could do a lot worse for yourself Travis, so come on, what do you say?"

The sound of the auctioneer's hammer signalled the sale was about to reconvene and it refocused Travis's resolve.

"Well it's a tempting offer Tony and I sure do appreciate it but . . . now how can I put this? See, I'd rather bottle my own piss and try to sell it as Champagne before workin' for a horse's ass like you."

"You're not still angry with me over old Jack Wilson's pawn shop are you? That happened years ago Travis; besides, it was just business, nothing personal."

Travis was incensed. "Business had nothing to do with it and you know it. Hell, you didn't even want the man's shop; you sold it remember!"

"He was a competitor Travis; plain and simple," DeVito retorted, raising his voice.

"No DeVito; he was just a frail old man." Travis turned to Cheryl. "C'mon honey, let's go find those seats."

But Tony DeVito had one last surprise up his sleeve. "Alright have it your way but I think it fair to warn you this ain't gonna be no two-horse race. Do you see that guy over there?" He gestured towards a smartly dressed man in a black Stetson making himself comfortable on a long pew. "It would appear our little secret's out the bag."

Travis took Cheryl by the hand and led her into the main hall to a couple of empty chairs. She glanced back at the man in the black hat. "That guy DeVito's going on about? He's another dealer ain't he?"

"So what if he is. Relax sweetheart. DeVito's just trying to scare us off that's all."

The man noticed Cheryl staring at him from across the crowded room and acknowledged her with a tip of his hat. Cheryl quickly turned away. "Well from where I'm sitting he's doing a damn good job."

"Now don't you start worrying your pretty little head over him. You see, unless he's got a whole bunch of money hidden under that fancy black hat of his, he's got as much chance of outbidding me as a one-legged man has of winning a butt-kicking contest."

"Ain't you ever heard of a credit card?"

"Take a look around you honey. Does this look like the kind of place that takes credit cards for Christ's sake?"

Cheryl surveyed the room and shrugged. "No, I guess not."

Travis watched as DeVito, Carl and Wayne took their seats at the other end of the hall. "Your damn right; and as for our fat friend over there," he whispered in Cheryl's ear, "my hunch is that all the cash he has on him is tucked away in that little envelope of his." Travis pulled his briefcase onto his lap and stroked it lovingly. "Whereas I, on the other hand, have enough greenbacks in here to buy me this whole god damn town. Cash talks in these parts sweetheart so just sit back, relax, and enjoy the ride."

"But what if . . . ?"

"No buts… Trust me honey, I know what I'm doing."

The auctioneer stood on the rostrum and shuffled his papers in preparation for the next lot. Leaning his wiry body over the pulpit he jabbed the microphone with a bony knuckle.

"Here we go again then folks with the last lot from Ma Dillon's old ranch. Lot forty-five; a fine collection of paintings. Alright then, who'll give me two hundred dollars to start things off?"

The hall fell silent. "Okay; one-fifty then." The auctioneer waited but no bid was forthcoming. "Come on folks, the frames alone gotta be worth more than that!" Finally, a hand belonging to a woman in an unflattering flower print dress popped up. "Thank you mam. Any advance on one-fifty?" A man in a baseball cap tapped the side of his nose. "One-sixty. It's with the gentleman in the cap at one hundred and sixty dollars." The auctioneer took a final look around and raised the hammer. "Fine, if we're all done then? Going once…"

Travis waited; his heart thumping so hard it threatened to rip through his denim shirt. He loosened his tie and, for the benefit of Tony DeVito, sat back and tried to look relaxed.

"Going twice…"

DeVito cracked first and his hand shot up into the air.

"We have a new bid in the room at one-seventy. Thank you sir. I'm now looking for one-eighty."

Coolly, Travis raised an arm. He fixed his eyes on DeVito who quickly responded with a nod to the auctioneer. "One-ninety. Now we're cookin'. Do I hear two hundred dollars?"

Travis tipped the rim of his hat.

"Yes I do," shouted the auctioneer. "Two-ten anybody?"

The bidding rally was relentless and the auctioneer was soon jumping up in hundreds.

The bid was with Travis at five thousand dollars.

"Going once, going twice . . ."

His eyes glued to the hammer twirling between the auctioneer's fingers, Travis allowed himself a momentary glance at the only other possible contender. But the man in the black hat just sat there, steely-eyed and motionless. Travis felt Cheryl's hot breath on his neck. "Come on," she whispered, willing the auctioneer to bring the hammer down.

DeVito shifted in his seat and turned to Carl and Wayne. "We're just burning daylight here. Let's find out what that smart ass is really made of." He stood up just as the hammer began to descend.

"Twenty thousand dollars to get this thing over with!"

The auctioneer jerked his hand back up and the crowd delivered a gasp. DeVito looked over at Travis with a grin that threatened to split his melon face as he flopped back down into his seat. Numb with shock, it was now Travis who sat steely-eyed and motionless as his brain tried to take in what had just happened.

"Sir, just to be sure I ain't hearing things," the auctioneer enquired, "you've just bid *twenty thousand dollars.* Is that correct?" The hushed crowd turned to face DeVito. He stood up again and straightened his jacket.

"There is nothing wrong with your hearing sir. That is my

bid."

Cheryl jabbed him in the ribs. "Not enough cash on him huh?"

Travis felt his throat begin to close, his mouth desiccated. He swallowed what adrenaline infused spittle he had left but it gave no relief. This was not going to be as easy as he thought.

The auctioneer narrowed his eyes and cocked his eagle head in Travis's direction. "I don't suppose you would like to counter that bid would you sir?"

The crowd hummed with anticipation and waited for his response. Terrified at the prospect of this going the full fifteen rounds, Cheryl tugged on Travis's sleeve, her eyes pleading with him not to continue. But when she saw DeVito sniggering at her husband from across the room, any thought she had of Travis throwing in the towel quickly evaporated.

"There's no way that horse's ass is gonna get the better of me," Travis said, jumping to his feet. "Thirty thousand!"

Cheryl's head slumped into her hands as the crowd put theirs together to applaud the stranger's tenacity. DeVito responded with the cock of a stubby finger and so began another fiery rally. Within minutes the bidding hit a new milestone - fifty thousand dollars.

The perspiration glistened on DeVito's brow and a blotchy red flush advanced up his bullfrog neck like an army of fire ants. Travis was gleeful. "Look at him; he's sweating like a hog on a barbecue. I think we got him on the run now honey."

"I'm selling at fifty thousand dollars," the auctioneer bellowed. "Going once... going twice ..."

Travis's eyes flashed across to his rival. "I got you now you son of a bitch," he mouthed, waiting for the inevitable crack of the auctioneers hammer. Then it happened.

"Sixty thousand dollars!"

Dozens of eager eyes scoured the rows of seats in search of a hand but Travis and Cheryl knew exactly where to look. "Shit. DeVito *was right* about that guy after all."

"Quit your griping will you," Travis snapped. "This ain't my first rodeo."

But things were about to get a whole lot worse. Having assumed DeVito was out of the race, Travis's jaw dropped when the fat man stood up and countered Black Hat's bid. The big guy in the white suit was not out of this yet and the crowd cheered its approval.

Cheryl grabbed hold of Travis's ascending arm and pushed it back to his side.

"Just think real hard about this Travis," she said, her voice threatening to break. "Are you really sure you wanna continue with this?"

"What? Are you out of your tiny mind? That painting is worth tens of millions of dollars and you're suggesting I should quit? Dream on honey; hell, I only just got started." Travis thrust his arm into the air and reached for the sky.

"Eighty thousand dollars!"

Cheryl stood up and began to inch past the knees of her ecstatic neighbours.

"And just where the hell do you think you're goin'?" said Travis, his eyes still glued to the auctioneer.

"I feel sick. I need to go outside and get some air."

Cheryl weaved through the forest of captivated onlookers not daring to look back. Stumbling out of the double doors and onto the steps of the church hall, she reached into her bag and pulled out a cigarette. Coopersville looked deserted and she knew why; the whole community was now gathered inside the church hall watching the best show in town. Only one man remained in the parking lot, whistling contently as he worked beneath the hood of a tractor. Cheryl wondered if he had any worries other than to breathe life into the wreck before him and she settled down to watch him work; anything to take her mind some place else.

Her daydream was interrupted by the piercing ring of her phone. The voice at the other end of the line was unmistakable and Cheryl's mother, Nancy, got straight to the point.

"Honey, that cookie recipe you gave me? Are you sure you didn't miss anything out 'cause I don't think they look quite right? Better give it to me again just in case."

The heavy doors of the church suddenly bounced open, slapping against the walls of the building with a loud bang. Startled, Cheryl spun around to see a man stumble past her as he rushed down the steps.

"Earl," he shouted across the parking lot, "get yourself in here, you gotta see this!"

Earl squinted over the hood of the tractor, his oil-streaked face set in a grimace.

"Darn it Marv. Can't you see I'm busy here? I ain't got time for none of your foolin'." He ducked back into the engine.

"Foolin' my ass!" Marv chortled. "Three city boys are biddin' like crazy for Ma Dillon's old stuff. Two hundred thousand - *and it's still goin' up!*"

The loud clang of Earl's spanner hitting the ground was masked by the sickening thud of his head bashing the underside of the tractor hood. Although somewhat dazed, Earl managed to stagger up the steps and follow Marv inside.

"Are you still there honey?" said Nancy.

With the words 'two hundred thousand' ringing in her ears, Cheryl was in no mood for confectionery chatter. "Sorry mom, I'm in the middle of something important right now. I'll call you tonight. Love you, Bye."

Cheryl's mind was in turmoil. Of course she wanted Travis to succeed, but not at any cost. All their assets were tied up to secure the obscenely high interest loan from Danny Bakula and if Travis didn't manage to acquire the painting for the right price…

An hour later, Cheryl took a final drag on her last cigarette and flicked it with the rest of the stubs scattered at her feet. Feeling a rumbling underfoot, she quickly grabbed her bag, ran down the steps and turned to face the door.

The crowd exploded from the confines of the stuffy hall like a burst dam and a stampede of boots and sneakers cascaded down the steps into the parking lot.

"Hell, that's the best fun I had in years!" declared Earl, slapping Marv on the back.

An outraged woman wagged a finger in Earl's face. "It's immoral, that's what it is! Payin' all that money for a box of old paintings when there are folks starving in the world."

Swept aside by the last of the Coopersville throng, Cheryl stood alone and waited. Finally Travis emerged from the gaping doors, his dark shoulder length hair framing the dimpled grin on his roughly shaven face. In his hands he carried a slim rectangular package wrapped in brown paper and twine.

"Well, ain't you gonna congratulate me?" he said, jogging down the steps.

Cheryl had only one thing on her mind. "How much?" she asked, quietly following him back to the car.

"Hell, you should have seen DeVito's face when the hammer came down," Travis laughed. "He was angrier than a swarm of bees that just found out Winnie the Pooh was coming to dinner."

"How much god damn it!"

Travis thrust the painting at his wife and reached for the phone in his back pocket. "If you'd stuck around while I was fighting for our future in there you'd know how much! Now hold on to this while I make a phone call. And be careful!"

* * *

Danny Bakula threw down the shovel and climbed out of the hole he had been digging for the past half an hour. Stretched out before him lay hundreds of square miles of desert wilderness; this place was everywhere and nowhere. His phone rang and a client's name flashed up on the display.

"Yo, Travis what's happenin'?" he said, using his shoulder to pin the phone to his ear while he wiped his hands on a stained rag.

Travis's upbeat voice flowed down the line. "Good news Danny. That deal I was telling you about? It came off!"

Bakula tossed the rag into the hole and marched over to

his car. "So when do I get my money back?"

"Soon," Travis chirped. "I already got a buyer hooked and landed in the boat so we'll be all squared up by the end of the week." He winked at Cheryl and she allowed him a half-hearted smile.

Bakula dragged a bound and gagged man from the trunk and ushered him to the edge of the pit. A blow from the shovel to the back of the man's legs brought him to his knees. "I'll see you at the end of the week then. Oh, and Travis . . ."

"Yeah Danny?"

"Don't let me down."

Bakula hung up, casually pulled a gun from his jacket pocket and shot the man in the back of the head. He rolled the corpse into the pit with the heel of his boot.

With Danny Bakula's veiled threat still bouncing off his ear, Travis took his trophy from Cheryl and carefully placed it in the trunk of his car.

Cheryl gave him a discreet nudge. "Hurry up with that," she whispered, "DeVito and his boys are heading this way."

Travis slammed the trunk and locked it.

"I suppose congratulations are in order," said DeVito, marching across the car park with an outstretched hand. Travis shook it firmly.

"Why thanks Tony," he gushed, unable to conceal his smugness. "I make that four in a row; guess that makes me top dog around here now don't it?" To rub even more salt in DeVito's wounds, Travis set his phone to camera mode and handed it to Cheryl. "Here honey, I want a photograph to celebrate my victory." He turned to DeVito. "I'm gonna hang it on the wall when I get my new downtown office."

DeVito reached for the phone. "Here, let me take it. I'm sure you'd like to be in the picture too wouldn't you darlin'?"

"Gracious in defeat," said Travis, "now ain't that somethin'?"

DeVito smiled. "Win some, lose some; you know how it is. There'll always be another time."

"Hell, I can't wait," laughed Travis, pulling Cheryl in close by her small waist.

Carl's stomach turned as he witnessed his boss fawning over the loud-mouthed prima donna and he spat out a phlegm ball in disgust. "Why the hell is DeVito letting that son of a bitch talk to him like that," he whispered in Wayne's ear.

"Who knows Carl? Maybe Travis was right. Maybe DeVito is losin' his touch."

DeVito held the phone high. "Okay you two, big smiles now!"

CHAPTER FOUR

THREE WEEKS LATER

Travis surveyed Dallas's glittering high-rise real estate from the window of a twenty-fifth floor office block in the city centre and pushed out his chest with pride.

In the distance the Reunion Tower rose like a sceptre towards the cornflower blue sky, sparkling in the early morning sunlight. He walked his fingers along the arm of the green antique leather chair, sat back and savoured the moment.

This is what it's all about.

A light knock on the mahogany panelled office door heralded the entrance of a pretty secretary. "Mr Lawson, Mr DeVito's here now," she said softly.

Travis stood up, brushed the lapels of his neat jacket and readied himself to meet his old business rival.

"Travis! Good to see you," said DeVito, swaggering into the room. "Hey, you're lookin' great." He pointed a finger and held it there for a moment like a cheesy game show host.

"Nice office you got here," said Travis.

"Thanks, business has been good." DeVito took his place

behind the vast antique oak desk and eased himself onto his green leather throne. Travis had to make do balanced on the edge of a small swivel chair designed for the proportions of a petite secretary.

"I hope I haven't kept you waiting too long," said DeVito. "Now then, what can I do you for?"

Travis twisted uncomfortably in his seat. "Well Tony, I've been thinking about what you said and… the thing is…" He swallowed what little pride he had left and blurted it out. "I'd like to take you up on that job offer of yours."

DeVito reclined back in his chair and lit up a fat cigar. "Sorry, I must have missed something," he drawled. "What the hell are you talkin' about?"

Travis squirmed with embarrassment and gripped the arms of the chair. "Don't you remember Tony? A few weeks back you offered me a job; at the auction in Coopersville?"

DeVito thought for a moment. "Oh that," he said, snapping his fingers. "Yeah, now that you come to mention it, I think I may have inferred somethin' along those lines." DeVito smirked and leaned forward across the table. He looked Travis straight in the eye. "I er, I take it that piss Champagne idea of yours didn't quite work out then huh? Never could see a market for it myself. Still, what do I know? I mean, I'm just a *'horse's ass'* ain't I?" Relishing the moment, DeVito drew on his cigar until the end glowed like hot coals and slowly blew the smoke into Travis's stunned face.

Travis coughed and stood up. "I can see this was a mistake so I won't waste any more of your precious time."

"Sit down Travis," said DeVito, forcefully. "I ain't

finished yet."

DeVito got up out of his chair and waddled around to the front of the desk. He bent down and tapped the side of his snout nose. "That painting of yours; it turned out to be a fake didn't it?"

"Cost me my business," said Travis, avoiding eye contact. "Bet that made your day."

DeVito straightened up and smiled. "Laughed so hard I almost dirtied my shorts. But the truth of the matter is you did me a big favour. See, if you hadn't of outbid me, I'd be the one asking *you* for a job!" He paused for a moment and looked at Travis critically. "Alright Travis, unlike you, I'm not one to bear grudges so I'm gonna cut you some slack; give you a break."

DeVito's flow was rudely interrupted when Carl and Wayne flung open the door and frogmarched a terrified dishevelled man through the room towards an adjacent office.

"What's this all about Tony?" The man whimpered, as Carl tightened his grip on the back of his collar.

"God damn it!" snapped DeVito. "Haven't I told you two morons to knock before stepping into my office?"

Wayne looked Travis up and down suspiciously. "Sorry, I didn't know you were talkin' to this assho . . ."

"Never mind, never mind," bawled DeVito, waving him away. "Just take that double-crossin' piece of shit in there. I'll deal with him in a minute."

"Now just hold on a minute Tony," the man protested. "You got it all wrong."

"It's Mr DeVito to you," growled Carl, punishing his disrespect with a slap around the back of the head.

DeVito cocked his little finger and his boys bundled the cowering man into the next room.

Tranquillity returned. "Now then, where was I?" smiled DeVito.

Travis leaned forward. "I think you were about to offer me a job."

"Whoa, now just hold your horses for a minute there Travis. See, there are a few things we need to get straight if I'm to seriously consider taking on a loose cannon like you. *Firstly*, as a buyer for my organisation, you gotta agree to play by my rules; do things my way."

Travis nodded enthusiastically. "Absolutely."

"*Secondly*", said DeVito, bending a finger to drive home the point, "everything you buy *must* go through my company. The consequences of doing otherwise will be severe, as my ex-employee in there is about to find out. Do I make myself clear?"

The groans of the man being beaten in the next room punctuated DeVito's words. Travis did not flinch. "Crystal," he said coolly.

DeVito walked back around the desk and poured two drinks from a finely cut carafe. He handed a glass to Travis who accepted it gratefully.

"Alright then Travis, let's get down to business. Now I heard on the grapevine you got a keen interest in showbiz memorabilia; music, films, that kind of thing. Would that be correct?" DeVito took a sip from his heavy glass and savoured the warmth as it sank down his throat.

Travis smiled confidently. "Some of the best pieces in Planet Hollywood came from me. Why it's my area of expertise!"

DeVito approached the back of Travis's chair and squeezed him firmly by the shoulders. "Now that's what I wanted to hear." The smell of fine malt hung on DeVito's breath. "Welcome to my organisation Travis. I think I got the perfect assignment for you."

CHAPTER FIVE

LIVERPOOL, ENGLAND – PRESENT DAY

"When you said we were going to Europe I thought you meant Paris or Rome, not some godforsaken industrial town in the north of England." Cheryl pulled her suitcase hard sending its wheels skittering across the car park of Liverpool John Lennon Airport.

"This is Liverpool for Christ's sake. Lighten up, you're gonna love it."

Travis stopped at the taxi rank and inhaled the intoxicating aroma of newly cut grass and jet fuel as he waited for the obliging driver to load their luggage into the back of the cab. Driving out of the airport he spotted a huge Yellow Submarine beached in the middle of a roundabout against the backdrop of a Lennon self-portrait. Running along the top of the image were the words; 'Above Us Only Sky'. Travis had been to Liverpool before and the prospect of exploring this colourful town again brought a much needed smile to his face.

The cab came to a stop in Ranelagh Street outside one of Liverpool's most historic buildings, the elegant Adelphi

Hotel. Built in 1912 to accommodate wealthy passengers travelling to North America including those of the ill-fated Titanic, The Sefton Suite, a replica of the Titanic's first class smoking lounge, still remained and attracted maritime enthusiasts to the hotel from around the world. But it was not the history of the White Star Line's ill-fated ship that enticed Travis to stay there; it was the fact Roy Rogers and Trigger were amongst its many famous patrons.

* * *

Cheryl stumbled into the room and immediately flopped down on the bed. A few paces behind, an exasperated Travis followed her inside struggling with their luggage. "Thanks for helping," he complained, peeling off his Stetson and throwing it down. It glided to a halt on the highly polished coffee table. He stood at the window and stretched his arms out wide to embrace the cityscape before him. "Ain't it great?"

Jet lagged and grouchy, Cheryl was in no mood for small talk and remained silent.

"Ah come on honey, what's your problem?" asked Travis.

Cheryl sat up. "Look," she huffed like a spoiled child, "sloshing around some Beatles Convention for trashy pop relics just ain't my idea of fun alright?"

"*Memorabilia...* is big business honey," he replied, defensively. "Remember those leather pants I brought back from my last visit?"

His wife's eyebrows knitted together and she shot him a killer glare. "How could I forget? I had to get the whole house fumigated!"

"You didn't turn your nose up at the seven grand I got for 'em though did you? That trash brings serious money from the right buyers, especially back home."

Cheryl jumped off the bed. "Has your IQ taken a rain check or something? It'll make serious money for DeVito. You work for him now remember!"

"You don't think I'm just gonna hand everything over to that horse's ass do you?" Travis argued. "Sure I'll find him some nice pieces, but I'll sure as hell be lining my own pockets first."

"That ain't gonna be enough to pay Danny Bakula the rest of his money though is it?" said Cheryl, her complexion taking on a distinctly crimson hue. "Three hundred thousand bucks you still owe him, not to mention all the interest that bloodsucker's charging!"

Travis snapped. "Alright, so I made a bad call! Shit happens in business and you brooding over it ain't gonna change a damn thing!"

"What do expect me to do? You've heard all those rumours about Bakula; what are we gonna do when that psycho catches up with us? Have you thought about that?"

"I've been trying not to," Travis muttered under his breath.

"What was that?"

"Nothing," Travis replied, softening his tone. "Listen honey," he said, brushing a finger gently across her cheek, "why don't you go freshen up. I know a great place we can eat."

Cheryl dragged her aching feet into the bathroom and sat in front of the brightly lit mirror. Travis put his head around the door as she scrutinised her tired face.

"While you're getting ready I'm gonna run into town and grab an itinerary brochure for the convention. I wanna make sure I'm first in line to snap up any bargains."

"Well, how long are you gonna be?"

Travis smiled. "The time it takes you to get ready? I'll be back before you've even started applying the second coat."

Cheryl looked up at him, her eyes full of concern. "Everything is gonna be alright ain't it Trav?"

Her child-like expression filled him with dread. The honest answer was that he didn't know. The unexplained disappearance of a number of Danny Bakula's ex-clients was more than a cause for concern and Travis knew that, unless he could make some serious money, and fast, it was only a matter of time before his name was added to the list. Travis brushed aside her fine blonde hair and kissed her gently on the forehead. "'Course it is sweetheart. I'll figure things out just like I always do."

No sooner had Travis clicked the door shut behind him the confident smile drained from his face. He had been in some tight fixes before but never like this. The assets from his business had raised enough to keep Bakula off his back in the short term but on the eve of flying out of Texas he issued Travis with a final ultimatum; find the rest of the money or face the consequences.

CHAPTER SIX

Barry jumped off the bus at the bombed-out ruins of St Luke's Church and ran along the busy shopping streets which swept down the hill towards the River Mersey. Dashing along Bold Street, he joined the tide of commuters as they swarmed towards Central Station and home. He passed the entrance to the station and soon found himself fighting against the multitude coming at him from the opposite direction. Like a salmon swimming upstream, he bounced off rocky shoulders and sharp-edged bags as he waded through the crowd. Then, something hooked his arm and reeled him from the hordes into the doorway of a jewellers shop. It was Brenda, his good friend and licensee of the Atlantic pub.

"And where are you off to in such a hurry?" she said, with a work-weary smile. "I've never seen you moving so fast."

Barry laughed politely and looked at his watch. It was almost five. "Sorry Bren, I'd love to stop and chat but I'm in a bit of a rush right now." He untangled his arm from hers and turned to walk away.

"You are still coming back to the pub for your dinner

later aren't you?" she said, with a hint of concern.

Barry fidgeted as he struggled to find the words to let her down gently.

"It's your favourite; fish and chips," she added, with a persuasive lift in her voice.

But Barry had bigger fish to fry. "To be honest Bren, I don't think I'll be able to make it tonight. Something's come up. Sorry."

Brenda did not disguise her disappointment. She was very fond of Barry and his optimistic outlook on life never failed to raise her spirits. Having spent months waiting for him to make the first move and turn their platonic friendship into something more serious, tonight was going to be the night she took the bull by the horns and told him how she really felt. "Oh, that's a shame. I was looking forward to showing you a box of old family photos I found in the cellar."

"Maybe tomorrow eh," said Barry, rejoining the stream of commuters. "I'll give you a call?"

"Alright love!" shouted Brenda, as he was jostled down the street. "You mind how you go!" She waved until he had melted into the crowd then turned for home.

In Mathew Street, tables and chairs were set out along the walkway and the smell of tapas and mezze hung in the air. The coffee machines which had served the city slickers earlier in the day had ceased their grinding and now optics drained into long chilled glasses as the invasion of the night crowd got underway.

But with The Beatles Convention looming, the possibility of an early finish was a non-starter for retailers preparing to capitalise on the army of dealers and Beatles fans set to descend upon the city.

Steve Benson finished the display in the shop window of The Beatles Store impervious to the growing carnival atmosphere in the town. He was tired; tired of relentless hours working behind the counter and the ever increasing arguments with his older brother Joe. Standing back to check his handiwork, his eyes were drawn down the long narrow thoroughfare. Overhead, colourful banners bridged the street and a neon Cavern sign crawled up the side of a red brick building heralding where it all began for the four lads who shook the world. A line of pretty girls caught Steve's attention, clipping along the cobbles in high-heeled shoes giggling arm in arm. It was the tall redhead in the middle that took his fancy and he followed her sleek fake tanned legs up to her short skirt which flicked out with each prancing step. Skipping past the window, they disappeared into Flanagan's Apple, an Irish music bar directly opposite the store. Steve looked back down the street in search of another distraction…and found one.

Shit. He ran to the door, flipped the open sign to closed and vaulted over the counter. Joe nudged open the kitchen door carrying two mugs of tea to find his brother cowering at his feet. "What are you doing down there?"

"Barry's coming!"

Joe slammed down the mugs and quickly joined him under the counter.

"That Barry's becoming a right pain in the arse," said Steve accusingly. "You're gonna have to have a word with him you know. I mean, he is *your mate* after all."

"What? He's no mate of mine."

"Well that's not what he thinks is it?" Steve retorted.

When Barry first entered the store three years ago, Joe was more than happy to accommodate him. It was not that he enjoyed listening to Barry's constant ramblings about a group that twanged its last chord over four decades ago; no, Joe's reasoning was more calculated than that. He thought that if he was nice to Barry, the tour guide would encourage his magical mystery punters to come and visit the store. Despite this never happening, the one-sided friendship blossomed and Barry had treated the place like a second home ever since.

The familiar tinkle of the door opening gave way to the sound of pounding feet then... silence. Steve and Joe held their breath and waited.

"You two are not going to believe what I've found!" rang a voice from above.

The brothers winced and looked up. Barry's full moon face beamed down at them, his eyes twinkling with delight.

Joe and Steve dragged themselves to their feet. "You're right Barry," Steve sighed, "but you're gonna tell us anyway aren't you?"

Unperturbed by their attempt to hide from him, Barry pulled out a letter and waved it triumphantly in the air like Neville Chamberlain on his return from Munich. "Take a look at this."

Steve plucked it from Barry's fingers and examined it.

"Look at the signature," Barry urged.

"John," said Steve, dismissively. He looked at it again. "Not John Lennon?"

Barry could hardly contain his excitement. "Yeah, and look who it's addressed to; *Stuart Sutcliffe*, the fifth

Beatle!"

Sutcliffe, a brilliant art student and Lennon's best friend, joined the band in 1960 after John and Paul persuaded him to buy a bass guitar with fifty pounds prize money he had won in a painting exhibition. They argued that they could never call themselves a 'proper band' without a bass guitarist in the line-up. Stuart knew he was not cut out to be a musician but went along with their scheme to help them out. The trouble was, despite their attempts to teach him, he never mastered the instrument and consequently had to endure John and Paul's unforgiving taunts during his time with the group. In 1961, after another gruelling stint in Hamburg, Stuart made the decision to leave. He was to marry his German girlfriend, Astrid Kirchherr, and continue his studies at Hamburg Art College under the tutelage of pop artist, Eduardo Paolozzi.

Joe snatched the letter from Steve. "Give it here. It'll be another fake," he said, squinting at the dog-eared page.

"Not this one," Barry gushed. "It's definitely genuine; I'd put me life on it. Look at the postmark, 1962." Joe shrugged his shoulders and tossed the letter on the counter.

"Aren't you going to read it?" stuttered Barry.

"No chance," said Joe. "The match is on tonight."

Barry was stunned. "But it could be the discovery of a lifetime."

"Bollocks," scoffed Joe, his deliberate voice negating Barry's enthusiasm from across the counter. "Alright, so it might have been written by John Lennon; that doesn't make it the discovery of a bloody lifetime does it?"

"No you don't understand," said Barry. "I'm not talking

about the letter; I'm talking about *Julia's Banjo*; the one Lennon's mum taught him to play when he was a kid. I think I might know where it is!"

John was the only child of Julia's brief marriage to Alf Lennon, a seaman who was rarely at home. When the marriage ended, Julia, a high spirited and impulsive young woman, couldn't cope with the pressures of bringing up a young son on her own and five-year-old John was packed off to live with her older sister, Mimi.

John's aunt strongly disapproved of Julia's free spirited attitude to life and she discouraged contact between mother and son. Despite this, when John was a teenager, he re-established a relationship with Julia making secret trips to her home just a few miles away at 9 Newcastle Road. It was during these visits she taught him to play 'That'll Be The Day' on her banjo and turned him on to Rock 'n' Roll.

On 15th July 1958, after visiting Mimi at her home in Menlove Avenue, Julia was knocked down and killed by an off-duty policeman. John never got over her death and in later life immortalised her in his songs, 'Julia' and 'Mother'. Shortly after Julia's death the banjo went missing; never to be seen again.

* * *

"Oh God, here we go," Steve laughed. "Barry, that banjo hasn't been seen for over half a century!"

Barry was smiling too. "Yeah, and I know why. John hid it! It's all here, in this letter."

Joe did nothing to hide his scepticism. "Go on then where? Where did he hide it?"

This direct line of questioning caught Barry off guard. "Well, it doesn't say *exactly* where", he admitted limply, "not in plain English anyway. You see, John has written part of it in 'Jabberwocky'."

"Jabber 'bloody' wocky?" Steve sniggered.

"Yeah," Barry continued unfazed. "It's a kind of jumbled up poetry, like you get in Alice in Wonderland. John loved all that Lewis Carroll stuff."

Barry spent the next ten minutes educating the brothers on how Lennon initially developed his Jabberwocky style of writing to prevent his prying Aunt Mimi from reading his letters and poetry. When he became a Beatle, John used Jabberwocky to write two best selling books, 'In His Own Write' and 'A Spaniard In The Works' together with songs such as, 'I Am The Walrus'.

"I see," said Joe, fighting back the laughter. "So what you've *actually* got is a letter that only the Mad Hatter can understand? Very convenient." He clapped his hands together to signal the end of the discussion. "Come on Steve, let's lock up. We're going to miss the kick off."

While Joe busied himself tidying things away behind the counter, Steve switched off the music and put on his leather jacket. Barry retrieved the letter from the counter and waved it at them. "John didn't write this for just anyone to read you know. He wrote it for Stuart. *He* would have understood what it meant."

"Good for Stuart," said Joe flatly. "Check the back door's locked Ste'."

Barry pushed on undaunted. "Come on lads, this isn't a pair of old winklepickers John might have worn at The Cavern you know. It's the holy grail of pop memorabilia. Just think about it, without that banjo The Beatles would never have happened; *and without them*, everything we know today would be different!"

Barry's well chosen words achieved the desired effect and the brothers stopped what they were doing. "So what's all this got to do with us?" asked Steve.

Barry came straight to the point. "I reckon if the three of us put our heads together and work out what this letter actually means; we can find it."

"Forget it," said Joe. "We've got a business to run. We haven't got time to go off on some wild goose chase have we Steve?"

Steve held up a hand and gestured for his brother to keep quiet. "Hold on a minute Joe. Just for argument's sake," he asked Barry, "if it was found, what do you reckon it would be worth?"

At last, a question Barry could answer with confidence.

"Okay, the Lennon piano that went under the hammer at Sotheby's in 2000? It sold for one and a half million pounds didn't it? Now, when you consider that it fetched that price over ten years ago, plus the fact Lennon owned more than one piano...You can see where I'm going with this can't you? The thing is; this banjo is unique; it's in a completely different league. Don't forget, it was also the first instrument the greatest rock 'n' roll legend ever learned to play. Taking everything into account, I reckon if it came up for auction today you'd be looking at, ooh at least *five million*."

*   *   *

Travis could not believe his ears. Eavesdropping from behind a bookshelf with a Beatles Convention itinerary brochure clutched in his sweaty hand he had heard every single word.

Five million; my God.

'Sweet Home Alabama' suddenly rang out from Travis's phone and stopped Barry's conversation in mid-flow. Travis grappled it from his pocket and saw the name flashing up. *Cheryl.* Cursing her under his breath, his finger stabbed at the off button faster than a woodpecker's head.

"Shit," whispered Joe. "I forgot he was still here." He shouted across to Travis. "Anything I can help you with sir? We're closing up now!"

Masking his anger and frustration with a constipated smirk, Travis emerged from behind the bookshelf and tipped his Stetson politely. He waved the itinerary brochure in the air. "No thanks, just browsing. I got what I came in for."

The eyes of the three men followed Travis up the stairs and they remained silent until he was out of the door. Barry waited for Steve to lock it before jumping straight back in. "So what do you think then lads? Are you going to help me find this banjo or what?"

*   *   *

The Grapes pub was only a stones throw from The Beatles Store and Joe and Steve arrived to find Barry standing at the bar ordering the drinks. They sat at a table and Joe checked his watch. "You do know the match has started," he sighed.

"Sod the bloody match Joe. What if Barry's right?"

Joe leaned forward. "And what if he's talking through his arse eh? I mean, let's be honest, it wouldn't be the first time would it?"

Before Steve had a chance to retort, Barry returned with a tray of drinks and sat down.

"Alright Barry, you've got our attention," said Joe indifferently. "What does this bloody letter of yours *actually say*?"

Barry took a furtive look around before spreading the letter out on the table. He cleared his throat. "Dear Stu," he whispered.

"Just get to the part where he mentions the bloody banjo!" Joe shouted, his patience now reaching breaking point.

Barry's finger zigzagged down the page and stopped at the relevant passage. In a hushed voice he began to read:

". . . *'I've stashed the banjo and all my stuff in an old haunt of ours for safe keeping. You know what Aunt Mimi's like, as soon as my back's turned she roots out my things and throws them away. She'll regret it when I'm famous!'"*

Joe was stunned. "Is that it?"

Steve picked up the letter and studied it for more clues. "Hang on, what's this bit here?"

". . .'*Talk to the bridge where the river meets the ocean. There, lying between Chaplin and Keaton. . . is*

Mother.'"

Barry sensed where the conversation was leading and took a long slow slurp of his beer to buy himself time to think. "That's some of the Jabberwocky stuff I was telling you about," he burped. "Or it could be part of a poem or something?"

Directly below the verse, a comic drawing jumped out from the page. It was the profile of a grotesque face with huge bulging eye and long upturned chin.

Very Lennon, thought Barry.

Steve pointed at it. "Looks like Joe after a night on the piss," he laughed.

Joe was not amused. "Right, I've had enough. We're just wasting our time here," he said, picking up his car keys.

"No we're not Joe." Barry protested. "John says quite clearly that he stashed the banjo in one of their old haunts for safe keeping didn't he? All we have to do is find out which one."

Joe threw his keys back on the table. "Do you honestly expect me to believe something like that could still be hidden somewhere after all these years?"

Barry was quick to answer. "'Course it could. People do that. They hide stuff away, forget about it; years later someone else comes along and discovers it. That's what happens with memorabilia."

"But how can you be so certain John didn't go back and get it?" grilled Joe.

Barry provided him with a textbook answer. "'Cause if he had, it would be hanging up in a museum somewhere and we'd all know about it wouldn't we? Besides, when

Love Me Do hit the charts later that same year Lennon couldn't go anywhere without being mobbed, especially in Liverpool."

"Hang on a minute," said Steve, spotting a flaw in Barry's argument. "Aren't you forgetting something? What about Stuart? He could have picked it up for him?"

Barry smirked back at them. "No he couldn't. Look at the date on the letter. April 9th 1962. The day after that letter was written...Stuart Sutcliffe died."

Joe broke the uneasy silence. "So, if John was the only person who knew where the banjo was hidden…"

"And he's dead…?" added Steve.

"That's right," Barry concluded. "We must be the only people alive who know John's secret."

Joe and Steve glanced at one another with a look of realisation.

"Alright," Steve said, his voice adopting a serious businesslike tone, "if we help you to find the banjo, it's got to be a three way split when it's sold. Agreed?"

Barry spat in his palm and thrust it out for the brothers to shake. "Agreed."

"So, where do we start looking then?" Steve asked.

Er . . . Good question. The logistics of actually searching for the banjo had not even entered Barry's head so it came as a relief when the most sceptical of the trio offered up the first line of enquiry.

"What year did John and Stuart meet?" Joe asked.

The date tripped off Barry's tongue. "1957. They attended the same art college in Hope Street."

"Okay," Joe continued, "so if they met in 1957; and Stuart died in 1962, then that narrows the timescale down to around five years doesn't it?"

"Brilliant!" beamed Barry. "And if I draw up a list of the old haunts they hung out in between those years we can start looking can't we?" Barry jumped from his seat and hastily finished his pint. He wiped the foam from his mouth with the back of his hand. "Right," he said through a stifled burp, "I'm going to get off home and start working on that list." He snatched the letter from the table and slid it back into his jacket pocket. "God it's dead exciting this isn't it?" he warbled. "It's like that Da Vinci Code."

"Hey!" Steve called after him as Barry headed for the door. "This is just between the three of us? Not a word about it to anyone else. Do you understand?"

Barry zipped a finger and thumb slowly across his mouth. "My lips… are sealed." With that, he bounced out of the door and was gone.

Joe started laughing. "Did you hear him? The bloody DaVinci Code? What's he like eh?"

Steve cracked a smile. "Hey, I don't know what you're laughing at. This could be our ticket out of here. Tenerife here we come!"

Barry strutted along Mathew Street with a spring in his step. Tomorrow, the search for the holy grail of pop memorabilia would begin. With his head crammed with thoughts of the banjo and old Beatle haunts, he failed to notice the man in a Stetson following ten paces behind.

CHAPTER SEVEN

Travis rushed into the hotel room to find his wife lying asleep on the bed still dressed for dinner. Cheryl groaned and rubbed her Alice Cooper eyes. "I've been trying to call you. What time is it?"

"Sorry honey, battery's dead. It's nine-thirty." He plugged his lifeless cell phone into the charger, ran over to the bedside phone and punched in a number.

"Where the hell have you been?" she said, struggling to a sitting position.

Travis put a finger to his lips in a gesture for her to keep quiet. "Hi there, this is Travis Lawson. Would you put me through to Tony DeVito?"

"Will you please tell me what's going on?" demanded Cheryl.

Travis held his hand over the receiver while he waited. "I've just lucked into something real big that could make us a whole bunch of money. If I play this thing right I'll be able to pay off Bakula and tell DeVito where he can go shove his job."

DeVito's voice boomed down the line. "Travis? I wasn't expecting to hear from you so soon. What's up?"

"Nothin' Tony, everything's fine. Listen, I'll come straight to the point. How would you like to be the proud owner of the most important piece of pop memorabilia that ever existed? I'm talking about a banjo; a very *special* banjo."

DeVito laughed. "A banjo huh? Have you been at the duty frees?"

"Hell no. I'm sober as a judge and serious as a heart attack. You see Tony; this ain't no ordinary plain Jane banjo. This one belonged to John Lennon."

"What? The Beatle guy that went and got himself shot?" DeVito reached for the decanter and poured himself a drink.

"That's the guy. And get this; it was the first instrument he ever learned to play. It's worth a fortune Tony."

DeVito lit a cigar and took a sip from his glass. "Go on, I'm listening."

Travis drew a deep breath. "The seller wants five hundred thousand pounds - cash."

"Forget it!" DeVito spluttered. "Hell, I wouldn't pay that if the Lord himself used to own it. You go tell that seller of yours he can shove it up his ass …sideways!"

"Okay Tony, you're the boss. Just thought I'd let you have first shot at it that's all. I reckon he won't have much trouble finding himself another buyer. Hell, you'd have to be pretty dumb to turn your nose up at five million now wouldn't you? Sorry to disturb you. I'll catch up with you soon big fella. Bye for now." Travis ended the call and glanced down at his watch. "Ten, nine, eight…"

Cheryl glared at her husband suspiciously. "Just what the

hell are you up to?"

"All in good time honey. All in good time. Five, four, three…"

The phone rang out and Travis snatched it to his ear. "Hi Tony, forget something?" Travis gave Cheryl a knowing wink.

DeVito slid forward and hunched over his desk. "Five million you said. That's gotta be dollars right?"

"Pounds Tony; pounds," Travis oozed, sensing his boss was about to take the bait.

DeVito fell back in his chair. "Jeez," he gasped, "that's one hell of a lot of money. Are you absolutely sure about that?"

"'Course I am. That's what you're paying me for ain't it? Check out the Lennon piano that sold at Sotheby's for one and a half million in 2000 if you think I'm talkin' bullshit," Travis retorted, sounding slightly offended.

DeVito tapped 'John Lennon piano' into the Google search engine.

"Look Tony, you sent me all the way over here to buy memorabilia to sell back home didn't you and believe me; this is the holy grail of pop memorabilia."

DeVito smiled when the search results popped up. "Okay I'm listening. What's the deal?"

Travis took the bull by the horns and proceeded to spin a yarn Hans Christian Anderson would have dismissed as a fairytale. "The guy selling the banjo is up to his armpits in crocodiles and he's desperate to make a quick cash sale. No cheques, no bank drafts and no letters of credit. This guy's smart and don't plan on handing over a big slice of money to the taxman here."

"How do you know he's on the level?" DeVito quizzed.

"You just leave that to me. I got excellent contacts over here so I'll see to it that the banjo is fully authenticated before parting with any of your money. Believe me Tony, this is the biggest thing to come down the turnpike since they found that Egyptian fella's tomb."

DeVito did not need a calculator to figure out he stood to make millions on the deal if Travis could pull it off.

"Alright," he said firmly. "Go for it. I'll send Carl and Wayne over on the next flight with the cash."

Awkward. "Whoa, slow down Tony; I wouldn't do that. See, this seller's a nervous little weasel, a real panty waist. Your guys would scare the shit out of him and blow the whole deal. Besides, by the time they get here someone else will have beaten us to the draw. Better to wire the money to an account I have over here."

Travis gripped the phone and waited.

"Alright," DeVito drawled, "we'll do this your way. But a word of advice; if you get a sniff of anything suspicious, *anything at all*, you pull the deal. You got that?"

Travis's voice was reassuring. "Trust me Tony; I know what I'm doing."

"You'd better; 'cause your balls are riding on this. Make sure you keep me informed every step of the way."

"No problem Tony. I'll text you with those bank details first thing. Bye."

Travis replaced the receiver and sat on the edge of the bed. "God I'm good."

Cheryl's voice was pained. "What the hell is goin' on Travis?"

"Fix me a scotch and soda and I'll tell you all about it?"

Cheryl pulled her feet back into her high-heeled shoes and tottered reluctantly to the mini-bar on the other side of the room. "This here banjo you've promised DeVito; you are absolutely sure you can get a hold of it ain't you? I mean, you don't want to be disappointing him, this being your first assignment an' all."

Travis stood up and paced the room like a politician about to deliver a manifesto.

"Honey," he said, spinning on his heel, "when Neil Armstrong made that epic voyage and stepped off the Lunar Lander, was he *absolutely sure* he wasn't going to sink up to his ass in god damn moon dust?"

Cheryl swallowed hard and blinked back at her husband. "What?"

Travis reinforced his next line with the point of a finger. "Was Christopher Columbus *absolutely sure* he wasn't gonna fall off the edge of the world when he sailed out into the uncharted ocean?"

Cheryl felt her legs buckle and she leaned against the refrigerator to steady herself. "Oh my God," she said, her voice faltering. "What the hell have you done?"

Travis rushed over and grasped her by the shoulders. "Honey, if I can pull this off I'll be right back in the fast lane."

The devious glint in her husband eyes confirmed her worst fears. "Holy shit I knew it!" she squealed, shrugging him away. "DeVito will have you ended if you double-cross him; that's assumin' of course Bakula hasn't already killed you first!"

"Double-cross him? How can you say that? You don't even know what I got planned yet."

"And I don't wanna know you stupid son of a bitch!" she shrieked, tears welling up in her crystal blue eyes.

"Honey, just hear me out will you? All I have to do is find the banjo before someone else does and all our problems are over."

Cheryl sat back on the bed, her snuffles turning into hysterical laughter. "Find it for Pete's sake? Are you saying...?" She was now laughing so hard she could hardly speak. "Are you saying you *don't even know where the freakin' thing is*?"

Travis winced. "Well, er, sort of. See, I overheard this guy talking and... well, he's found this letter and.... ah shit honey, it gets real complicated and I'm too tired right now to explain all the details. The point is; DeVito won't know he's actually buying the banjo from me so I'll get to keep his money. And, with the twenty percent commission I'll get when he sells the damn thing, I will come out of this with well over a million bucks!"

"Bullshit!" Cheryl screamed. "He ain't that dumb."

Travis raised his voice. "As long as DeVito gets the banjo and makes his millions he will be as happy as a hog in slop."

Cheryl pulled a handkerchief from her bag and wiped the mascara from her eyes. "Alright smart ass; then tell me this," she snuffled. "If you're so sure about finding this thing, why bring DeVito into it at all? Why not simply sell it and keep all the profit for yourself?"

Travis paced the room. "Hell, do you think that ain't already crossed my mind? Trouble is it takes time to find the right buyer and with Danny Bakula baying for my blood; time is something I don't have on my side right now. No, the way I figure it; the sooner I get my hands on that banjo, the sooner I can use DeVito's cash to pay Bakula off. I mean, that is what you want ain't it?" Travis had struck a nerve.

"And what if you don't find it?" she said hesitantly. "What happens then?"

Travis sat on the bed next to her and brushed a stray lock of hair from her eyes. "Look sweetheart, if that happens I'll just give DeVito his money back and tell him the deal fell through; no harm done."

"All of it?"

"Every cent."

"Do you promise?"

"'Course I do. Hell, you don't think I want Carl and Wayne breathing down my neck too do you?" Travis wrapped his reassuring arms around Cheryl's shoulders and squeezed. "Now come on, what do you say we give it our best shot?"

Cheryl pushed him away. "What do you mean... *we*?"

* * *

The following morning was warm and the forecast of more sun had brought the rain hardy inhabitants of Liverpool out in their hordes. Sefton Park rang with the sound of yapping dogs, kids playing football and the feet of joggers pounding the footpaths. Barry strolled to the local bus stop with his head buried in a Beatles magazine happily munching his way through a large bag of crisps. Having arranged with Joe and Steve to start their search for the banjo at two o'clock, the day was full of excitement and promise.

Sitting in his hire car a hundred yards from the bus stop, Travis familiarised himself with the gadgets on the dashboard while Cheryl fixed her makeup. "I don't know why the hell I let you talk me into this?" she complained, thrusting the lipstick back into her bag.

Travis prodded a button on the built-in satellite navigation system. "Look, all you got to do is be friendly to the guy and find out what's in that letter of his."

Cheryl's brow furrowed. "How friendly?" she demanded.

"Well not *too* friendly. Just, you know, be nice." Travis looked through the windscreen and sat up when he recognised Barry's bulky frame ambling down the road. "Right, get ready honey. Here he comes now."

"Where?"

"Over there look; the guy wearing the cap."

Cheryl's mouth dropped open. "That mountain man is *him*! Christ, he looks like a god damn rain barrel. You must be crazy if you think I'm gonna get cosy with a slob like that. I ain't goin' through with it. Do you hear me? I ain't goin' through with it!" She brought her fist down on the dashboard to emphasise the point.

Travis leaned across her lap and grappled the passenger door handle. "Oh yes you are," he said, bundling his wife out of the car. "Texas gals ain't stuck together with spit. Hell, it's not as if I'm asking you to marry the guy."

Flicking back her hair, she shot Travis a glare that would have killed any other man at twenty paces. "And what if he's some kind of weirdo?" Cheryl hissed, as she watched Barry load his mouth with another handful of crisps.

Travis shook his head in disbelief. "Weirdo? What the hell are you talking about honey? The guy likes The

Beatles for Christ's sake."

Cheryl bent down and glared at Travis through the passenger window. "Yeah, so did the guy who shot John Lennon you dickhead."

"Look," said Travis casually, "I'm gonna be sitting right here keeping an eye on you so you ain't got nothing to worry about." He wafted her away with his hand. "Now go on, hurry up and get yourself over there."

Cheryl's powder pink jacket perfectly complemented her short denim skirt and calf-length boots and with sunglasses nestled on top of her carefully styled hair, she fixed her eyes on the target and strode towards the bus stop. Sidling up behind the unsuspecting tour guide she took a cigarette from her bag and made her move.

"Say mister, do you have a light?" Cheryl waited expectantly, the cigarette perched between perfectly painted nails.

Barry looked up from his magazine, his mouth bulging with crisps. "Sorry," he crunched, "I don't smoke."

Cheryl smiled and reunited the cigarette with its box. "What the hell," she said, letting out a delicate laugh. "I've been trying to give up anyway."

Now most red-blooded men in this situation would have jumped at the chance to make small talk with a beautiful woman but not Barry. He just acknowledged her with a polite nod and buried his nose back into his Beatles Monthly. Cheryl was nonplussed. This had never happened to her before. She looked over to Travis sitting in the car and shrugged her shoulders. He gesticulated wildly pointing at the item in Barry's hands. Cheryl finally got the message. "Say, what's that you're reading?"

Barry looked up again. "Oh, it's just a magazine" he said casually, "about The Beatles."

Cheryl grabbed his arm. "Well ain't that something. I just *love* The Beatles!"

Barry's eyes widened. The woman clinging to him was a Beatles fan and, as he now noticed, a very pretty one too. "Do you?" he said, unable to believe his luck.

She offered her hand. "I sure do. I'm Cheryl by the way."

Barry screwed up the empty crisp bag and buried it into his pocket. "Barry," he said, shaking it gently, "Barry Seddon."

Cheryl plucked a tissue from her bag and discreetly rubbed the greasy residue off her fingers.

"You're a Yank aren't you?" Barry said, through a cheesy grin.

She let out a small shriek. "A Yank? Man, you gotta be kidding!"

"Sorry," Barry faltered, "but I thought you were American."

"Well, you got the American part right but I'm from the Southern United States, you know, the Great State of Texas."

"Oh," said Barry, slightly confused. "What's the difference?"

"What's the diff...? Hell, didn't you learn anything in school? The Yanks are those thieving carpetbaggers from the Northern USA." *Is this guy taking the piss?*

Barry looked deflated. "Sorry, no offence; I wasn't in school that much." He opened up his magazine again and lowered his eyes.

Fearing she was about to lose his attention, Cheryl

gently pulled the magazine down and blinked her spidery lashes at him. "No, me neither," she said in a soft voice.

Reassured that he had not offended her; Barry cracked a smile. "Actually, I suppose calling you a Yank is a bit like calling a 'Red' a 'Blue Nose'," he said thoughtfully.

"A what?"

"Oh, it's a football thing," Barry replied. "You see, we have two football teams in this city, Liverpool and Everton. Liverpool are red and Everton are blue. I'm a red. We refer to the Evertonians as Blue Noses."

"Is that so? Well I must remember never to call you a Blue Nose then mustn't I?" The ice now broken, Barry and his new friend burst out laughing.

Watching from the car, Travis felt a gnawing twinge in the pit of his stomach, an uneasy churning sensation he had not felt since high school eating away at his hard outer shell like rusticles on a sunken shipwreck. As he witnessed his wife giggling and flirting with this complete stranger, the pangs of jealousy wracking his body were an uncomfortable reminder of the lengths he was prepared to go to make a fast buck. He thought of something else to take his mind off it. *Danny Bakula.*

Barry looked at Cheryl properly for the first time. She was a stunner alright.

Late thirties perhaps? He looked at her left hand. *Good. No ring.* He curled his Beatles Monthly into a tight tube and shoved it into his pocket. "Are you going into town?" he enquired politely.

Cheryl had not noticed the bottle green bus decelerating at the bus stop and it now obscured her view of Travis across the road. Biting the bullet, Cheryl made the decision she knew her husband would want her to make.

"I guess I am," she said sweetly.

Travis watched the bus move off fully expecting to see his wife standing in its wake but she was gone. *That's my girl.* Before the bus had a chance to disappear around the corner, Travis fired up the engine, swiped at the indicator stalk and screeched off in hot pursuit.

Cheryl dug deep in her pocket and picked out enough loose change to pay for her fare into the city centre. She then followed Barry to the back of the bus.

"Do you mind if I sit with you?" she said, pointing to the window seat next to him. "I hate riding alone."

Barry sucked himself back into the seat. "Be my guest."

Cheryl squeezed past his knees and lowered herself daintily onto the green leatherette.

"So, what brings you to Liverpool then?" he probed.

"Oh, er, I've had a pen pal here since I was a kid and, er, every couple of years we visit one another. This year it's my turn."

"I see. So where is she today? That's if your pen pal is a 'she'," Barry laughed, nervously.

"Oh she's working so I decided to take a trip into town and do some shopping. And what about you; what's your reason for being alive?"

"I'm a Beatles tour guide, on the Magical Mystery Tour bus," he announced proudly. "We take tourists around the city and show them where it all began for the Fab Four."

"Wow, is that so? I remember watching that film when I was a kid. Couldn't make head nor tale of the damn thing."

After the success of the critically acclaimed Beatle films, 'A Hard Day's Night' and 'Help', the third celluloid offering from the Fab Four had everyone's expectations running high. 'Magical Mystery Tour' was the first major project The Beatles had undertaken since the death of manager Brian Epstein a few months earlier but, when the movie was broadcast on British TV on Boxing Day 1967, the critics and public alike slated it. Designed as a madcap psychedelic romp, the multi-coloured fifty minute home movie fell flat when it was broadcast in black and white. So bad were the reviews in fact, Paul McCartney felt obliged to make a public apology. Over time, critics warmed to the originality and inventiveness of the film and no one argues that the songs featured in it are amongst some of the groups finest.

"So what was it all about anyway?" Cheryl asked. She was to regret opening her mouth.

CHAPTER EIGHT

Within the densely packed battalions of terraced houses lining the streets of Dingle, the working class suburb of Liverpool in which Ringo Starr once lived; one house still had its curtains closed to the world. Filtering through the window of the front bedroom the sound of a car horn infiltrated the deep slumber of a man hung over from the night before. Steve Benson's eyes flickered open and his irises pulled painfully as the light struck them. This, accompanied by a dull thud at the base of his skull, made for a less than ideal start to the day. The impatient owner of the car horn shouted through the letterbox. "Steve! Get up you lazy bastard!"

The bedroom resembled a changing room in a cheap department store. Ladies clothes had been flung over the back of a wicker chair and a wardrobe door hung open to reveal racks of shirts and neatly folded jeans. Over the bed hung the pungent smell of halitosis and cheap perfume. The duvet wriggled and a woman's head, complete with smudged lipstick and tousled peroxide hair, emerged like a monster from the deep. "Who the hell's making all that noise at this time of the morning?" she groaned.

Steve's gluey eyes slowly focused in on the apparition lying next to him and the events of the previous evening came flooding back. *Oh Christ.* He sat bolt upright, threw back the covers and vaulted out of bed. "Quick, you'll have to get up. It's my brother. He's giving me a lift into work."

The brassy blonde swung her corned beef legs to the floor and bent down to collect her scattered underwear. "Thank God for that. For a minute there I thought it might have been my bloody husband."

Steve averted his eyes to avoid peering into the crevice of the woman's thonged rump as she reached down to pick up her bra. "Husband? You never said you were married!"

"You never asked," she replied, matter of factly. She lay back on the bed and shoehorned herself into a tight black pencil skirt then stood side on to the mirror to admire the result. Another series of loud thumps on the front door ricocheted off Steve's fragile ear drums. "Come on love, hurry up or he'll have the door off the bloody hinges." Hurriedly he picked up her coat, dumped it on her shoulders, threw back the curtains and banged on the window. Joe stared up at him and jabbed an impatient finger at his watch before wandering back towards his car.

Steve turned to his one-night stand and wafted a ten pound note in her face. "Here, this should cover it."

The woman glared at the money and slapped him hard around the face. "What kind of a girl do you think I am?" she protested.

Steve rubbed his jaw. "It's for a taxi!"

"Oh sorry," she said, giggling with embarrassment. "I thought you might have thought I was…well you know…"

"Whatever." He pushed the money into her hand,

grabbed his jacket and bundled her down the squeaky staircase.

"You couldn't give me a lift could you love?" she panted, as Steve slammed the front door behind them. He avoided making eye contact and checked his watch.

"Which way are you going?" he asked.

"Oh just back into town."

"Ah, wouldn't you know it eh? We're going the other way. Sorry love." He ran across to Joe's revving car and jumped into the passenger seat.

"Hey! What about me?" she shouted after him.

"Go down to the bottom of this road and take a right. There's a taxi rank next to the chip shop. See ya!"

The window slid to a close and the car pulled away from the kerb. Joe couldn't help sniggering as he watched his brother's most recent conquest wobbling down the street on white stiletto heels. "Who's the one-woman hen night?"

"I had to take one for the team last night," Steve replied in a detached tone. "I didn't catch her name."

"I've had to get Frank to open up for us again you know," said Joe, as the car sped off towards town and The Beatles Store. "Why can't you just go home after work instead of going out on the piss all night?"

"Don't start Joe, my head's banging enough as it is," Steve complained. "Stop off at Bridy's Café will you. I might feel better when I've had a bite to eat."

* * *

Barry was in his element. Finally, he had met someone with the same interests. "But it's like Lennon said, 'Pete Best was a great drummer, but Ringo was a great Beatle'."

Cheryl tried to break into the one-sided conversation. "Say Barry, speaking of John Lennon?"

"And everybody at the Cavern hated Ringo when Pete Best got the chop you know. There were fights, riots and everything."

"Really?" said Cheryl, through a stifled yawn.

"God, I wish I'd been around to see them playing at The Cavern," said Barry dreamily. "Hey, did you know it used to be a Jazz club? Yeah, back in the late fifties…"

Cheryl leant her head against the vibrating window of the bus and watched the leafy avenues merge into one another as Barry rambled on and on.

Three cars behind, Travis had the bus firmly in his sights and the signs for Albert Dock flashing past told him it was nearing its destination.

"…But Paul wasn't dead," laughed Barry, "someone just started that rumour because he wasn't wearing any shoes on the cover of Abbey Road. Hey, side two of that's brilliant isn't it? Did you know that it was made up from different bits of old songs that The Beatles never finished? Yeah, and Golden Slumbers is actually a nursery rhyme. Well, the words are. Paul wrote the music for that at his dad's house over on the Wirral…"

* * *

Sid manoeuvred the Magical Mystery Tour bus around the potholes of Regent Road, past Stanley Dock and over the iron bridge into the heart of docklands Liverpool. Up a cobbled side street, wedged between a scrap yard and timber merchants, was Bridy's Café; clean, neat and honest. Inside, the homely ruddy-faced proprietor greeted and served her customers as if they were family.

"Morning Sid, the usual is it?" Bridy gave him a welcoming smile and rooted in the front pockets of her gingham apron for a notepad and pencil.

"Yeah, go on," he said, his eyes still fixed on a scantily clad woman adorning the centrefold of a tabloid rag.

"No Barry today?" enquired Bridy.

"Not yet thank God."

Bridy leaned over the red Formica counter and prodded a finger at the newspaper. "You two haven't had another row have you?"

Sid's dismissive grunt and irritable shake of the newspaper gave Bridy her answer.

"Go on. What's he done this time?"

Sid folded his newspaper and looked up. "On the way home after work yesterday, there I was just trying to give him some friendly advice and he bit my bloody head off."

Bridy cracked an egg into a pan and whisked it firmly with a fork. "You haven't been having a go at him again about getting a girlfriend have you?"

Whether it was female intuition or just downright nosiness, Bridy's knack of sussing out a situation always caught Sid off guard. *How could she know that?*

"Oh don't look so surprised Sid. I get to hear all the gossip in here. Look, I know you mean well, but Barry's a grown man. You can't keep telling him what to do with his life. He's got to make his own way in the world."

Sid looked over his shoulder at the other customers and lowered his voice.

"Yeah, but he doesn't seem interested in women. Don't you think that's a bit odd?" Sid gestured for Bridy to move in closer. "You don't think he might be licking the other side of the stamp do you?" he whispered in her ear.

"What? Gay?" Bridy laughed.

"Sshh...." Sid cringed, checking to see no one was listening.

"Well what if he is?" she said turning the eggs out onto a plate. "As long as he's happy why should you care?"

"Because Bridy," said Sid through clenched teeth, "I'm with him all day, every day and people might start thinking that we are... that I'm his..."

Bridy pulled her head back sharply. "You're his boyfriend?"

Several lorry drivers glanced over and looked Sid up and down. "Thanks for that Bridy," he hissed.

"Oh stop being paranoid. Barry's not gay. He just hasn't found the right woman yet that's all. Not all fellas are like you you know."

"And what's that supposed to mean?" challenged Sid.

"Nothing. See, there you go again, jumping to all the wrong conclusions. You just get on with your own life and let Barry get on with his."

* * *

"... So then John said .... 'Turn left at Greenland!'." Barry slapped his hand down on the back of Cheryl's seat and roared with laughter.

"Oh my," said Cheryl checking her watch discreetly, "that's so witty ain't it?"

"Hey, I've just had an idea," said Barry excitedly. "Seeing as you like The Beatles so much, why don't you come on a tour with me?"

Cheryl squirmed uncomfortably. "Hmm, well I don't know about that. See I've got quite a bit of shopping to do and…"

"Ah come on Cheryl, you'll really enjoy it, I know you will."

Barry's cheery face beaming back at her made it difficult for her to refuse. Besides, she had not managed to get a word out of him about the letter or the banjo.

"Hmm, well I suppose I could use a little fun right now. Okay, you got me," she said chirpily, "where do I sign on?"

The bus came to a stop outside Liverpool One, the sleek shopping quarter of the city, and Barry stood up to let Cheryl off. He pointed to the opposite side of the road. "The pickup point is over there, right outside the Albert Dock. Just look for the Magical Mystery Tour bus, you can't miss it."

"Great," she said squeezing past. "I'll see you there at eleven then."

Cheryl disembarked and the bus moved off. From the back window she saw Barry grinning at her and she afforded him a polite wave. A rental car screeched up alongside and the passenger door swung open. Travis leant across. "Well honey, how did it go?"

Cheryl climbed in and fastened her seatbelt roughly. She took out a cigarette. "Give me a god damn light."

Travis dutifully flicked at his Zippo and held it out for her. He could not fail to notice Cheryl's fingers trembling as she probed the flame with her cigarette; a sure sign she was not in the best of moods.

"Well? Did he say anything or what?"

Cheryl took a long deep draw and held the smoke down to achieve the maximum nicotine hit. She looked at Travis with contempt before blowing the smoke slowly into his face. "Sure he did. Did you know that Ringo never actually played drums on the seven-inch version of Love Me Do? No, he only played on the album version. And it was Paul McCartney, *not John Lennon*, who first used tape loops as an art form."

"No shit? Well ain't that just fascinating. Now, did he say anything, *anything at all*, about the letter or the banjo?"

Cheryl avoided eye contact. "No."

Travis's irritation was beginning to get the better of him. "Could you be a little more specific?"

"Sure. He didn't say a freakin' thing about the letter or the banjo. Christ, I never got the chance to ask him nuthin'. The guy just wouldn't shut up!"

Travis smashed his hands down on the steering wheel. "Damn it! What the hell are we gonna do now?"

"Relax will you; I'm meeting him again at eleven o'clock. He's taking me on a freakin' guided tour to show me where The Beatles used to play."

"He's what?"

"Oh, didn't I tell you?" she said, through a plume of smoke. "He's a Beatles tour guide for Christ's sake."

Travis's face lit up and he flashed a white smile. "A Beatles tour guide? Why that's just perfect!"

Cheryl grabbed his arm. "No Travis, it ain't. What if Barry starts to get the wrong idea?"

"Oh, so his name's Barry is it? You see, he did tell you

something after all. Look honey, if he's a tour guide he'll be expecting you to be asking lots of questions won't he? Just use some of that Southern Belle charm of yours, that'll get him talking."

He leaned across and opened the passenger door. "Go grab yourself a coffee or something," he said, stuffing a ten pound note into her hand. "I'll catch up with you later."

"Wait a minute; you ain't just gonna leave me here all alone are you?"

"Afraid so honey. While you're on the tour with your new friend, I'm gonna see what I can find out about that banjo. Give me a call when the tour's over and I'll come and pick you up."

Cheryl pulled the collar of her jacket up around her neck as she watched Travis's car speed off. *Asshole.*

* * *

Barry waded through the door of Bridy's café with the poise and swagger of a gunslinger. Joining Sid at the counter he pushed back his cap. "Sausage butty please Bridy."

With an expert stab of a fork, Bridy hooked three fat sausages from the frying pan and piled them between two slices of buttered bread. She handed the sandwich to Barry. "You look pleased with yourself love. Have you won the lottery or something?"

Barry waited until Sid had raised his steaming mug of tea to his lips before delivering the killer line. "I think I've found myself a girlfriend."

Like a spouting gargoyle, Sid sprayed the counter with

tea before coughing his disbelief into his newspaper.

Bridy shot Sid an accusing glance. "Good for you love. I'm very pleased for you."

Barry and Sid adjourned to a table and Barry filled his colleague in with the details of his brief encounter.

Sid scratched his head. "So let me get this straight. You're saying that this beautiful American bird just walked over to you at the bus stop and started chatting you up?"

"Well, I wouldn't have put it quite like that," chewed Barry, his hamster cheeks bulging with food, "but yeah, I suppose she did." He plopped a third lump of sugar into his mug of tea and slurped the spillage from the saucer.

Sid rubbed his chin and arched an eyebrow. "Did she seem, you know . . . normal?"

Barry stared at him over his round rimmed glasses. "And what's that supposed to mean?"

"Nothing," replied Sid, as he watched Barry stab a sausage onto a fork and shovel it sideways into his face. "So she, er, she wasn't carrying a white stick or anything?" Sid began to laugh.

"Oh, I get it," Barry gagged, wiping his greasy mouth with the cuff of his sweatshirt. "You don't think someone like Cheryl could be interested in a person like me. Is that it?"

Sid shook his head. "To be perfectly honest with you, no I don't. Alright, so she might have talked to you at the bus stop. So what? She was probably just being polite."

Barry drained the last of the tea from his cup and slammed it noisily on the table. "Do you want to put your money where your mouth is?"

Sid looked surprised. His colleague was rarely this

forthright. "A bet do you mean? No, I wouldn't want to take your money off you mate."

Barry reached into his pocket and slapped a note onto the table. "Come on, I bet you twenty quid that everything I've told you is true."

Sid stared at the money. "Alright you're on!" He threw a twenty pound note on top of Barry's and rubbed his hands together excitedly. "So how are you going to prove it then?"

"Easy, I'm going to introduce you to her. She's coming on a tour with me."

Over at the counter, Joe and Steve were collecting their breakfast orders to take away. Sid spotted them and shouted across. "Hey lads! How would you like to make some easy money?"

* * *

Barry looked out of the window of the Magical Mystery Tour bus and gripped the handrail with unnecessary force. The loss of twenty pounds he could bare; giving Sid a reason to ridicule him for the foreseeable future, he could not.

Steve was as curious as Sid when the driver told him about Barry's alleged new girlfriend and he too could not resist taking a twenty pound punt on the chance that the tour guide was making the whole thing up.

"Have that money ready Joe!" shouted Sid, as he geared down for the entrance to the Albert Dock. Although anxious to get into work, Joe was persuaded to join them on the bus and hold on to the bet money. He looked down the aisle at Barry fidgeting nervously, his nose pressed up against the window. "You and Sid shouldn't be taking advantage of him like this you know."

"Couldn't resist it bro," Steve smiled back.

Joe looked at his younger sibling disdainfully.

"Ah come on Joe, it's only a few quid."

"And that makes it right does it?" he reprimanded.

The bus lurched to a stop outside the pickup point and Sid cut the engine. "Here we go lads," he announced. "It's show time!"

The four men jumped off the bus and eagerly scanned the waiting crowd of tourists. The queue was full; bursting with expectant punters of all nationalities. Some fans wore Beatles costumes while others stepped out in a more generic sixties style. With digital cameras and camcorders at the ready they were set to capture all things magical and mysterious.

"Well come on then Barry. Can you see this new girlfriend of yours or what?" Steve cackled.

"Not yet, no," Barry replied subdued, his words peppered with doubt.

Sid patted Barry on the back. "That's because she's just a figment of your imagination. Go on, admit it," he laughed.

Barry stood up on tiptoes. "Wait a minute. I think; yeah, here she comes now!" he said, his voice gaining an octave. Sid and Steve fell about laughing when they saw a huge ball of a woman ambling towards them, smiling as she waved her ticket in the air.

"Bloody hell Barry," spluttered Sid, "are you taking the piss? You said she was attractive and sophisticated. That's what he said, wasn't it Ste'?"

Steve wiped a tear from his eye and nodded. "Yep, that's what you said. If nothing else, you're in breach of the trades description act."

Feeling a snigger brewing, Joe bit into his lip in an attempt to kill it at birth.

Sid thrust out an open palm. "Come on Joe, we win. Hand the winnings over."

Barry meanwhile, oblivious to Sid and Steve's misguided conclusion, continued to wave at his Texan beauty further down the queue. When she reached him she put a friendly hand on his shoulder. "Phew, I made it!" she said, catching her breath.

Barry spun around to face his stunned companions. "Lads, I'd like you to meet Cheryl. Cheryl, these are my mates, Steve, Joe and Sid."

She held out a well-manicured hand and shook each of theirs in turn. "Nice to meet y'all guys," she said in her softly lilting Texan accent. Her arm linked Barry's. "Mister Tour Guide here has promised to show me a really good time. Ain't that right Barry?"

"Has he now," Steve cursed under his breath.

Sid just stood there, his mouth hanging open like a dead fish as he watched his fat friend cuddling up to his new girlfriend. Cheryl smiled at her starry-eyed tour guide and snuggled in closer. "It is still okay for me to ride up front with you ain't it Barry?"

"Wouldn't have it any other way," he replied. With a chivalrous swoop of his arm he gestured for Cheryl to climb aboard. As she mounted the steps, he whispered to Steve and Joe. "I'll meet you back at the store at two o'clock." He turned to his dumbstruck colleague. "Come on Sid, we don't want to keep the lady waiting do we?"

Sid boarded the bus, climbed into his seat and started the engine.

"Hold on Barry," said Joe, as the tour guide turned to follow Sid onto the bus. "I think this belongs to you." Joe stuffed the sixty pounds bet money into Barry's top pocket and patted it gently. "Well played mate."

As Steve watched the bus pulling away, Joe thrust a bunch of keys into his brother's hand. "I'll see you later."

"Later? Where are you off to?"

"I'm going to the store to do a couple of hours work before Barry drags us off on some daft treasure hunt. You're walking back to Bridy's to pick up the car."

CHAPTER NINE

Research, research, research. That is what separates the wheat from the chaff, the quartz from the diamonds and the winners from the losers. Back in Coopersville, Travis had learned this lesson the hard way and he had no intention of making the same mistake again. He knew that if he was to come into contact with Julia's banjo he would have to recognise it as the real McCoy. The Beatles Story, a museum packed with artefacts and memorabilia, was the perfect place to begin.

Travis meandered through its maze of narrow corridors which were lined with brightly lit display cases; all laid out in a chronology of key events that shaped the lives of the Fab Four. At different points, the corridors opened out into feature areas; the interior of the Yellow Submarine, a favourite with young children who chimped around pushing brightly coloured buttons which let out satisfying honks and hoots. Further along, a scene from the claustrophobic Cavern Club, its brick arches and cosy nooks reverberating to the pulsing sound of Mersey Beat. Travis eventually came across a white baby grand piano standing on a raised plinth, cordoned off by a crimson rope. Printed in a ghostly ethereal font on the surrounding walls were the words to Lennon's most famous song, 'Imagine'.

Travis noticed the curator of the museum walking out of an office. "Excuse me mam," he said, doffing his hat. "Does this museum of yours happen to have any information about the banjo John Lennon's mom taught him to play when he was a kid?"

The curator smiled. "Certainly; please follow me."

She led him back towards the main entrance and stopped in front of a tall glass display case. Inside, song sheets, photographs, letters and other pieces of memorabilia were arranged around the main item. "Is this what you're looking for?" she asked.

Travis looked up and a chill coursed through his veins. The instrument was beautiful, its glistening mother of pearl inlay contrasting sharply with the deep rich tones of its rosewood veneer. Below it, printed on a piece of small white card were the words, 'Julia Lennon's Banjo'.

Travis fought hard not to show the curator the bottom had just fallen out of his world. *How could that dip-shit Beatle guy get it so wrong?*

"But I thought this thing was supposed to be missing?" he said, his voice quivering like a kid who had just been denied a candy bar.

"It is," she said, "this is only a replica. But, based on descriptions we've managed to acquire from John's family, we're confident it's an accurate representation."

Travis looked up, puckered his lips and kissed the air. "Thank you baby Jesus; thank you."

She took a step back. "I beg your pardon?"

"Sorry mam; just a little overwhelmed that's all."

"Right, well, I'll leave you to admire?" The curator

scurried back down the corridor glancing over her shoulder as the mad cowboy began taking photographs of the banjo from all angles.

* * *

Each Beatle home had been visited, each venue explored. Cheryl had to hand it to the guy; Barry certainly knew his stuff. His encyclopaedic mind had captivated the bus full of enthusiasts for over two hours and at the end of the tour he was treated to a rapturous round of applause. But she still hadn't got what she came for so when Barry invited her for a drink at The Cavern she did not hesitate in accepting.

He returned from the bar and put two glasses down on the table. "Sorry, they didn't have any iced tea," he said, apologetically.

Cheryl raised the glass to her lips and sipped politely. "That's okay. Coke's just fine."

"So, which part of the tour did you like the best?" Barry asked.

Cheryl thought for a moment. "I suppose seeing where they all lived when they were kids; especially John Lennon. I didn't realise his childhood home was so . . ."

"What, posh?"

Cheryl laughed. "Yeah, he wasn't a working class hero at all was he?"

Unlike the other members of the band who were city kids living in council houses, Lennon was a well-heeled suburban boy by comparison. He lived with his Aunt Mimi in a neat semi-detached house in the affluent area of Woolton, situated on the outskirts of Liverpool.

Cheryl, having manoeuvred the conversation onto the subject of John Lennon, seized the moment and began her interrogation. But she would have to tread carefully. After listening to Barry's skilful banter on the tour she realised he was no fool. The information in his head would have to be plucked like seeds from a pomegranate with pinpoint precision if his suspicions were not to be raised.

"So, let me in on the skinny Barry. Just how did John Lennon get into music? I guess he started off on guitar, right?"

"It wasn't the first thing he learned to play."

"Really? What was it then?"

"Have a guess," Barry teased.

Cheryl bit her tongue. She was in no mood to play games but what choice did she have? She leaned her head to the side and placed a finger to the corner of her mouth. "Okay, I guess it was...a harmonica!"

"Not even close." Barry gloated. "You're not gonna believe this but..."

Sid appeared from nowhere and pulled up a chair. "Ah, so this is where you've been hiding. Don't mind if I join you do you?"

Yes I do you ignorant ass wipe, thought Cheryl, the moment now lost.

"Get us a drink will you Barry; I'm skint," said the bus driver, as he made himself comfortable.

"Skint?" Cheryl enquired.

"It means he's got no money," Barry explained.

"Yeah, I lost it on a bet didn't I Barry," said Sid, with a mischievous glint in his eye. "You see love, I was in the café this morning having breakfast when..."

Barry sprang up from his chair like a jack in the box. "A pint of bitter then is it Sid?"

"Yeah. Oh, and a packet of cheese and onion. Don't worry; I'll keep your lady friend amused while you're at the bar."

As soon as Barry was out of sight, Sid moved in closer.

"So, Barry tells me you met him at the bus stop?"

"That's right," Cheryl replied, keeping her response to a minimum.

"Look, don't take this the wrong way love, but I've known Barry for years and he's not really your type. Don't get me wrong, he's a lovely bloke alright, but you strike me as the sort of woman who needs a man with a bit more… experience."

Oh God, I think I'm going to be sick. "I see," said Cheryl, folding her arms. "Someone like you I suppose?"

"Got it in one." Sid replied, checking over his shoulder to ensure Barry was still out of earshot. "So, now that we've got the formalities out of the way, how do you fancy coming on a private tour; just you and me? I'll make it worth your while." He winked and placed a wandering hand on her thigh, his deluded smirk worthy of first prize in a gurning competition.

Cheryl smiled back at him, casually lifted her drink and poured it over his head. Sid leapt up, yanked the shirt from his baggy corduroy trousers and shook out the ice cubes that had fallen inside the open neck. "Jesus Christ! What the hell was that for?"

Cheryl stood up and eyeballed him. "I wouldn't go out with a greaseball like you if you were the last man on God's green Earth. Tell Barry thanks for the tour." She picked up her bag, slung it over her shoulder and stormed out.

* * *

The visit to The Beatles Story had gone better than expected and with a cell phone full of images, Travis now knew what the elusive pop relic looked like. But he had one small problem to overcome before he could search for it. DeVito had sent him over to attend The Beatles Convention and was expecting Travis to bring back a haul of memorabilia, *including* the banjo he had promised him the night before. There was only one guy in town up to the task of acquiring all the memorabilia he needed and that was Billy Sheridan. Travis and Billy had crossed paths a few years earlier in a Manchester sale room. A collection of Georgian Toby Jugs had caught Travis's eye but after a hard fought battle he lost out to another buyer. Sheridan, who had witnessed the whole thing, knew a kindred spirit when he saw one and when Travis adjourned to the refreshment area to lick his wounds Billy Sheridan was hot on his heels. Business cards were exchanged and within a few days Travis Lawson was the recipient of six Toby Jugs at a very reasonable price. Funny, they bore a remarkable resemblance to the sale room collection; but Travis asked no questions. He made a healthy profit offloading them to a New York dealer and on subsequent visits to Liverpool, Travis made sure Billy's establishment was his first port of call. With renewed confidence and fire in his belly, Travis marched along Upper Parliament Street keeping his eyes peeled for Billy's shop, 'Seconds Out.'

The window display boasted an eclectic feast of desirable

second hand items; satellite navigation systems, televisions, electric guitars; everything bought and sold for hard cash. Billy leaned back in his shoddy leather chair and rested his muddy trainer-clad feet on the counter. At forty-two years old, his thin face bore the marks of a difficult life. A white scar underscored his left eye and his high sultana cheeks and thin nose served to convey the furtive, cunning nature of a small rodent. He sank his yellow teeth into a cheeseburger as he watched his young apprentice sort through some of their latest acquisitions.

Franny, a nervous youth with an irritating compulsion to blink before speaking, had been taken under Sheridan's wing after his bungled attempt to rob the shop a few months earlier. Billy had opened up early one morning to discover a pair of legs hanging out of the toilet window. Scurrying outside to the yard, he found the terrified sixteen-year-old wedged fast still clinging to a bag full of swag.

After giving Franny the kicking of his life, Billy treated him to a hot brew and a piece of toast. He saw in Franny a boy with a similar philosophy to his own, a boy he could train and mould to his own design in the same way Fagin trained the Artful Dodger.

Billy observed Franny with a critical eye as he pondered over which items he should display in the shop window. Eventually, he chose a laptop computer.

"Don't put that in the window you tit!" Billy scolded. "It was only robbed last night; it's hotter than my ring piece after a Vindaloo."

"Where shall I put it then?" blinked Franny nervously.

"Do you really want me to answer that? Go and make me a brew; and take that thing with you!"

Billy shook his head and consoled himself with a soggy chip dripping with tomato sauce. Settling back, he pulled his hood over his eyes and prepared to take a nap. By the time Travis entered the shop Billy was fast asleep, snoring and twitching like an overfed bloodhound. Travis smiled, sneaked over to the slumbering wide boy and knocked his feet off the counter.

"It wasn't me; I was nowhere near the place…" Sheridan bleated, as he was jolted rudely from his bad dream and into consciousness. He took a moment to pull his vision into focus and sat up.

Travis smirked at his old acquaintance. "Howdy, Billy boy. Still up to no good?"

Billy leapt from his resting place and patted Travis on the back. "Bloody hell, if it isn't the Lone Ranger. How are you mate? When did you ride into town?"

"Yesterday." Travis replied, eyeing up the merchandise lining the shelves.

Billy joined him out front and put a friendly hand on his shoulder. "So how's business?"

"It's been better."

"I see, like that is it? So what brings you into my humble establishment this time?"

Travis took down an electric guitar hanging on the wall and checked the name plate. "Beatles memorabilia."

"But you usually buy at the convention don't you?"

"Yeah, but something important has come up and I ain't got time to go rooting around like I'd normally do."

Billy narrowed his weasel eyes and stroked his tapering chin. "I see. And you want me to source a few nice items for you. Is that it?"

"That's right, but they gotta be good. Not like this piece of crap." Travis put down the guitar and wiped his hands on his jacket.

Billy held out his arms as if to embrace him. "Travis, have I ever let you down?"

"Nope, can't say you have Billy. That's why I'll be counting on you to come up with the goods."

"No problem, but I'll need some cash up front."

Travis shook his hand firmly. "I knew I could rely on you Billy boy." He pulled a pen and a scrap of paper from his back pocket and began writing. "Now then, here's a list of the type of things I'm looking for."

* * *

Standing on the corner of Mathew Street, Cheryl clicked her nails over her cell phone and wondered how she was going to break the bad news to Travis. *If only that Sid asshole hadn't burst in and messed things up, Barry would be singing like a canary by now.*

"Cheryl!"

Cheryl spun around and saw a red-faced Barry wheezing towards her, the armpits of his shirt dark with sweat. She quickly slipped the phone into her bag and walked back down the street to meet him.

"Where are you going? I thought you were staying for a drink?" he asked, gasping for breath.

"I was, 'til that creepy friend of yours started slithering all over me like a damn rattlesnake. He's lucky he ain't wearing his balls as earrings."

"With a face like his they'd probably suit him. What

d'you reckon?" Barry joked.

Cheryl cracked a smile.

"Look, do you see that pub over there?" Barry pointed at The Grapes across the road.

"Yeah. What about it."

"Come on, I'll show you. There's something in there no true Beatles fan would want to miss."

Barry led her into the welcoming atmosphere of Liverpool's most famous pub. After ordering drinks he pointed to a photograph hanging on the wall above a wooden bench seat. Taken circa 1962, the photo was of four young leather-clad Beatles sitting on, what appeared to be, the very same seat.

"Well, what do you think?" said Barry with pride, gesturing for Cheryl to sit down.

Cheryl studied the photograph in more detail. "Wait a minute, how can you be so sure this picture was taken here? All the pubs in Liverpool must have old seats like this."

"Because," Barry argued, "a few years ago, when the builders were taking down a false ceiling, the wallpaper you can see in the photograph was still up there." Barry pointed up towards the ceiling. "Look, there it is."

Cheryl looked up and saw a metre thick strip of the original 1950s paper clinging to the upper part of the walls. Her eyes flitted from its dirty orange pattern back to the photograph.

"Wow, I see what you mean." She looked up at the wall again. "But why is it covered with Plexiglas?"

"To protect it," said Barry. "After the building work was finished and the pub reopened, the fans started peeling it off to take home as a souvenir."

Cheryl seemed genuinely impressed. She sat back and stretched her arms out along the back of the seat. "I guess this must be a very special place for someone like you then huh?" she mused.

Barry nodded and took a sip from his glass. "Don't laugh, but sometimes after work I'll sit here, close my eyes and imagine that The Beatles are sitting right beside me."

"Hah, now I can see why you're a tour guide," she laughed. "You really live the part don't you?"

Barry's eyes were drawn back to the photograph, his face oozing with emotion. "God Cheryl," he said dreamily, "I wish I'd been there. Hey," he suddenly perked up, "I'll bet you'll never guess why The Beatles sat in this particular seat?"

Cheryl did not bother to answer; she knew he was going to tell her anyway. He pointed down a tiny corridor which led to the ladies toilets. "Back in the 60s, all the office girls would come in here after work and get changed in the toilets before going down to The Cavern."

"Ah, I get it," said Cheryl, "and from here the boys had a perfect view of all the pretty girls going in and out."

"Exactly!"

Cheryl took a sip of her cola and shivered a little inside. Barry's uncanny ability to bring the past back to life was impressive and before she knew it she was listening to his life story.

"But when mum died, my two step-sisters put the family home up for sale."

Cheryl looked shocked. "What; even though you were still living in it?"

"I can't say I blame them really. They were both married and had already left home. Anyway, with my share of the money I was able to buy a little place of my own."

"And what about your dad?"

"Which one? My real dad died when I was nine; an accident at work. And my step-dad, well, the less said about him the better."

"You two didn't get along then huh?"

Barry showed no hesitation. "Hated him. He only married mum to get his hands on dad's insurance money."

"But surely your mom must have suspected…"

"It wasn't as simple as that," he interrupted. "Eighteen months after dad died, mum told me she was getting married again; said a boy of my age needed a father. A couple of weeks later she got wed and, two months after that, my sister was born."

"Ah, now I see what you're getting at."

"Yeah, and in those days it was still frowned upon to have kids out of wedlock so I don't think she felt she had much choice. It was only when the pig moved in with us that we both realised what he was really like. He was a drunk you see, and violent with it. I had to spend most of my teens hiding up in my bedroom to keep out of his way."

"Poor kid. And there was no one in the family you could turn to for help?"

"Mum wouldn't let us breathe a word to anyone. She said it would only make things worse although I think my Auntie Pauline might have known what was going on. Whenever I got home from school she always seemed to be there, sitting in the kitchen talking to mum."

"Probably checking to see everything was alright," said Cheryl.

Barry nodded. "She was great my Auntie Pauline. It was her that got me into The Beatles. Before she moved to Australia she gave me her collection of old Beatles albums; said they'd cheer me up. She was right. As soon as I heard my step-dad coming in from the pub, I'd run up to my room, stick my headphones on, and disappear into my own little world until the shouting stopped."

"So why didn't your mom tell this step-dad of yours to go take a hike?"

"You're joking aren't you?" Barry snorted. "She was terrified of him, I was too. Give him the slightest excuse to start a fight and he'd..." Barry picked up his pint of bitter and took a deep gulp. "Well let's just say he wasn't the nicest guy to be around."

"Yeah, I know what you mean. A cousin of mine had a husband that sounds just like him. God, when I think of some of the things he used to do to her. It's just as well she ended the relationship when she did."

"Divorced him did she?"

"Shot his head clean off," said Cheryl casually. "See, that's one thing I will say about the good ol' USA. At least back home you're allowed to defend yourself if some asshole starts beating up on you. Not like here where it's usually the victim that winds up dead or behind bars."

A fleeting image of his dear old mum standing at the top of the stairs in her dressing gown and curlers wielding a double-barrelled shot gun flashed through Barry's brain.

Cheryl looked into his glazed eyes and shook a bag of peanuts at him to reclaim his attention. "So, this step-dad of yours, what happened to him?"

"Drank himself to death," Barry replied coldly. "Anyway, let's not talk about him anymore. Tell me about yourself?"

"Not much to tell really. Left high school at seventeen, married by eighteen; divorced a year later."

"Any kids?" asked Barry.

Cheryl thought for a moment. "No," she said quietly. "Anyway, Mr Tour Guide, you were about to tell me something at The Cavern before we were interrupted by your slithery friend. I was asking you about the first instrument John Lennon learned to play?"

Cheryl's fears that she might raise his suspicions were unfounded. It was a question Barry had been asked hundreds of times and he answered it without hesitation. "It was a banjo. His mum taught him how to play it; talked about it in interviews all the time, right up to his death."

Cheryl feigned her surprise. "Wow, a banjo huh; who'd have guessed it?"

It was time for her to probe a little further. "Funny, I don't recall seeing any photos of him with it. Why is that do you think?"

If the cogwheels in Barry's brain had been allowed to turn a little further he may very well have smelt a rat. Fortunately for Cheryl, another timely interruption stopped that happening when the afternoon light from the open doorway dimmed and a long shadow fell on the stone floor of the pub. Steve leaned on the door frame.

"Hey, Romeo! We said two o'clock didn't we? You'd better get your arse over to the store before Joe changes his mind." The shadow retreated and Barry checked his watch.

"Bloody hell," he said in a panic. "I didn't realise it was

that late, I'm gonna have to leave."

Cheryl's heart sank. The result of her three hour ordeal had ended with a big fat zero. As she watched Barry draining the remaining inch of his pint her thoughts turned to Travis, probably sitting in the car right now waiting for her return with a treasure map complete with an 'X' marking the spot.

"Oh, you can stay just a little while longer can't you Barry?" she said persuasively, placing her hand on his.

Barry let out a regretful sigh. "I'd love to but I've got to go somewhere with Joe and Steve."

Cheryl grabbed her coat. "Great. Then what say I come along for the ride. Your friends won't mind will they?"

Barry faced a dilemma he was ill-equipped to deal with. For the first time in his life he had to choose between the two things that mattered most; the woman of his dreams, or the prospect of finding the most important pop relic that has ever existed.

He made his decision. "Well, actually; they might," he said, with a pained expression.

"Oh," replied Cheryl, unable to hide her embarrassment. "Then, you go right ahead, don't worry about me." Her next line was a masterstroke. "I mean, I'm sure I can find someone else in this town who can tell me all about John Lennon."

Barry took the bait. If anyone was going to educate the beautiful Cheryl about The Beatles it was going to be him. He ripped the back off a beer mat and pulled a worn pencil from the depths of his trouser pocket. "Here's my phone number. If you give me a ring in a couple of hours we can meet up again. That's if you want to?" he added, shyly.

Cheryl blinked up at him. "Alright," she said forcing a smile. "You got yourself a date."

CHAPTER TEN

Brenda leaned against the bar of the Atlantic pub, gazed through the open door and out into the potholed street. "Penny for your thoughts Bren," boomed Sid as he closed the door behind him, dampening the distant rumble of lorries and the pungent smell of a recently unloaded cargo of fish.

"Hi Sid," Brenda sighed. She gathered together a pile of freshly chopped lemon segments and threw them into a bowl. "Sorry I was miles away there," she said, wiping her hands on a bar towel. "Pint of bitter is it?"

"Please love. Oh, and can you put it on the slate? I lent Barry my last twenty quid this morning."

Brenda threw down the bar towel. "I'm running a pub not a bloody charity shop," she chastised, waving a finger at him. "No money, no drink."

"Ah, go on Bren, I'm bloody parched," Sid pleaded. "I'll give you the money when I come in tonight."

Against her better judgment she relented. "Just this once Sidney, but don't start making a habit of it."

Sid gave her a wink and rubbed his hands together with anticipation. "Cheers Bren, you're a star."

"Where's Barry?" she asked. "He was supposed to be giving me a call last night."

As Sid watched Brenda filling his glass, a worrying thought crossed his mind. Revealing that the man of her dreams was out canoodling with a tasty piece of crumpet from the other side of the pond might not be such a good idea. Bereft of cash, Sid had been banking on Brenda's good nature to keep him supplied with ale for the rest of the afternoon so the last thing he needed to do right now was upset her.

"Barry?" he said, casually. "Oh, you know what he's like Bren. He's probably rummaging around at a car boot sale or something."

Brenda's half-born smile proved unconvincing.

"What's the matter love? You're not your usual cheerful self."

"Oh it's nothing," Brenda sulked, handing Sid his drink. "It's just me being silly."

"Go on," he prompted, licking the froth from his top lip, "I'm listening."

Brenda leant across the bar towards him. "Well, have you ever had the feeling that the best times of your life have already happened; that there's nothing left to look forward to anymore? I don't know what brought it on, but when I looked in the mirror this morning it suddenly dawned on me that I've got more years behind me than I have in front. Quite frightening it was."

Sid put down his pint authoritatively. "Look, why don't you look on the positive side Bren? You've built up a great little business here, *and,* you own the place. So what have you got to worry about eh? Your future is as safe as houses."

Brenda straightened up. "But I don't want to be working behind a bar for the rest of my life," she said, shooting the bus driver an incredulous stare. "When I was a girl I dreamt about becoming a doctor, or a vet."

Sid laughed. "I thought you have to be clever to do that."

Brenda slapped him playfully on the back of the wrist. "Hey, I left school with ten 'O' Levels you cheeky sod. I could have gone to university."

"Yeah, so what stopped you then?" Sid fired back, pushing his luck.

Brenda's mind flashed back to her teenage life in Liverpool during the political turmoil of the 1970s and her heart sank. "Oh, the same thing that stopped most people from a working class background getting a decent education; money. Remember, you had to be well off to go to university in those days, not like today with all these student loans and grants. And as for my mum and dad; well they just couldn't afford it. They needed me out of school and behind this bar as quickly as possible to help put food on the table. So that was the end of that. I've been pulling bloody pints ever since."

Sid handed his empty glass back to Brenda and smiled. "Yeah, but no one can pull 'em quite like you though Bren."

* * *

Resplendent in Beatles Store sweatshirts and furnished with ID cards, Barry, Joe and Steve were set to gain access to all the main Beatles sites across Merseyside. Their first foray as intrepid investigators, however, had not gone quite as expected. A wasted journey into Crosby had just been made; a gentile northern suburb of Liverpool guarded by a strange otherworldly presence – iron men. Antony Gormley's famous art was usually the main draw for visitors to this town, but not for Barry and his comrades. They had planned to visit Alexandra Hall, a regular on the early Beatles gig circuit, but it was gone, recently demolished and replaced by a bland box of apartments for the discerning property virgin. Barry was devastated. "Look what they've done!" he cried, staring at the ugly red building from the back passenger seat of Joe's car.

Joe did not hide his impatience. He stamped his foot on the accelerator and they sped back up Moor Lane, past the tall white mill and on towards the traffic lights.

Steve twisted around in his seat and addressed a disgruntled Barry. "Where to now then Sherlock?" he asked curtly.

Barry fumbled amongst an array of scrawled notes and papers in the back of the car. "Take a right at the next set of lights."

Litherland Town Hall was located in an unlikely arboreal cul-de-sac on the edge of a semi-industrial district. Sutcliffe and The Beatles played their debut gig there after returning from Hamburg in the December of 1960. The brown bricked building with its distinctive arched windows was used as a Beatle venue no less than eight times and, on one memorable night, the group joined up with Gerry and the Pacemakers and performed as 'The Beatmakers'. Rumour has it, after one raucous gig there Stuart Sutcliffe was set upon outside and severely beaten. After receiving a vicious kick to the head Stuart's health quickly deteriorated and local historians claim it was this act of violence that eventually led to him having a fatal brain haemorrhage.

Annie, the elderly cleaning lady, allowed Barry and friends to peruse what fragments remained of the original building. "You're thinking of adding this place to your tour are you?"

"Well, er…" Barry stumbled.

Steve's irritation got the better of him. "You must be joking love; there's hardly anything left of it. Tell me; just how long has this health centre been here?" He squinted through narrow eyes at the person the question should have been directed at…Barry.

* * *

Travis met up with his wife at the Marina Yacht Club. They sat outside to enjoy the last of the day's warmth and planned their next move. While Travis studied the banjo photographs he had taken that morning, Cheryl cupped her hands around a hot mug of black coffee and looked out across the water. The forest of masts swayed gently in the breeze and the clinking of the tillers echoed like distant cowbells. "Wouldn't it be great if we could just climb aboard one of those boats and sail off into the sunset; make a new start somewhere else, away from all this… crap?"

Travis looked out at the marina and watched as a happy couple sipped wine on the bow of a small but perfectly formed schooner. He turned back to the photographs. "Well if you'd have found out what was in that letter instead of listening to Beatle boy's life story, maybe we might have been able to do just that."

She grabbed her husband's hand. "Oh Trav, can't you figure out another way to do this. I don't want to see Barry getting hurt. He's such a nice, genuine sort of a guy."

Travis didn't look up. "There *is* no other way. We just gotta stick to our plan."

Watching Travis squinting at the photographs for the past half hour was now grating on her nerves and she slammed her mug down on the table. "Your plan you mean! Hell I hate all this lying and sneaking around. It just don't seem right."

Travis looked up and pushed back his hat. "Alright honey, you win. Let's just forget the whole thing."

Cheryl was taken aback. "You don't really mean that…do you?"

"Sure I do; if that's what you really want. The house should fetch a reasonable price; enough to pay off Bakula anyway. Hey, and if we sell the cars too, we might be able to afford a little place in one of those trailer parks you grew up in. How's that sound?"

Cheryl let fly. "Don't you start twisting things around and making out this is all my fault you sarcastic son of a bitch. It was you that got us into this mess, not me!"

Travis's phone began to ring. "Yeah," he said, glancing at the name flashing up on the screen, "and I'm trying to get us out of it!"

"Well ain't you gonna answer that for Christ's sake?"

"Are you kidding? It's DeVito."

"Dammit Travis, you can't just ignore him!"

Travis stood up. "And just what the hell am I supposed to tell him huh? That the seller he thinks he's buying the banjo from doesn't actually exist? That the whole cockamamie story was just somethin' I cooked up so I could pocket his five hundred grand to pay off a psychopathic loan shark? Get real Cheryl. I can't talk to that son of a bitch until I have that banjo in my hands."

Cheryl picked up her coat and walked to the door of the clubhouse.

"Where the hell are you going now?" Travis shouted after her. "We ain't taken care of the bill yet?"

"You take care of it," she snapped, refusing to look back. "I've got to get ready to go out on a freakin' date!"

* * *

For Barry, Joe and Steve the morning had been nothing short of a disaster. Barry sat in the back of the car cowering like a scolded dog while the Benson brothers came up with reason after reason why they should forget the whole thing.

"You're gonna have to do a lot better than this," moaned Steve.

"Yeah," Joe chipped in, "'cause it's costing us a bloody fortune having to get Frank to cover for us while we're wasting our time with you."

Barry had no argument. He knew he should have checked the venues he chose to visit that morning were, at the very least, still there. "I know lads, I'm really sorry. I realise now we've been going about this the wrong way."

"How do you mean?" Steve asked.

"Think about it. The banjo was the only physical thing John had left of his mother so he would have put it somewhere very special; with someone he could trust."

"Oh well that narrows it down a lot doesn't it eh," scoffed Joe.

"Actually, it does," Barry retorted defensively as he pored over the letter. "The clues are all here; we just need to get inside Lennon's mind to figure them out."

"How?" Joe and Steve asked, simultaneously.

"Pete Best. I spoke to him last night and he has agreed to meet up with us. He was still in The Beatles when John wrote the letter so he might be able to point us in the right direction."

At last Joe felt he was driving with a purpose and by the time The Casbah came into view Barry had treated him and Steve to a potted history of the club.

It was in early 1959 when Pete Best's mother, Mona, heard about a coffee bar in London called the Two Eyes. It was proving to be incredibly popular with the youth of the day and had a constant stream of beat groups providing all the entertainment. Mona thought she could emulate this success in Liverpool; the venue being the cellar of her large Victorian home which she was able to buy after pawning all her jewellery and placing a bet on 'Never Say Die'; the 1954, 33-1 Derby winner. Pete Best and a host of friends got down to work and cleared out the cellar to create their very own club.

The Casbah opened on 29th August 1959 with a gig from The Quarrymen whose line up included; John Lennon, Paul McCartney and George Harrison. When Pete Best joined a few months later, the group changed its name to The Silver Beatles and subsequently, The Beatles.

Joe pulled up outside the Grade II listed building in Haymans Green, situated in the picturesque suburb of West

Derby village, and cut the engine. Strains of beat music could be heard coming from inside The Casbah and the three men got out to investigate. "That'll be Pete's band," said Barry excitedly. "He told me they were rehearsing today."

They followed the music to the back of the house and down a set of narrow steps to a small doorway. After ducking down under the squat lintel to avoid a 'Casbah kiss', a term used by clubgoers to describe cracking one's head on it, they entered a warren of dark basement rooms.

Black walls covered in stars, shadowy murals and spider webs harked back to a time when the primordial soup of pop culture was simmering; ready to burst into life. They eventually found the band thrashing out the last chord crescendo and with hands held aloft above his drum kit; Pete Best clicked his sticks together to signal the final deafening beat.

Barry, Joe and Steve put their hands together in appreciation as Pete disentangled himself from his drums and joined them. He greeted Barry enthusiastically having got to know him through their mutual Beatles ties.

"Alright Barry; lads." The four men shook hands and Barry could see from the expressions on their faces that Joe and Steve were impressed.

"These are the guys I was telling you about on the phone Pete." The brothers acknowledged Barry's words with a friendly nod.

"I was just telling Joe and Steve on the way here, this is the place where you and the other Beatles signed your management contract with Brian Epstein isn't it?"

Pete pointed at a small wooden table. "24th of January

1962. We were sitting right there."

Barry regarded the spot with reverence, his eyes wide with wonder.

"Anyway," said Pete, "Barry told me on the phone you were putting a fanzine together and that The Casbah was going to be its first major feature."

This revelation was news to Joe and Steve and nervous glances were exchanged between them. *Barry; you little liar.*

"Er, yeah, that's right," said Steve hesitantly. "We also think the fans would be interested in learning more about the early days…"

Joe came straight to the point. "Like where you all used to hang out; that sort of thing."

"Fine," said Pete. "So, what do you want to know?"

"Everything," Barry gushed.

Pete invited the researchers to sit around '*the table*' and for ten minutes explained The Casbah's significance in the making of The Beatles. Afterwards, he invited them to *"come and have a look at the artwork"* and they followed him dutifully as he led them to the famous 'Lennon ceiling' which John painted in 1959. Black stars, moons and diamonds peppered the white background in a style that would have been deemed radical at the time. In another room, a mural by John's first wife, Cynthia, depicted a young quiffed Lennon in a rock 'n' roll stance. The white silhouette emblazoned on the black wall conjured up in Joe's mind the ghostly Hiroshima shadows left behind after the nuclear blast. Above the image of John, on the shiny black ceiling, were more stars this time individually painted and mounted by Lennon and McCartney; each one now worth tens of thousands of pounds.

"They treated this place like a second home," said Pete, as the memories came flooding back. "John even slept here sometimes after a late gig. He was terrified of waking his Aunt Mimi."

The thought of Lennon, the tough leather-clad rocker and self-confessed rebel being worried about his finger wagging Aunt Mimi was hard to imagine and it brought a smile to everyone's face.

"Have you ever found anything in here that belonged to John?" Steve blurted, amidst the laughter. Pete pondered over the question. There was something in the squeaky tone of Steve's voice that betrayed him and his comrades shot him an incredulous stare. How could he have been so indiscreet?

"Ah, so that's what this is all about," said an enlightened Pete. "You've heard about my latest Lennon find have you? Look lads, if you wanted to see it, all you had to do was ask."

"It's here then is it?" Steve asked flatly.

Pete nodded. "A little beauty it is too; mother of pearl, very rare. Found it about a year ago when we were renovating the place; between the joists above the Lennon ceiling. I haven't got a clue how it got up there."

I bloody have, thought Steve, quietly fuming.

"Can we see it?" asked Barry, hardly able to contain his excitement.

"Wait there; I'll have to fetch it from the safe."

Pete disappeared into the depths of the club while Barry looked around in awe at the richly decorated chamber. It all made sense now. If ever there was a fitting resting place for

Julia's banjo, this was it. As he waited for Pete to return, Barry knew how Howard Carter must have felt the moment before gazing upon Tutankhamen's treasure for the first time.

Joe and Steve swooped on the dreamer like harpies. "What the hell are you so excited about eh?" Joe sneered in Barry's face. "You do know what this means don't you?"

Steve did not wait for Barry's brain to process the question. "It means we've just lost five million quid you bloody idiot!"

Pete returned hiding something behind his back. Since The Casbah Club reopened its doors to the public in 2002, the ex-Beatle liked nothing more than to delight and surprise fans with fascinating titbits of new information, especially the 'so called' experts.

"Come on then Pete, where is it?" asked Barry, craning his neck like a puppy dog on a leash.

"Now remember," said Pete, racking up the tension, "other than me, no one has set eyes on this since 1960."

Barry felt his heart thumping against his rib cage and his toes curled in anticipation.

"Alright," Pete said, "feast your eyes on that."

Silence.

"It's definitely John's," Pete announced with pride.

Steve couldn't contain himself any longer. "A guitar pick?"

Pete took a step back when Steve flung his arms around his brother's neck, pulled him down and planted a sloppy wet kiss on his balding head. Sure, Pete had witnessed this kind of hysteria hundreds of times during his time with The Beatles, but not from a middle-aged man.

The sound of the band striking up again was the ex-Beatle's cue to bid farewell to his guests and with the promise of a copy of the new fanzine once completed, Barry, Joe and Steve thanked him for his time and made their way to the exit.

Back in the car, Barry remained silent. Unlike his friends, who were only in it for the money, he was bitterly disappointed the banjo had not been found. Just to have held the relic in his hands for even a few brief moments would have been enough. With a heavy heart he retrieved his notes from the glove compartment and quietly scrubbed the third old haunt from the list.

CHAPTER ELEVEN

On the other side of the Atlantic, Tony DeVito had not wasted any time. Since transferring the money to Travis's account, he had busied himself trying to secure a buyer for Julia's banjo. To avoid paying a big slice of the profit in commission, DeVito had made the decision not to involve any of the public sales rooms, preferring instead to seek out a private collector with no limits. His research finally paid off when he received a call from none other than Diego Fernandez, a multi-millionaire oil baron and Texas royalty.

Fernandez had invited DeVito to his summer retreat on the waterfront of Rockport excited at the prospect of filling a gap on the wall of his 'Heroes' gallery between Elvis's white Vegas costume and Jimi Hendrix's Fender Stratocaster.

Diego, a music fanatic and international collector, fitted the bill perfectly and he welcomed DeVito with open arms when he arrived to discuss the deal.

After sipping drinks on the veranda, they made their way down to the private jetty and boarded a sleek speed boat. Diego treated his guest to a tour of the old harbour before launching into the bay and heading east towards St Joseph

Island. Trussed up in his business suit and sporting a wide-brimmed Stetson, DeVito swallowed his nausea and clung on to the side rail as the speeding vessel bounced off the waves like a skipping stone.

Diego was in his element. Kitted out in Jesus sandals, Bermuda shorts and capped sleeved T-shirt, the bronzed millionaire rode the boat like a bucking bronco, whooping as he took on another breaker. "I'd hang on to that hat if I were you Tony!" he shouted, flashing his unnaturally white teeth. "If the wind doesn't take it, the herons will! What say we go 'round again?"

From the vantage point of the paragliders weaving through the air fifty feet overhead, the boat circled like a Catherine wheel; fizzing white waves arcing from its savage propeller blades as it made another three hundred and sixty degree turn. Diego waited for his guest to respond. He took DeVito's flapping arms as a sign of enthusiasm and pulled hard on the throttle. The engine responded and the sleek craft swerved into the next available wave.

DeVito's guts churned in protest at the idea of prolonging this hell ride and he turned his bloodless face to the ocean to liberate his breakfast.

Back at the house, DeVito politely declined the oyster brunch and headed straight for the bathroom to clean himself up.

"I'll have the maid send you up some clean clothes!" shouted Diego, as he watched his guest make an uneasy ascent up the ornate grand staircase.

An hour later, a self-conscious DeVito emerged sporting a large pair of knee-length khaki shorts and open-necked shirt decorated with a bold palm tree print. Diego escorted him through the Baroque interior of the mansion and into the gallery.

"Sorry about my dad's clothes Tony, they were the only ones I could find that would fit you. I'll have your suit cleaned up and sent on to you."

"Much obliged," said DeVito, taking in the magnificent collection of showbiz memorabilia on display in the ambient marble-lined space of the exhibition hall.

Diego ushered him towards a mannequin in a cowboy suit. "You remember this guy don't you Tony? Roy Rogers. That's one of the costumes he wore in that TV series of his. And that dress over there," Diego oozed pride and pointed to a sequinned red low cut evening gown, "Marilyn Monroe wore that little number in Some Like It Hot!"

"I'm impressed," nodded DeVito, as one of Clint Eastwood's ponchos caught his eye.

"You should be," Diego boasted. "I got clothes worn by Elton John, Michael Jackson, Britney Spears. I've even got one of Lady Diana's cocktail dresses for Christ's sake. You see Tony; I want this to be the best private collection in the world!"

"What about musical instruments?" asked DeVito.

"Hell I got enough of those to fill Madison Square Garden twice over. Beach Boys, Hendrix, Dylan, Bon Jovi, Bowie. I got stuff that belonged to all those guys."

"And what about The Beatles?" said DeVito, steering the conversation back on track.

"I'm still working on that," Diego confessed. "But I do have one of George Harrison's twelve-string guitars *and* a numbered White album, signed by all four Beatles."

"I guess the Lennon banjo would be a significant addition to your collection then huh?"

"That would depend on the price," said Diego, getting down to business.

DeVito made his move. "Can I be honest with you Diego? All this stuff you have here is great; truly remarkable…"

"But?" said Diego.

"But . . . it just ain't unique my friend." DeVito wandered over to the Elvis collection and pointed at his iconic white Vegas costume. "Take this for example. There's another one just like it hanging up in Gracelands." DeVito moved on to Jimi Hendrix's Fender Stratocaster. "And this guitar; every collector on the planet has got one of those. Hendrix owned hundreds of the damn things. Same goes for all this other stuff too. And as for Elton John; hell, he sells off his entire wardrobe every year to raise money for charity!"

DeVito put a friendly arm around Diego's shoulder. "Look, don't take this the wrong way, all this stuff is really great but, if you're truly serious about this collection being the best, what you need here is something no one else on the planet has got; something that can't fail to impress all those business clients and high-flying showbiz friends of yours. Do you hear what I'm saying?"

"Alright," said Diego. "How much do you want for it?"

DeVito rubbed his chin and paced the floor. "That's a difficult one. How do you put a price on something that is, quite frankly, priceless?"

"Try," said Diego.

"Seven million. How does that sound?"

Diego reeled. "What? You must be out of your mind!"

DeVito remained composed. "I don't think so my friend. You know better that anyone just how much Lennon memorabilia is worth, not to mention something as unique and special as this. Most of the rock stars you got in here wouldn't have been around if it hadn't have been for Lennon and this banjo of his... and you know it!" DeVito moved in closer. "So let's cut to the chase; if you want your collection to be the best you gonna need the holy grail of pop memorabilia hanging on *your* wall not someone else's. I'm letting you have first shot at it Diego but there are plenty of wealthy Russians and Chinese out there who'd love to get their hands on this too. Just think about that for a moment." DeVito leant on a display case and allowed the millionaire to absorb his words.

Diego walked through the gallery and stopped at the vacant spot between Hendrix's guitar and Elvis's white Vegas costume. He turned to DeVito.

"I'll give you five million for it."

"Seven," DeVito fired back.

"Six..."

"Done!"

The two men embraced like Russian comrades and gave each other a congratulatory slap on the back. "So when can I expect delivery?" Diego asked.

"Soon," DeVito replied confidently. "One of my guys is bringing it back from Europe as we speak."

Diego raised a bushy brow. "Hell, I assume you can trust this guy? I sent someone out to collect something for me once; never saw the son of a bitch again. Cost me millions."

The fat man's guts became acquainted with his throat for

the second time that day. It had never occurred to him that his new employee might be tempted to run off with the banjo once he had acquired it.

DeVito arrived back in Dallas with mixed feelings; elated at the deal he had struck with Diego, but increasingly twitchy at the fact Travis had not returned any of his calls.

'I assume you can trust this guy?' Diego's words had sliced his confidence like a hot knife through butter. He remembered what his dear old pa said to him before handing the DeVito family firm over to him. '*Never assume anything. It makes an 'ass' out of 'u' and 'me'.*'

Pacing his oak panelled office in a haze of blue smoke, he listened again to the message drawling from the speaker on his desk. Travis Lawson was sincerely apologetic.

"Hi, I'm sorry but I can't take your call right now. Please leave a message and I'll get back to you..."

"Travis, you son of a bitch! What the hell are you up to?"

It was time to take action.

CHAPTER TWELVE

Outside Strawberry Fields, Barry, Joe and Steve peered through the thick unkempt foliage beyond the scruffy red iron gates. Supported by sandstone pillars daubed in graffiti, the gates were an irresistible pilgrimage for Beatles fans but cried out for the care and maintenance they rightly deserved.

"How do we get in?" asked Steve, tugging at the rusting padlock.

Barry checked to see that the coast was clear. "Quick, we're gonna have to climb over."

Joe gawped back at him. "Climb over. We've got passes haven't we?"

"Not for Strawberry Fields. Our bus stops outside; just to let the tourists take photographs."

"I don't believe this. Are you saying we need permission to get in?" Steve asked, with an incredulous glare.

"Get in the car Steve," Joe ordered. "We're going back to work."

"But why?" Barry whined, chasing after the brothers as they walked briskly across the road.

Steve blasted the hapless tour guide with both barrels.

"How can we search a building if we're not even allowed inside it you bloody idiot?"

"But we weren't going to go inside the building anyway," Barry argued. "John only ever hung out in the woods around the back."

Joe's voice was filled with derision. "Oh. So where do you suppose he hid the banjo then eh; up a bleedin' tree?"

"No", Barry retaliated, "in the air-raid shelter. A gardener who used to work in there brought his wife on a tour a few months ago. He told me all about it; said it was tucked away at the back of the main building, near the edge of the woods. Now I don't know about you two, but when I was a kid, that would be just the sort of place I would have wanted to explore."

"Somewhere special you said!" Steve barked. "Do you honestly think Lennon would be daft enough to hide his precious heirloom in some manky old air-raid shelter?"

"Why not? The location's perfect. It's right next to Mimi's house so John would have been able to keep an eye on it whenever he wanted. And don't forget; this place was special enough for him to write a song about wasn't it?"

Joe had deep reservations. "Look mate, when we agreed to help you with this we didn't expect to be breaking the law. What if we get caught in there eh? We could get done for trespass."

"Yeah we could," Barry conceded, "and I could lose my job. Come on Joe, you don't think I'd risk that unless I really believed the banjo could be in there do you?"

Joe thrust the car keys back in his pocket. "A quick look; then we're out of there."

Strawberry Fields was once a children's home run by the

Salvation Army. It was there that a young John Lennon would squeeze through his Aunt Mimi's back fence to join the orphaned children at play. With his own mother and father now absent from his life, John found it easier to bond with kids who never had reason to talk about parents. Although the original home was bombed during World War Two and a 1970s building now stood in its place, Lennon was on record as saying he only ever frequented the woods, spending every spare moment he had climbing trees; hence the line in The Beatles classic song, 'Strawberry Fields Forever': *'No one I think is in my tree...'*

Joe jerked his thumb in the direction of the gates. "Over you go Barry."

With well-timed precision, the brothers ushered Barry's dead weight up off the ground and over the gate. But with his trouser pocket snagging on a jagged piece of iron work, Barry hung over it like a half-filled sack of potatoes and it needed a violent shove to send him over the top. He found himself lying on his back staring up at the sky through the floppy-fingered leaves of a chestnut tree. "Piece of cake," he groaned, getting to his feet. Joe and Steve conquered the gate with ease and joined Barry under the cover of a rhododendron bush.

"Okay," whispered Steve, adopting a commando stance, "where to now?"

Barry rubbed a muddy hand across his clueless face. "Er..."

"You do know where this shelter is don't you?" Joe chided.

Sensing his brother was about to snap, Steve took control of the situation. "Follow me," he whispered, "the woods are over there."

Barry and his comrades darted through the bushes hugging the perimeter of the lawn until they reached the back of the main building. A last dash saw them jumping over a small barbed wire fence, through a neglected allotment patch and into the relative safety of the secluded wood. Steve noticed an unusual hillock protruding from a copse of unmanaged sycamore trees which seemed to jar against the natural contours of the landscape. On one side, the hillock sloped off gently into a field of tall grass; on the other, partially obscured by a dense thicket of gorse bushes, it looked more angular in appearance; a tell-tale sign that whatever lay beneath was probably manmade. "I'll bet you a pound to a pinch of shit that's it," announced Steve confidently. Tentatively they advanced; squeezing past the tangle of thorny armoured branches which punctured skin and clung to clothes like cruel Velcro. Eventually the bushes surrendered to a crumbling concrete path where roots and tendrils had fought in vain to penetrate. Beyond lay a corrugated iron door which had been assimilated by knotted braids of creepers and vines. It gave little resistance when Steve lunged at it with the sole of his boot.

Barry suppressed a shiver when he parted the curtain of foliage and peeked inside.

"Jesus Christ," baulked Steve, pressing a hand over his nose. "Either Barry's shit his pants or something's died in there."

Joe spotted a rusty ladder descending into the bowels of the shelter. "Do you reckon that will take his weight?"

Barry recoiled as foreboding filled every fibre of his

body. "I'm not going first," his voice quivered.

"Oh yes you bloody well are," said Joe, adamantly. "This was your idea remember."

Barry turned to Steve in the hope he would continue to lead the way but all he got was a contemptuous stare. "Down you go mate."

Joe and Steve watched as Barry clumsily negotiated the dilapidated ladder before disappearing into the darkness. "I'm inside!" he shouted, his voice reverberating from the void.

"Alright, keep your voice down," hissed Steve. "Shine the torch on the ladder; we're coming in."

The reinforced concrete Stent air-raid shelter had stood its ground since the Second World War and was a credit to the Liverpool city engineers who constructed it. Nestling within the grounds of the old orphanage, it remained a legacy to those children unfortunate enough to have experienced the evil warmongering of 'Madalf Heatlump' and his 'Nasties' who bombed them during the war years.

Barry's torch flicked across the dank mossy walls and into small rooms which ran off the main corridor. The cold blue halogen beam strobed across rusty bunks, tables and chairs which had been left stacked at teetering angles; their oxidised metal legs clinging together as if a long forgotten fear still gripped them.

Huddled around their one and only torch, the twenty-first century invaders crept through the putrid slurry which washed over the floor of the wartime maze. "It's like Aladdin's cave in here," Barry declared, as his fingernails embedded themselves in the torch's rubber handle.

Joe picked up a salt box from one of the many shelves

lining the walls; its spotted foxed label promising to add flavour to any wartime meal scraped together from meagre rations. The apron-clad mother, her hair tied on top of her head in a neat head scarf, looked back at him with a homely smile.

"Wait!" yelled Steve as he broke ranks and snatched the torch from Barry's grasp. He moved the saucer of light down the wall and brought it to a hovering stop. "Over there, under that bunk bed."

In a heartbeat the others were at his side, crouching down beside a long rusting metal box. The three men fell silent, barely breathing. Steve hurriedly aimed the beam at the corroded lock. "Let's get this thing open."

Outside, the grassy slope of the shelter made an ideal secluded spot for two young lovers and Jason's hopeful hand wandered up Leanne's leg. She pushed him away and suppressed a nervous giggle. "Cut it out, someone might see."

"There's no one here; it's private property." He rummaged in his pocket and produced a packet of strawberry flavoured condoms.

Leanne sat up and folded her arms. "Well you know what you can do with those don't you," she huffed, extinguishing the glint in Jason's eyes in an instant.

"But you told me you liked strawberries?"

"I do," she said haughtily, "out of a bloody bowl!"

Jason put his arms around her and whispered gently. "Come on Leanne, I do love you, you know."

Leanne reached for his hand and squeezed it. "Do you really mean that?"

"'Course I do," he said.

"And you'd never leave me?"

"Never. I'll always be here; right by your side," he cooed, cuddling up to her.

His words achieved the desired effect and she kissed him deeply on the lips.

"It is quiet around here isn't it?" she said, pulling back to take a breath.

Jason knew his luck was about to change. *Game on.*

Several feet beneath the lovers, Steve examined the lid of the box. Despite the rust he could just make out the blue paint of a trade sign, but the words were illegible. "Go on, open it then," Barry urged.

"Here, use this," said Joe, handing his brother an iron bar he had found whilst rooting around in one of the rotting cupboards. Steve kicked the box on its side and attacked the lock.

"Careful!" Barry winced, as the lid cracked ajar. The corroded hinges groaned in painful defiance as Steve forced them apart for the first time in decades. Neatly packed inside the cork-lined chest was a stock of medical supplies, all in pristine condition. One by one, the treasure hunters removed brown ribbed iodine bottles, calico bandages and an assortment of tinctures eager to find out what lay beneath.

"Look, there's another compartment underneath," said Barry, brushing aside an assortment of triangular bandages and safety pins. He lifted the loose wooden board from the box and ceremoniously revealed its contents.

Barry slowly blew out his breath in an effort to control

his frustration. "Gas masks."

"Oh, for God's sake; I told you this was a waste of bloody time," Joe ranted loudly, not caring who might hear.

Suddenly, a feeling of unease crept up Steve's spine and all senses were on high alert. He lowered his voice as he strained to pick out details from the gloom. "Did you see that? Over there by that piece of corrugated iron; I think something's in here with us." The calm in Steve's voice belied his inner panic.

Armed with the crow bar, he bravely edged his way towards the large sheet of corrugated metal leaning against the wall. Very slowly, he reached out and peeled it back. "Shine that torch over here will you?" The wall beneath writhed like wet leather before fragmenting into a thousand pieces. With a piercing high-pitched screech it swooped suddenly, enveloped Steve's body and sent him crashing to the ground.

Numb with fright, the torch slipped from Barry's hand, fell into the muddy water and plunged them all into dreadful darkness.

Barry bolted for the hatch, his Cuban heeled boots slipping and skating on the slimy floor like a grizzly bear's paws on a frozen pond. On reaching the foot of the ladder he was unceremoniously dragged back by Joe who was desperate to reach daylight and freedom before the unseen menace caught up with him. It was Steve, however, surrounded by a storm cloud of irate bats, who emerged first from the shelter. His brain on autopilot and body wired with adrenaline, he pushed his way through the undergrowth and sprinted down the grassy slope towards the woods.

*   *   *

Jason kissed Leanne on the forehead and lifted his head to take a breath. He froze. Running towards him was a man streaked with mud thrashing his hands wildly above his head. Too terrified to speak, Leanne's lover whipped up his trousers, jumped to his feet and fled. Leanne could only watch as the man who promised never to leave her galloped down the hill towards the main building. "Jason?" she called after him. "Jason!" She felt the rumble of boots and quickly turned around.

"It's alright love," Steve panted, leaning over her as he gasped for breath. "I'm not going to hurt you."

The bloodcurdling scream that followed pierced the air and echoed from every corner of the grounds. Even Jason stopped to take a look as he frantically punched 999 into his phone.

The woods flashed past as Barry, Joe and Steve sprinted through the foliage; branches thwacking back in their muddy faces as if punishing them for their uninvited intrusion. They soon reached the high sandstone wall which marked the perimeter of Strawberry Fields and followed it until they found themselves back at the iconic red gates. Amidst the glares of tourists and passers-by, Barry, Joe and Steve bundled themselves over the gates and ran for the car; the putrid stench of the shelter slurry following them across the road.

"Nice one Barry," Steve said, shooting the breathless tour guide a dirty look from the visor mirror as he scraped the stinking mud from his hair.

"Sshh," Joe hissed. "Listen."

The unmistakable whirring of a police siren could be heard floating on the breeze; and it was getting closer. Joe launched into action twisting the ignition key so hard it threatened to snap. Leaving Strawberry Fields behind in a cloud of smoking rubber, the car made a hard left onto Menlove Avenue and ducked into a driveway. The three men held their breath as they watched the police car speed past on the opposite side of the dual carriageway. "Christ that was close," Joe wheezed.

Barry wiped his hands on the back of the passenger seat and reached for his notes. "Well, I suppose that's another one we can cross off the list."

Joe and Steve could find neither the energy nor the words to respond.

CHAPTER THIRTEEN

When Travis arrived back at the hotel he made straight for the mini-bar. Pouring himself a large one, he sat on the bed and tried to rid his mind of misery that had dominated his life since the auction in Coopersville three months earlier.

Sweet Home Alabama rang out from his phone and a name flashed up which compounded his despair. Tony DeVito. "Shit," he muttered, tossing the phone on the bed like a hot potato. Cheryl returned from the bathroom and put the finishing touches to her makeup. "Who was that?" she asked.

"Sales call," Travis lied. He looked her up and down and winked his approval. "You look great honey."

"I hope Barry thinks so." Cheryl curled the corner of her mouth as she swiped the red lipstick across it.

Travis tried to keep the conversation positive. "Any idea where he's taking you?"

Cheryl threw the lipstick tube into her bag and zipped it up hard. "It doesn't really matter does it," she retorted bluntly. "Just as long as you get what you want?"

Travis rolled his eyes. "Look honey…"

The hotel telephone rang and Cheryl picked it up. "Okay thanks. I'll be right down." She replaced the receiver and reached for her coat. "Taxi's here, gotta go." She flung her bag across her shoulder and marched to the door.

Travis held out his arms. "Well don't I even get a kiss?" he asked.

"Don't bother to wait up," she said flatly, before slamming the door behind her.

Travis stared into his empty glass. Suddenly he felt drained as the magnitude of their predicament thumped into his brain like a jackhammer. He hurled the glass at the wall and watched with a modicum of satisfaction as it shattered into tiny pieces.

Back in the sanctuary of his flat, Barry peeled off his stinking clothes and carried himself off to the bathroom. Using the spouting shower head as a microphone, he bellowed "she loves you yeah, yeah, yeah!" as he prepared himself for his date with Cheryl. When the last remnants of mud had been eradicated from his body, he wrapped himself in a towel and ran a comb through his thick wavy hair. He rarely wore aftershave but managed to squeeze a few drops from a bottle Brenda had bought for him last Christmas. His thoughts turned to the warm-hearted landlady as he buttoned up the only formal shirt he possessed. *That reminds me, I must give Brenda a call.*

Brenda had prepared the pub for the evening ahead and, with a popular live act booked to provide entertainment; she was expecting it to be busy. As the first of the punters began to wander through the door and secure their seats the telephone rang out behind the bar. Brenda answered. "Hello, The Atlantic."

"Hi Bren, it's me," said Barry cheerfully.

Brenda's face lit up. "Oh, hello love, where have you been hiding? I was starting to get a bit worried. Is everything alright?"

"Couldn't be better. Listen Bren, there's something I want to talk to you about." Barry took a deep breath. "Do you remember me telling you how I was waiting to find the right girl?"

Brenda gripped the phone until her palm tingled. "Yeah?"

Barry rushed his words down the line. "Well, what are you doing tonight?"

Brenda looked at herself in the glass beyond the optics and tidied the unruly russet locks from her slim face. "Well, I'm supposed to be working," she giggled, "but I suppose I could always ask one of the girls to cover for me."

"Great," he blurted. "Because there's someone I want you to meet. Her name's Cheryl."

Brenda's heart sank. She looked back at the gaunt, freckled reflection staring back from the glass and lowered her eyes. "Cheryl?" she said quietly.

"Oh she's great Bren. I met her on the bus this morning. And guess what, she's a Beatles fan! Brilliant eh? Sid and Steve didn't believe me when I told them about her. Bet me twenty quid each that I was making the whole thing up. You should have seen their faces when I trousered their money; a bloody picture it was!"

Later that evening, Barry entered the Atlantic sporting Cheryl on his arm like a trophy. It may just have been her imagination but Cheryl was certain the background chatter from the locals dipped in volume as they strolled over to the bar. Brenda had not noticed them coming in and was busily taking orders and serving drinks.

"Hi Bren," Barry shouted across the bar.

Brenda recognised his friendly voice and instinctively spun around with a beaming smile. It was short-lived. Barry turned to his beautiful date. "This is Cheryl, the lady I was telling you about on the phone. Cheryl, this is a good friend of mine, Brenda."

Brenda studied her nemesis with interest. Squeezed perfectly into her snug fitting red dress and with beautifully styled hair she looked a million dollars. Barry too had made an effort; his brand new shirt still bearing the tram lines of the packaging. Self-consciously, Brenda adjusted her supermarket bargain frock before extending a polite hand. Cheryl shook it limply. "Hi there. Nice to meet you." Before Brenda had a chance to respond, Cheryl turned to her date. "Say, I'd like to go freshen up. Where's the bathroom?"

Brenda jumped in. "You'll find *the toilets* down the corridor on the right," she said, in a dignified businesslike manner.

Barry pulled Cheryl in close. "What would you like to drink?"

"Oh, anything; whatever you're having," she said, fluttering her lashes at him. "I'll be back in a minute."

Barry's eyes followed Cheryl's stunning curves until she was out of sight.

"Two pints of bitter then is it?" said Brenda abruptly.

Barry shrugged. "Er, yeah, I suppose so." He drummed his fingers on the bar while she filled the glasses. "So, what do you think of her then Bren?" he said with a cheesy grin.

"How the hell should I know?" Brenda replied coolly, "I've only just met the woman."

"She's from America you know," trilled Barry.

"Is she really?" the landlady replied, not bothering to look up. "I'd never have guessed."

Barry looked at her inquisitively. This wasn't like Brenda. But then the penny dropped. "Sorry I didn't call you last night. I was a bit busy."

Without ceremony she thrust the pints down on the counter and held out her hand for the money. "So I see."

"You wanted to show me something didn't you?" asked Barry, handing her the cash.

"Nothing important," Brenda replied, offhandedly. "Just some old photographs I found in the cellar."

"I'd really like to see them though Bren."

She turned to face him and peered through the scratched lenses of his round rimmed glasses. The look in Barry's eyes confirmed his words were sincere and her mood lifted.

"Would you?"

"'Course I would. I love looking at old photographs."

Brenda wiped her hands on the front of her frock. "Stay right there, I'll go and get them."

This was not quite what Barry had in mind. "Er, yeah, alright," he said, shifting uncomfortably with one eye fixed on the ladies toilets.

The back room of the pub was neatly laid out in the style of an old parlour. A small occasional table was draped with a crisp white cloth and a large brown teapot presided over finely painted china cups, saucers and side plates. On the wall, taking pride of place amongst a selection of family portraits, was a large framed photo of Barry and Brenda standing beside the Magical Mystery Tour bus. She pulled out a stubborn drawer from an old oak writing desk and lifted a shoe box from the neatly ordered paperwork.

Brenda hurried down the dimly lit hallway and followed the chatter of customers back to the bar. "Here they are," she said excitedly, holding out the box. But Barry was gone.

"What's up Bren? You look like you've just swallowed a wasp," cackled Sid, as he squeezed his way to the bar through the heaving front line of customers.

Brenda thrust out her palm. "Eight pounds forty three please," she demanded, before he'd even had chance to order a drink.

"Eh?"

"For the drinks you wheedled out of me this afternoon," she said, angrily. "You lied to me Sid. You didn't lend Barry any money at all; you lost it on a bloody bet!"

"But how did you…?"

"Barry told me. He's sitting over there with his… fancy woman."

Sid followed her gaze to a cosy corner on the far side of the room where Barry and Cheryl sat laughing and joking.

"Look love," he said, grasping her hand, "I know how you feel about him; that's why I didn't want to tell you about the bet. I knew it would only upset you."

"I thought he liked me," said Brenda in a small voice.

"He does like you," Sid reassured her, fearing she was about to start crying. "He just hasn't had the bottle to ask you out that's all."

Brenda snatched her hand back. "Is that right? Well it

didn't stop him asking 'Ellie May' over there did it?"

"What? You don't think...? Christ Bren, didn't you know? Barry never asked her out, *she asked him!*"

Brenda took a moment to absorb Sid's words.

"I know. I couldn't believe it either," laughed Sid. "Why do you think I lost the bloody bet? Let's face it Bren; a woman would have to be really desperate to want to go out with a tit like Barry wouldn't she?"

"Thanks very much," said Brenda, rapping him on the back of the knuckles.

"Sorry love, no offence. What I meant was; she's really good looking isn't she; she could have any man she wanted?"

Brenda looked over at Cheryl and shrugged. "Well she seems happy enough from where I'm standing."

"For now maybe, but you mark my words," he said, tapping the side of his nose, "as soon as he starts reciting the sleeve notes from A Hard Day's Night you won't see her arse for dust."

"Bloody hell Sid, he's not that bad. I know he goes on a bit, but underneath all that is a very warm and caring person. I know that's what I like about him."

"Well you should have told him then shouldn't you?" replied Sid, forcefully.

"Yeah well," Brenda mumbled, "it's too late now isn't it?"

"Look, let me give you a bit of friendly advice."

Brenda put her head in her hands. "Christ, do you have to?"

"Just hear me out will you. If you're really serious about Barry, all you've got to do is snap him out of his infatuation and make him see what he stands to lose."

"And just how am I supposed to do that?" asked Brenda.

"Easy. Make him jealous."

* * *

Cheryl's mom dusted the flour from her hands and stood back from the smoking oven. "Well if that don't work nothing will." With a look of satisfaction, she unstrung her apron and hung it up on a peg next to the refrigerator. She had heard the chime of the doorbell a few moments earlier and hurried down the hall just as it rang for the third time. Leaving the chain on the door she squeezed her voice through the gap. "Yes, may I help you?"

The smartly dressed man, hair slicked back and side-parted in vintage style, stepped back and looked at the number on the front porch. "Sorry mam, I think I must have written down the wrong address."

Nancy put her hand on the chain catch and it dropped loose. She pulled the door open and faced the benign looking visitor. "And who might you be lookin' for?"

"Travis Lawson," he replied.

Nancy folded her arms and looked the stranger up and down. "Well you got the right address son but he's not at home right now. And you are?"

The man placed a shiny black shoe on the doorstep and thrust his hand forward. "Oh, the name's er, Ray, Ray Jackson. Trav and me; we were at high school together but we ain't seen each other in years. As I was in town on business, I thought I'd look him up and surprise him."

Nancy relaxed and smiled. "Oh, now that's a shame.

You see Travis and Cheryl; that's my daughter; they're in Europe right now."

Ray tried to filter the surprise from his voice. "Europe?"

"Yeah, he got some business over there. I'm just minding the house while they're away."

He blinked up at Nancy like a wounded deer. "Looks like I came all this way for nothin'?"

"Guess you should have called him first huh?" she said sympathetically.

"I've been trying mam but his phone just kept going to voicemail."

She hesitated for a moment. "Strange? I don't seem to be having any problems getting through. Look, tell you what; why don't you come on inside. I usually give them a call about now anyway. I'm sure he'd be pleased to hear from you."

Ray laughed. "I'm sure he would."

The Lawson's home was tastefully decorated in delicate shades of primrose. Its dark hard wood floors were softened with large rugs and the light drapes billowed like clipper sails in a soft breeze. Ray browsed the living room and plucked a vase from a shelf. "Moorcroft isn't it?"

Nancy was prideful. "Yeah, Cheryl collects it."

"Expensive taste," he said, juggling it from hand to hand. Nancy moved to his side and relieved him of the object, placing it carefully back on the shelf.

"Why don't you take a seat Ray? Make yourself at home."

"Thanks." He relaxed back in the large white sofa and rested his arms on the luxurious designer cushions.

"Now then," she said softly, "let me make that call."

* * *

Travis lay back on the bed and stared blankly at the TV screen. With only eighty-four channels to choose from, his thumb was beginning to feel numb as it poked at the remote in search of something decent to watch. His phone rang and he checked the name flashing up. It was safe to answer.

"Hi Nancy; everything alright?"

"Everything's just fine; 'cept for that neighbour of yours blocking the driveway again with that darned truck of his."

"Listen Nancy, I'm afraid Cheryl's at the beauticians downstairs gettin' her nails done right now. I'll get her to give you a call though as soon as she gets back."

"Thanks, but that's not why I'm callin'. See, an old friend of yours called Ray has dropped by to see you. I'll put him on."

Ray? Travis sat up. "Wait, Nancy just hold on a minute will you…"

Nancy passed the phone to her guest. "I'll fetch you a glass of lemonade and some homemade cupcakes while you're talking."

Ray waited a moment until she disappeared into the kitchen. "Yo, Travis, long time no see. Anyone would think you were trying to avoid me."

The blood drained from Travis's face as the psychopath's voice struck his ear drum. "Bakula," he gasped. "What in hell are you doing in my house?"

"Didn't I tell you I'd be paying you a visit if I didn't receive the rest of my money? Well, here I am."

"Come on Danny, I've paid you most of it ain't I? I just

need a couple more weeks to raise the other three hundred grand that's all."

"Three hundred and twenty five; you're forgettin' the interest."

"What? But I'll never be able to pay you back if you keep raisin' the bar like that!"

"You knew my terms Travis. Besides, you don't have much choice."

"And what's that supposed to mean?"

"Leaving a sweet old lady here all on her own while you're off havin' a fine old time. I mean, what if she was to take a fall in the middle of the night? It could be days before she was discovered."

Travis's anxiety turned to blind panic. "Now come on Danny, please. There's no need to involve Cheryl's mom in any of this. All I'm askin' for is…"

"Shut up! I'm still not gettin' through to you am I? Maybe I should kill the old lady right now; show you I mean business before movin' on to that pretty little wife of yours; Cheryl, that's her name isn't it?"

"Now look, Danny please, I'm working on something real big over here, I mean *really big*. You'll get your money as soon as I get back, I swear to God you will."

"You got 'til mornin' to wire what's owing to my account. If you don't; you know what's gonna happen."

"Mornin' for God's sake? But that's impossible; I need more time!"

"Time's up. You know what you gotta do."

Nancy entered the room carrying a tray of cakes and lemonade. Bakula acknowledged her with a smile.

"Anyway, it's been real nice talking to you again Trav.

Listen, I gotta dash so I'll put you back onto Cheryl's mom. Catch up with you soon. Bye for now."

Nancy took the phone from him and held her hand over the receiver. She pointed at the tray. "Take a couple of those with you for the drive home son."

Bakula smiled at her through a set of pearly white teeth and selected a cupcake. "Very kind of you mam, thank you. I'll see myself out."

What a nice young man. Nancy waved goodbye to her guest then turned her attention back to Travis. "Hello, Travis are you there...Hello."

Walking down the drive, Bakula lifted the offering to his lips and took a large bite.

Sweet Jesus. He blew the rubbery morsel out of his mouth and it dropped to the ground with a dull thud before bouncing to a stop under an Azalea bush.

* * *

"Are you sure this is going to work?" Brenda asked, cuddling in closer to Sid.

"'Course it is; now just smile and do what I told you." Sid put down his pint and rested his hand on Brenda's thigh.

A look of horror crossed her face. "What the hell do you think you're doing?"

"It's got to look real hasn't it?" argued Sid.

"Alright," she relented, "but any higher and you'll be wearing that pint."

Over in the opposite corner, Barry was in full flow. "Did you know that most of The Beatles vocals were double tracked?"

"No, I can't say I did," Cheryl replied, wrestling the large pint glass to her lips.

"Yeah," chattered Barry, "and if you look at the sleeve notes on the back of the Hard Day's Night album…"

A smirking craggy face leered at Cheryl from the other side of the room and caught her eye. She gave Barry a gentle nudge. "I don't know what the hell Brenda sees in that slimeball friend of yours. He gives me the god damn creeps."

Barry unglued his eyes from his hot date and followed her gaze to a table in the opposite corner. A smug wink from Sid as his hand wandered up and down Brenda's leg achieved the desired effect and Barry's jaw hit the floor.

"Okay, we've got his attention," Sid whispered. "Now, move your hand further up my leg."

"Don't push your bloody luck Sidney," Brenda hissed. "If I want nuts I'll get them from behind the bar."

Cheryl tapped Barry on the shoulder. "Hey, remember me?"

Barry pulled his eyes away and turned back to Cheryl. "Sorry. Yeah, as I was saying; albums like A Hard Day's Night had sleeve notes written on the back…"

Unable to comprehend what he had just seen, morbid curiosity soon got the better of him and his eyes were once again drawn to Sid and his unlikely admirer.

"It's working," Sid sniggered. "Just look at his bloody face. Okay; on to phase two." He turned to Brenda and planted a kiss firmly on her mouth. She responded with clamped lips and clenched fists. Whether it was jealousy or just sheer disgust that caused Barry to pour his pint down the front of his new shirt was debatable. Either way, a trip to the bathroom was necessary to mop up the spillage. Making his apologies to Cheryl, he squelched off in the direction of the men's toilets.

Sid grinned. "Just one more turn of the screw should do it." He threw Brenda a wink and followed Barry down the corridor.

Cold water trickled from Barry's chin as he squinted at his reflection in the mirror. He splashed another palm full over his face and shook off the excess.

Sid swung open the door and walked in with a Travolta strut. "Hey Barry, that Brenda's a bit of a goer isn't she?" His voice echoed off the tiled wall giving his statement the authority of an official announcement. He stood up against the urinal and unzipped his fly. "I reckon me and the one-eyed baldy fella are in for a bit of action tonight."

"I don't think so. Brenda's not like that," Barry replied quietly, mopping down the front of his shirt with a paper towel.

"What! You're joking aren't you? You saw her; she can't keep her hands off me. Anyway," said Sid, fastening his trousers, "once I've poured a few more Bacardi's down her neck she'll be up for anything."

An image of his bullying step-father crashed into Barry's thoughts as Sid's callous words struck home. A brief moment of hesitation preceded an unexpected reaction from the mild mannered tour guide and he lunged at Sid, pinning him up against the wall by his scrawny throat. He pushed his angry purple face into Sid's. "If you do anything to hurt Brenda, so help me I'll…"

"Me upset her?" yelped Sid, like a wounded dog. "You're doing a pretty good job of that yourself. How do you think she felt when you came marching into her pub bold as brass with that American tart on your arm? Gutted she was. You know how she feels about you."

Barry relaxed his grip on the quivering bus driver and took a step back.

"No I don't," he replied quietly.

"For God's sake Barry, I told you on the bus didn't I?" shouted Sid with exasperation.

"Yeah, but I didn't think you were being serious!"

With renewed bravado Sid straightened his tie and marched up to Barry. "That's your problem isn't it?" he said, poking him in the shoulder. "You *never* think." He moved in closer and looked Barry in the eye. "You had your chance mate and you blew it. Now it's my turn."

"Fine; well, I hope you'll be very happy together," Barry snapped, before storming out. Sid smiled at his reflection in the mirror and redistributed his thinning hair with a wet comb. Brenda would soon be looking for a shoulder to cry on and he would be on hand to supply it. Sid gave himself a congratulatory wink before leaving to break the bad news to the unsuspecting landlady.

Barry returned to his date and watched as Sid snuggled in close to his best friend. Grabbing his jacket from the back of the chair the jealous tour guide stood up and turned to Cheryl. "It's getting a bit stuffy in here," he said, trying to control the emotion in his voice, "do you mind if we go somewhere else?"

Thank God. Cheryl snatched up her handbag and followed him to the door.

"Oh well that's just great isn't it," Brenda huffed, as she watched them leave. "Now what?"

Sid took a sip of his pint. "I tried Bren," he sighed, "I tried." He returned his hand to her leg and squeezed it sympathetically.

Brenda looked down in disgust at the nicotine ingrained fingers pulsating around her thigh and for the second time that day, Sid found himself shaking out the ice cubes that had fallen into the open neck of his shirt.

The cold air of the evening cleared Barry's head as he and Cheryl linked arms and strolled along the promenade back towards the town.

"Are you okay Barry," she asked, her voice tinged with concern. "You seem a little quiet."

Barry smiled back at her. "Quiet? That's the first time anyone's ever said that to me. No, I'm fine, really I am."

"Anyway, aren't you gonna tell me why you had to rush off on me like that this afternoon?"

"Er…" Barry faltered. "Just a bit of business that's all." He tried to change the subject. "Wow, look at that," he said, leaning his body over the railings to take in the view. "We get some of the best sunsets in the world around here."

They watched as the setting sun poured its fire onto the Mersey estuary like a smouldering crucible. Dissolving below the horizon, the glowing embers rippled along the river before dying against the sea wall.

"It sure is pretty," Cheryl sighed, trying her best to sound interested. "So come on tell me; where were you and your friends going?"

Barry felt decidedly uncomfortable. Lying was

something he was not very good at and Cheryl's probing was met with a stony silence.

"I guess that means mind your own business huh?"

"Sorry, it's just that I promised the lads I wouldn't say anything about it that's all."

"Say anything about what?"

"That's just it, I can't say."

She gave him a playful push in the arm and giggled softly. "Oh come on Barry, surely it can't be that important."

Barry looked her in the eye. "Believe me Cheryl, it is. Look, I really want to tell you; in fact I'm dying to tell you, it's just that..."

She stopped walking and looked him in the eye. Her voice was intense. "Hey, we're supposed to be friends ain't we; or did I get that wrong?"

Cheryl was radiant, her blonde hair shimmering in the dying light of the sun. The piercing hurt in her eyes proved fatal and Barry fell for her Southern Belle charm hook, line and sinker.

He sat her down on a nearby bench seat and took her hand. "Can you keep a secret?"

* * *

No sooner had the hotel door creaked open and Travis was on his feet confronting his exhausted wife. "Well honey, how did it go? Did you find out what was in the letter?"

"I found out everything I could," Cheryl sighed, taking off her coat and throwing it over the arm of a chair.

"And?"

She sat on the bed and dropped her hands into her lap. "You ain't gonna like this but Barry and his friends can't make head nor tail of it. Apparently, Lennon used to write in some kind of jumbled up poetry, to stop his aunt from reading his letters or something. The bottom line is they ain't got a clue where the banjo's hidden."

"Hell, those Brits couldn't find their ass without a map," said Travis, pacing the room. "The clue's in there," he insisted. "I heard Barry say so with my own ears!"

"Well if it is, they can't find it."

"Did he show it to you?"

She sensed where his line of questioning was leading. "Well no," she said gawkily.

"Christ Cheryl, didn't you even ask to see it?"

"Of course I did. But he doesn't carry it around with him like a freakin' donor card; he keeps it in his apartment."

"Shit!"

"Look Travis, it's time you faced up to things. Nobody's going to be finding no banjo so I suggest you just forget the whole thing and give DeVito his money back."

Travis sat beside her on the bed. "I can't do that sweetheart," he said softly.

"Travis honey, it's over. Just call him and tell him the deal fell through. You don't want to risk getting him all riled up and end up losing your job now do you?"

Travis paused. "While you were out your mom called."

"Well I hope you didn't tell her I'd gone out on my own? You know how she worries."

"Someone had dropped by to see me."

"Who was it?"

Travis didn't cushion the blow. "Danny Bakula."

Cheryl got up and steadied herself against the wall. "That psycho... was in our house... with my mom! Christ Travis, is she alright?"

Cheryl rushed to the bedside phone and began frantically punching in numbers.

"What the hell are you doing?"

"Making sure she's still breathing."

Travis wrestled the phone from her grasp and replaced the receiver. "You don't need to do that. Bakula said as long as he gets his money by morning we ain't got nothin' to worry about."

"Mornin'! Hell, you'd have to rob a bank first!"

Travis walked to the window. "Not necessarily," he said slowly.

Cheryl rushed over and spun him around to face her. "No Travis. Now I know what's whirlin' around in that thick skull o' yours, but if you use DeVito's money to pay off our debts we'll be running from those two thugs of his for the rest of our lives!"

Travis turned to face her. "Tell me about it. I've seen those boys in action and I know they're just itching for a reason to score a home run with my head."

"Call that son of a bitch Bakula and ask him for more time."

"I tried that already."

"Then try again."

"It's not as simple as that."

"It never is with you! Christ Travis, what are we going to do? What about mom?"

"Quit worryin' about your mom!" Travis shouted

angrily. "Bakula's got his money alright! I had it transferred to his account while you were out."

It was not often Cheryl found herself speechless, especially when arguing with her husband, but at that moment in time she just couldn't find the right words to express how she was feeling. On the one hand, she was relieved Travis had done the only thing he could to save her mom from Bakula's murderous clutches; but on the other, he had landed them in an equally dangerous predicament by using Tony DeVito's money to do it. Eventually she mustered up the only sentence she could think of that bore any relevance to their situation.

"So, what do we do now then?"

"I ain't figured that out yet."

"Call DeVito," Cheryl sighed, her eyes welling up. "Just get it over with and tell him what's happened. Dragging this thing out is only gonna make things worse."

Travis handed her his phone. "It's too late for that sweetheart; I've just picked up my messages; read that text."

Cheryl's eyes bulged as she read it out loud. *'Where the hell are you? Have found buyer for the banjo. Take next flight home. Call me! T. DeVito'.*

"You think that's bad?" said Travis, coldly. "Read the next one; came in five minutes ago."

'Carl and Wayne flying over. Have banjo ready for collection.! T. DeVito'.

Cheryl threw the phone on the bed. "They're coming here! Oh my God, what are we going to do?"

Travis grabbed her by the shoulders. "We're gonna find that god damn banjo, that's what we're gonna do! I ain't out of this yet and I'm not giving up 'til I've seen that letter with my own eyes."

"You just don't get it do you huh?" yelled Cheryl, pushing him away. "If three Beatles experts from Liverpool can't figure it out, what makes you think a dumb ass cowboy from Texas can do any better?"

"Well you better start praying that he can otherwise he'll be flying back to Texas in a god damn box!"

Cheryl searched her husband's eyes hoping to find a hint of insincerity, a tell-tale glint that would convince her that he was exaggerating. She shivered inside. He was deadly serious. "Alright; so what next?"

"You said Barry keeps the letter in his apartment, right?"

"Yeah, so?"

"So here's what I want you to do."

* * *

Barry walked out of the bathroom with a toothbrush sticking out of his mouth and flicked open the CD player next to his bed. 'Goodnight' from 'The Beatles' (white album) was always the song of choice to help him on his way to a restful night's sleep after the antics of a busy day. Lying back on his bed, he threw the toothbrush on the bedside table and rinsed the minty foam from his mouth with a sip from a coke can. As the opening chords of the Lennon song caressed his ears, he switched off the bedside lamp, closed his eyes and sank his head back into the pillow. His phone rang.

Barry felt for the light switch and fished his mobile from the tangle of sheets. "Hello?" he said, scratching his head.

"Barry?"

"Cheryl? Is that you?"

"Look, I'm sorry for calling you at this time but I was wondering; how about dinner tomorrow night; just the two of us?"

Barry sat up. "Dinner? Yeah, that'd be great. There are some nice restaurants in the Albert Dock; we could go there if you like."

"Actually, I was thinking of something a little more intimate. How about making it your place?"

"Brilliant! It'll make a nice change cooking for two. What time?"

"How does seven-thirty sound?"

"Sounds great to me," Barry chortled.

"Fine; I'll see you tomorrow night then. Sweet dreams. Bye"

Barry jumped out of bed and looked admiringly at his reflection in the mirror. He raised both fists in triumph. "Yes!"

CHAPTER FOURTEEN

It was pleasantly cool inside The Jacaranda where the man who gave The Beatles away held court. To the delight of his spellbound audience, Allan Williams pulled anecdote after anecdote out of the hat like a wizard shaman. The enduring popularity bestowed upon The Beatles first manager was dear to him and he gladly fulfilled an important purpose for the fans during the days running up to the annual Beatles Convention. He was much more than a living, breathing eye witness to the early years of the fledgling group; he was the man who nurtured the band and sent them to Hamburg. Allan had leased the former watch repair shop and converted it into a coffee bar in 1957. Naming it The Jacaranda after an exotic flowering tree; 'The Jac' as it became affectionately known, opened one year later.

With John and Stuart attending the Liverpool Art College nearby, they soon became regular customers of The Jac and spent many an afternoon huddled around a table talking art and music over empty coffee cups. Allan grew fond of the penniless duo and, to help them out, put them to work painting the toilets in exchange for free food and drink. Along with running The Jacaranda and The Blue Angel, another club he owned in town, Allan was a promoter and booking agent for many local bands including Gerry and The Pacemakers.

It was during one of his promotions at The Liverpool Stadium that John Lennon asked if he could get some work for his own group. Allan was shocked; he knew John and Stuart as art students, not musicians. Having agreed to act as their manager, he allowed them to rehearse in the basement of The Jac until he felt confident enough to send them on a tour of Scotland to hone their talents.

In August 1960, John, Stuart, Paul, George, and the recently recruited Pete Best, set off from Liverpool in a small crowded van, driven by Allan, for a stint he had secured for them at The Indra, a seedy nightclub in the red-light district of Hamburg, West Germany.

A year later, it came as a great disappointment when he felt obliged to end his association with The Beatles over their refusal to pay commission to which he felt he was entitled. Brian Epstein took over as The Beatles' manager in 1962 and contacted Allan to make sure there were no remaining contractual ties. Allan did not pull any punches. *'Don't touch 'em with a barge pole,'* he warned, *'they will let you down.'*

In later years, Allan and The Beatles were back on good terms. Described by McCartney in 'The Beatles Anthology' as: *'A great guy; a good motivator and very good for us at the time',* Allan's popularity hit new heights. Although guilty of making the most foolish gaffe in showbiz history, Allan Williams seemed more than happy with his legacy.

When he received a phone call from Barry the previous night telling him all about a 'fanzine' he and his friends were putting together entitled, 'The Definitive Guide to The Beatles Old Haunts', Allan was only too pleased to be of assistance. If anyone had information about the era of Sutcliffe and Lennon, he did.

Barry, Joe and Steve pushed back the doors of The Jac and scanned the room. "There he is, over there," said Barry. "Now remember, I've told him we're working on a fanzine so be careful what you say."

"What do you want to drink Allan!" Joe shouted. Allan's head spun around like a barn owl. The offer of a free tipple was like holding a red rag to a bull and he quickly excused himself from his admirers and scurried across to join the trio at the bar. They all knew Allan as a fellow regular of The Grapes in Mathew Street and greeted him like a long lost friend before retiring to the basement of the club for a quiet chat.

"John and the lads rehearsed over there," said Allan, pointing to a dark corner of the room. "They didn't have the money to buy microphone stands so they had to tie the mikes to broom handles," Allan laughed.

Barry, Joe and Steve knew what was coming next and before the silver-haired old man had chance to reminisce any further, Barry retrieved the list from his pocket and handed it to him. "Have a look at this list of The Beatles old haunts please Al. Can you think of any we might have missed?"

Allan's finger meandered down the names. "Well, The Cavern's not on here for a start."

"No, that's right," acknowledged Joe. "We only want to know about the places they hung out when Stuart was in the band."

"Yeah, and Stuart died before The Beatles started their residency at The Cavern," Barry interjected.

Steve leaned forward intensely. "The thing is Allan, the post-Cavern days have been written about millions of times. What we're interested in are the places no one really knows about. That's why we came to see you."

Impressed by Steve's convincing banter, Joe gave his brother an approving nod.

"I see," said Allan, mulling over the list again. "Well, you seem to have everything covered." Then he spotted something. "No, wait a minute, Gambia Terrace is missing."

"Of course!" Barry said, chastising himself with a slap on the thigh. "I knew I'd missed something. It's opposite the art college. John and Stuart shared a flat there for a while."

Allan cast his mind back. "It was more of a squat from what I remember; a real shit hole. John told me he left all his gear there when he went to Hamburg."

Barry, Joe and Steve sat up. "Did he?" they replied in unison.

Allan handed the tatty piece of paper back to Barry. "Cheers Al," he said, patting him on the back. "Another drink?"

Over the next half an hour their line of questioning grew more adventurous as Allan knocked back the steady supply of free booze. Had he ever found any Beatles artefacts during his time at The Jacaranda? Had John or Stuart ever entrusted him with anything to look after while they were playing in Hamburg?

"I did have a pair of Paul's leather pants once," Allan revealed. "Well, they were supposed to have been Paul's. There was no way of proving it really."

"Wow, have you still got them?" asked Barry.

"No. I offloaded them a couple of years ago to some Texan guy. Five grand he paid me for them, the daft sod."

"And what about this place?" asked Steve. "Has it changed much?"

"That mural on the wall is original; John and Stuart painted it. The only other thing I can remember from my time here is that." Allan pointed through an open door to an old coal bunker, hidden behind crates and beer barrels in the corner of the cellar. "I used to hide the takings in it. Let's face it," he laughed, "if you were robbing the place that would be the last place you'd think of looking wouldn't it?"

On the other side of town, Cheryl sat in the hotel room fiddling nervously with a stray lock of her blonde hair. "Do you have any idea at all what time Carl and Wayne will be arriving?"

Travis was staring out of the window deep in thought. "Sometime tomorrow I guess; who knows?"

"God, what a mess. Didn't I tell you DeVito would panic if you didn't return his calls?"

"Yeah, so you keep sayin'. Now hush up will you, I'm trying to think. I need to find a way of keeping his apes off my back for a little while longer."

He glanced down at a 'What's On In Liverpool' guide lying on the table and an idea suddenly popped into his head. Quickly, he snatched up the phone and punched in a number. He drummed his fingers on the bedside table as he waited for a reply. "Come on, pick up for Christ's sake." Travis exhaled his relief when he heard Billy Sheridan's voice on the other end of the line.

"Hi Billy boy, it's me Travis. Listen, I know this is short notice but can you meet me in half an hour; I'll explain everything when I see you. You can, great. Okay Billy, this is where I'm going to be."

* * *

It was almost midday by the time Barry, Joe and Steve pulled up outside John and Stuart's old flat. Barry flicked through the pages of his Beatles Anthology book which he had brought along for reference and stopped at page fourteen.

"Here it is lads, Gambia Terrace." They huddled around the book while Barry filled them in with the details.

Lennon and Sutcliffe had lived there for about four months spending most of the time playing music and painting. Described by Lennon as, *'just like a rubbish dump',* the flat was in a terrible condition and had no furniture except for a couple of beds and an old piece of tatty carpet. But it was the final paragraph relating to Gambia Terrace that caught Barry's eye. "Bloody hell, Allan was right! Listen to this. Lennon said, *'I left all my gear there when I went to Hamburg.'*"

Steve rubbed his hands together and looked across the road to the large Georgian building. "Now we're getting somewhere. Which flat was it?"

"Number 3," Barry replied without hesitation.

Joe brought the conversation back down to earth. "It's a bloody dentist."

They looked up at the lettering etched into the glass of the window. G D Morgan Dental Practitioners.

"Bollocks," said Steve. "Well that's that then isn't it?"

Joe rubbed his unshaven chin, deep in thought. "Wait a minute. If I'm not mistaken, the attics in those houses are all interconnecting. They're Georgian you see; that's how they built them in the early eighteenth century."

Barry pushed back his cap and scratched his head. "How the hell do you know that?"

"Discovery Channel," sighed Steve. "If ever you need to know about sharks, the Titanic or property renovation, Joe's your man."

"And *where*," Joe mused, "is the most likely place John would have stashed his beloved banjo while he was over in Hamburg? In the attic; right?"

"So what?" whined Steve, like a bored child. "We can't just knock on the door and ask the dentist if we can search his loft can we?"

Joe pointed to a boarded up dwelling at the gable end of the terraced block. "No, but if we can get into the attic of that derelict house, all we've got to do is make our way along the row until we're in the one above the dentist's."

Barry was ready to burst. "Brilliant!"

* * *

Outside The Beatles Story, Travis glanced at his watch as he eagerly awaited the arrival of Billy Sheridan. "Strange place to meet isn't it?" said a voice from behind. Travis spun around and shook Billy's hand with the enthusiasm of a bank manager greeting a lottery winner.

"Come on Billy, let's go inside. There's something in here I need you to see."

Travis ushered a bewildered Sheridan through the museum and stopped at the display case housing the replica of Julia's banjo. "Billy my friend," said Travis pointing at the banjo, "I need you to get me one of those."

Billy stared at the instrument and drew an angry breath through his yellow bucked teeth. "Bloody hell Travis, have you dragged me all the way here just to show me that? I do know what a banjo looks like you know. You could have told me what you wanted over the phone."

"No I couldn't. You see, the one I want must be identical to this one in every minute detail. Look, see how it's got all that mother of pearl inlay on the back?"

"Alright, I'll see what I can do. When do you need it by?"

"Tomorrow morning."

"What? Are you taking the piss? Do you know how long it's going take me to source something like that?"

"Why no time at all Billy boy." Travis put his arm around his bony shoulder and pulled him in close. "You see, I've already done that for you." Travis turned to the banjo and gave Billy a nudge.

Sheridan shrugged him away. "What, you want me to…?"

"Yep," Travis replied casually. "That's if it ain't out of your league of course?"

Travis's goading had the desired effect. "Listen mate, nothing is out of my league. You name it, I can get it."

"Great," said Travis. "How much?"

Billy took a discreet look around, his weasel eyes shining like black beads in the half-light of the room. He paid particular attention to the array of CCTV cameras hanging overhead and in each corner. He walked over to Travis and whispered. "CCTV cameras, infra red, vibration touch sensors...Three thousand should cover it."

Travis pulled back. "Three grand! You gotta be kidding me right?"

"No Travis I'm not. And I mean *'pounds'* not that Mickey Mouse money of yours."

"I'll give you a grand and that's my final offer."

"Bye Travis; have a nice day." Sheridan showed the cowboy the palm of his hand and walked towards the exit.

"Alright, alright," said Travis, waving him back. "You're as crooked as a dog's hind leg Billy, do you know that? Where do I collect?"

"Do you remember me taking you to the Sound Bite Café the last time you were in Liverpool?"

"The place where you handed over the Toby Jugs? Sure, I remember. Christ, I didn't stop shitting for a week."

Billy pulled up his collar and turned to leave. "Meet me there tomorrow; twelve o'clock. Oh, and Travis; make sure you have the cash with you . . . all of it."

* * *

In the alleyway running along the back of Gambia Terrace, Barry, Joe and Steve took a final look around before forcing open the rotting wooden gate of the derelict property. The courtyard garden, once perfectly proportioned and symmetrically laid out by the keen eye of a Georgian designer, now lay festooned with brambles, thicket and unruly sycamore shoots. Beneath the undergrowth, the centre could still be picked out by a crumbling ornate fountain which now spouted cascades of weeds instead of the restful musical tones of tippling water. *A secret garden,* Barry thought, as snail shells crunched underfoot.

Steve approached a window and easily pulled away the wooden boards which had been haphazardly nailed across to offer some protection from the elements and unlawful squatters. With Barry leading the way, they climbed inside the gloomy house in search of the staircase. They found it in the centre of the Minton tiled hallway opposite the front door and tentatively negotiated their way up the creaking rotten treads to the top floor. The finely crafted mahogany handrail felt like silk under Barry's hand as he made his ascent. On reaching the top floor, his torch illuminated the hatch leading into the attic. "How the hell are we going to get up there?"

"We'll have to give you a leg up," said Steve.

"Hang on a minute, why is it always me that has to go first?" argued Barry, shining his torch light in Steve's face.

"Because," said Steve, wincing in the dazzling beam, "we need to be down here to lift you up don't we, you fat lump?"

Joe and Steve joined hands and prepared to take Barry's weight.

"On three then," said Joe. "One...two..." Barry positioned his dirty boot in their upturned palms and on the count of 'three' they launched him towards the hatch. Gripping onto

Barry's legs, they steadied him until he eventually managed to push back the hatch and haul himself inside.

"I'm gonna help Steve up now," Joe shouted. "Get ready to grab him."

Like a caber tossing Scotsman, Joe locked his hands together and catapulted his younger brother up towards Barry's outstretched arms. Joe looked up and saw two heads peering down at him like cuckoos in a nest.

"How are you going to get up?" Steve shouted down.

Joe scratched his head. "Good question. Tell you what, I'll wait in the car and keep a lookout while you two are having a look around."

"You conniving little git," said Steve through gritted teeth. "You had no intention of coming with us did you eh?"

Joe gave his brother a wave and headed back down the staircase. "Don't forget to count the chimney breasts on the way along; otherwise you'll be looking in the wrong attic. Have fun chaps."

Inside the velvet blackness of the loft space, the rafters looming overhead resembled the rib cage of a giant sleeping beast as they were picked out by the torch light. On hands and knees, Steve and Barry gingerly made their way forward.

One floor below in the dental surgery, Mr Morgan stripped off his rubber gloves and walked over to the sink to wash his hands. "Bye Mr Pinchin, see you in six months."

The patient dabbed at his dribbling mouth with a paper tissue and nodded politely before opening the door to leave. The overpowering aroma of the receptionist's perfume made the dentist's nose wrinkle as she entered the treatment room.

"Excuse me Mr Morgan, a gentleman has just telephoned suffering with severe toothache. I've had to give him an emergency appointment. Hope you don't mind."

"What time Janice?" he asked, drying his hands.

"He'll be here in about twenty minutes. He's coming straight from work."

Janice turned to leave. "Oh Janice, before you go; be a dear and hold the fort for me while I nip out for a sandwich will you?"

Steve felt another splinter dig into the palm of his hand and grimaced at Barry's fat backside wobbling along in front. "How much further is it?"

"We've passed four chimney breasts," panted Barry, "just one more to go."

They halted their advance in the fifth attic space and took stock of their surroundings. Stacks of cardboard boxes, packing cases and bundles of jaundiced newspapers littered the joists. "Alright, you start over there and I'll try here," whispered Steve, ducking down under the eaves in an attempt to revive the blood flow to his legs.

Barry held the torch in his mouth and prised open the first packing case. He stared down at the magazines contained within and grunted with disappointment before moving on to the next.

Steve was not having much luck either and after ten minutes of careful examination he began randomly tipping out the boxes as anger and frustration got the better of him.

"Nothing there?" asked Barry.

"Sod all. Just books; dental journals mostly. Come on, let's get out of here."

"In a minute," said Barry. "Let me check this last box before we go."

Panning his torch light back down the low eaves towards the hatch, something caught Steve's eye. Beautifully veneered with rosewood and adorned with brass inlay, a cabinet stood alone propped up against a water tank, its bun feet resting on a series of planks straddling the joists. Steve edged his way towards the antique and slid open one of the finely crafted drawers. Grinning back at him were sets of gleaming false teeth labelled with handwritten tags, presumably to identify the patient to which each set belonged? Steve looked over at Barry rummaging away on the other side of the attic and a mischievous thought entered his head. He removed a set of teeth from its protective plastic bag, ripped off the tag and slotted them into his mouth. Like a cat stalking its prey, Steve crept up behind the unsuspecting Barry and tapped him on the shoulder. On seeing the ghoulish warped face leering back at him, Barry instinctively jumped back, his feet landing hard on the delicate plaster and laths spanning the rickety wooden joists. Steve's offer of a helping hand came too late and he could only watch in horror as Barry's bulky frame succumbed to gravity and plummeted amidst a cascade of debris down to the floor below.

Steve spat out the false teeth and scrambled over to the jagged gaping hole. Below him, face up with arms and legs spread-eagled like Leonardo's Vitruvian Man lay Barry, silent and motionless.

"Jesus Christ Barry, are you alright?" said Steve, in a hushed, yet urgent voice.

Barry's eyes flickered open and slowly focused in on his friend's anxious face peering down at him from above. "I think so," he groaned. Tentatively, he moved each of his limbs. *No pain, nothing broken.* Barry pulled himself to his feet and brushed off the powdery plaster dust.

"You're one lucky bastard," said Steve, pointing at the stack of flattened cardboard boxes he had landed on. Barry picked up his cap and flipped it back on his head. "Where the hell am I?"

"Dunno. Looks like some kind of store room," said Steve. "I'll meet you back at the car."

"What? You're not just gonna leave me down here are you?" Barry pleaded.

"Well there's no way you can get back up is there? You'll just have to find another way out. Now hurry up before someone comes."

Steve's head pulled back from the hole and he scurried off into the depths of the attic. Barry was alone.

After the fiasco at Strawberry Fields, Barry was now beginning to think the elusive banjo must be cursed. *Maybe it isn't meant to be found*, he thought, as he moved stiffly to the door. He pressed an ear to it. Silence. *Good.*

Pushing it open a few millimetres, he peeped through the crack and his eyes fell upon an empty dental surgery. He spotted the doorway to the main corridor which lay a couple of metres beyond the dentist's black leather chair on the far side of the room. Barry inched his way inside. With his ears pulsing to the thumping rhythm of his heart, he tiptoed, step by agonising step, towards the door and reached for the handle. Then he heard the clicking of urgent footsteps moving towards him and promptly retreated back inside. The footsteps were now accompanied by voices and Barry's eyes darted around the surgery in search of a suitable place to hide. Suddenly, the door burst open. Frozen with fear, Barry found himself staring into the bewildered eyes of the dentist.

Mr Morgan glanced at his wristwatch. "My word, that was quick. I wasn't expecting you for at least twenty minutes." He looked Barry up and down; his gaze perusing Barry's dusty dishevelled clothes. "Had to come straight from work did you?"

What the bloody hell's he talking about? Disorientated and confused, Barry could only offer up a half-hearted nod.

"Too painful to speak is it?" Mr Morgan said, sympathetically. "Alright, hop into the chair and let's see if we can find out what the problem is."

Not wanting to raise any suspicion, Barry thought it best to do as instructed. Lying back in the chair, Mr Morgan proceeded to focus the medical spotlight into Barry's mouth before selecting an instrument from a tray. The hooked, scythe-like implement prodded at each of Barry's teeth until it eventually found a cavity to probe around in. Barry clamped his sweaty hands to the arms of the chair and let out a gurgling throaty groan in protest as the searing pain threatened to lift off the top of his head.

"Yes, it's a loose filling," declared Mr Morgan, pulling down his mask. "Don't worry my friend; we'll soon have it sorted out."

Barry quivered when he heard the high-pitched squeal of the drill firing up. Mr Morgan's face loomed over him once more. "Open wide please."

Fifteen minutes later, Barry bade a mumbled farewell to the dentist and clutching a paper tissue to his swollen mouth, made his way down the staircase to freedom. Making a speedy ascent *up* the stairs was a man in workmen's overalls; his face grimaced in pain. Putting two and two together, Barry bolted out of the door and ran like hell.

CHAPTER FIFTEEN

Barry would have joined Joe and Steve for the post-mortem of their most recent debacle but his throbbing mouth was not up to the challenge. Numb from the dentist's injections, the drooling tour guide was returned to his flat before the brothers headed for the Philharmonic pub in Hope Street.

Joe got straight to the point. "Looks like we're going to have to put Tenerife on hold for a while doesn't it bro?"

"Why do you say that?" asked Steve defensively.

Joe rested a finger on his lip. "Er, let me think," he jibed sarcastically, "Barry! How's that for starters? He's a bleedin' liability he is." Joe leaned forward and looked Steve in the eye. "Look mate, I only went along with his little scheme to keep you happy but don't you think it's time we called it a day and got back to work? The convention starts tomorrow."

Steve shrugged his shoulders as his brain searched for a plausible counterargument. "Can't we just give it one more day?"

"Why? There's nothing of any use in that letter of his. We just keep going around in bloody circles."

"But Barry's convinced we're close to finding the place we've been looking for."

"Bollocks," Joe retorted. "If we were looking for one of The Beatles old haunts from The Cavern onwards it would have been easy; but, before 1961, when the group was unknown? Come on Steve, Lennon and Sutcliffe could have hung out in every club and pub in Liverpool for all we know. What are we supposed to do; search every bloody one?"

Joe looked into his brother's sad face and a pang of guilt hit him in the pit of his stomach. Although the last couple of days had indeed been a complete waste of time, the quest for the banjo had lifted Steve's spirits and given him something to believe in once more.

"Alright, you soppy sod," Joe said, ruffling up his brother's hair. "We'll give it one more day."

"Thanks Joe." Steve smiled and watched as a steady stream of customers began to fill the bar. Then someone caught his eye. Seated on a tall stool sipping a mineral water, a beautiful blonde was turning more than one head. He looked at her for a moment before giving Joe a nudge in the arm.

"Hey, look over there. Isn't that Cheryl?"

They watched as a tall handsome stranger strode over and sat down beside her. She greeted him with a kiss on the lips before reaching for a menu.

"Did you see that?" Steve gasped. "That bloke just kissed Barry's girlfriend!"

* * *

Barry had spent the late afternoon tidying his flat and his arms ached from all the scrubbing, polishing and hauling of bin bags down two flights of stairs to the refuse collection point outside his flat. Now spotless, he stood back to admire his work. With Cheryl due to arrive for dinner at seven-thirty he paced the kitchen, checked and rechecked the food, then dashed into the living room to light the candles on a small table set for two.

The long awaited ring of the doorbell sent his heart into a cascade of panicky missed beats as he ran down the hall to open it. Cheryl stepped out of the darkness and into the stark glare of the security light hanging over the doorway. Barry opened his mouth to greet her but it was Cheryl who spoke first.

"Hi," she said, thrusting a bottle of wine into his hand.

The tour guide's eyes were drawn to her figure hugging dress and plunging neckline as she squeezed past his galvanised frame.

"Gee, something smells good," she said, following him up the stairs and into the living room.

Barry gestured to a small sofa. "Take a seat. Would you like a drink?"

The Texan beauty daintily perched herself on the edge of the sofa and smiled up at him, her large eyes perfectly framed by lush black lashes.

"A glass of that will be just fine," she said sweetly, pointing at the bottle in his trembling hands.

Barry shuffled nervously from foot to foot. "Right then; better get this open."

Back in the sanctuary of the kitchen, he eventually liberated the stubborn cork from the bottle and filled two glasses. He took a long sip from his and allowed the effects of the alcohol to permeate through his bloodstream before venturing back into the living room. Cheryl was on her feet with a photograph in her hands. She placed it back on the shelf and took the glass from her host.

"Thanks." She pointed at the photograph. "Who's the lady?"

"That's my mum," he said, gazing at it affectionately.

"I guess you must still miss her huh?" she said softly.

"She was more than just a mum; she was my best friend. 'Course, she'd still give me a clip around the ear if I stepped out of line."

Cheryl laughed and took another gulp of her wine before returning to the sofa.

Barry sat down beside her. "So, er, what did you get up to today?"

His inquisitive tone caused her to let out a small involuntary burp. "Oops, pardon me," she giggled with embarrassment. "Hmm, what did I do today? Nothing to write home about; just chilled out at my pen pal's apartment. What about you?" she added, trying to deflect the question.

The 'ding' of the oven signalled the end of round one and Barry stood up. "Sounds like dinner's ready. I'll go and get the food."

Half an hour later, Cheryl's arm was stiff from sawing at her unyielding slab of incinerated steak. She relaxed back, dabbed her mouth with a napkin and threw it onto the table. "That was a lovely meal. You're a great cook."

"Thanks," Barry replied bashfully, through the flicker of the glowing candlelight. "Would you like some strawberries for afters?"

Cheryl's cheeks blew out like a bullfrog's neck and she

patted her stomach. "Are you kidding?" she puffed. "I'm just about fit to burst."

"Maybe later then eh?" he said, optimistically.

Later? It was time for Cheryl to make her move.

"Say Barry," she said, reaching across the table and taking his hand, "how about letting me have a look at that John Lennon letter you told me about last night?"

The tour guide retrieved his hand and stood up. "What about a coffee then?"

"Not right now thanks." Undaunted, she pushed on. "Barry; the letter? I really would love to see it."

Barry searched her pleading eyes and came to a decision. "Alright, I'll show it to you." He walked over to the sideboard and pulled out an envelope from a top drawer. "Here it is," he said, holding it up for her to see.

Cheryl's saucer eyes gleamed. "Wow! Come on then bring it over," she urged. "I'm dying to take a peek."

He returned the envelope to the drawer and slid it shut.

"Barry? What are you doing? I thought you were going to let me…" Cheryl protestations were cut short.

"I'm keeping a promise," he replied coolly. "I said I'd show it to you and I have; but I gave the lads my word I wouldn't let anyone read it. I'm sorry."

"Ah, c'mon, what harm can it do? They don't need to know."

"I'll know," he said, raising his voice. Barry returned to his seat and fiddled with his napkin to avoid her gaze.

Cheryl felt her throat close in panic. *Think god damn it, think!* She eventually broke the embarrassing silence.

"Do you know something," Cheryl said casually, struggling to keep the lid on her inner turmoil, "I think you're absolutely right."

Barry looked up, her response to his rebuttal taking him by surprise.

"It's like my daddy always used to say," Cheryl continued, "if you make a promise to someone you've got to stick by it. Okay, you said something about strawberries didn't you?"

The tour guide's mood lightened and he gathered up the dirty plates. "But I thought you said you were full?"

"Oh, I think I can probably make room for a couple."

Barry sprang up from his chair. "Coming right up!"

Cheryl waited until he had disappeared into the kitchen before rushing over to the sideboard. She glanced at the photo of Barry's mum and shivered as the woman's face glared back at her accusingly.

My God, she thought, *how far have I fallen to be willing to steal from such a decent man?* But when her thoughts flashed to Travis; his body lying in a shallow grave riddled with bullet holes, her guilt quickly evaporated. With her heart racing, she mustered what little courage she had left and reached for the drawer.

"Cheryl!"

She jerked her hand back in fright and slowly turned around. Barry was nowhere to be seen.

"Do you want cream on your strawberries?" his voice reverberated from the kitchen.

Cheryl relaxed and breathed a long sigh of relief. "Just a little!" she shouted back.

The warped wood of the cheaply made drawer let out a painful squeak as she yanked hard on the brass handle. Plunging her eager hand inside, she grasped the only envelope in sight and took a brief glance. Stuart Sutcliffe's German address scrawled on the front confirmed it was the letter she was looking for and with the precision of a pickpocket she removed it from the envelope, stuffed it into her jacket and returned the empty envelope back to the drawer.

Barry returned with the dessert to find Cheryl where he had left her, sitting at the table casually puffing on a cigarette. She looked at him through a blur of mild intoxication, which the anxiety of the evening had been keeping at bay, and she let out a nervous girly giggle.

For Cheryl, the rest of the dinner date was a stressful affair. Fearful that Barry might relent and show her the letter after all, she deliberately avoided talking about The Beatles and kept the conversation focused on his culinary expertise. It came as a great relief when, half an hour later, she heard the honking of a taxi's horn outside in the street.

"Taxi's here," she said, jumping up from the sofa like a gazelle.

Barry wrapped Cheryl's coat around her shoulders and escorted her down the stairs to the front door. She stepped out into the night and the fresh air cleared her cluttered head. "Thanks for taking the time to show me around and everything," she said, forcing a smile. "It's been a lot of fun."

Barry didn't hide his disappointment. "So this is goodbye then?"

"I guess it is. See, I've got to head back to the States soon and there are some things I gotta take care of before I leave."

Barry seemed close to tears. "No need to explain; I

understand."

The taxi sounded its horn again.

"Listen, you take care of yourself now, do you hear me?"

Cheryl wrapped her arms around his thick waist and squeezed him tightly. "You're one of the nicest guys I've ever met Mr Tour Guide," she said, kissing him on the cheek. "I just want you to know that."

With the letter now in her possession and the prospect of making her husband deliriously happy, the drive back to the hotel should have been a pleasant one. It wasn't.

* * *

The hotel door clicked open and before Cheryl had time to open her mouth, Travis pounced.

"Well?"

"Here!" Cheryl pulled the letter from her bag and threw it on the bed. Travis rushed over and scooped it into his eager hands. His eyes darted hungrily down the page.

"My God you did it!"

"Oh I did it alright," she said, throwing her coat over the back of a chair. "Do you realise Barry's gonna be heartbroken when he finds out what I've done to him?"

Travis laughed. "Come on, get real. In a few days time you won't even remember his name. Now help me try and make sense of this bullshit will you. Who the hell could 'Jac' be?"

Cheryl looked at the letter over Travis's shoulder. The hours of lecturing from Barry had taught her something useful after all. "Jac ain't a person dumb ass. It's The Jacaranda, the club where The Beatles started off? Barry told me all about it."

"The Jacaranda? Yeah, I've heard of that."

"I wouldn't get too excited though," said Cheryl, pouring herself a drink, "it's bound to be the first place they looked."

"Then they didn't look hard enough. Check this out." Travis slapped the letter down on the coffee table and pointed to the relevant paragraph. "Get your coat back on honey. We got a banjo to find."

CHAPTER SIXTEEN

Cheryl pulled herself close in to Travis's side to shield herself from the breeze whistling up the hill from the river. Loitering in a secluded doorway behind The Jacaranda, they waited until a drunken reveller had finished relieving himself against a dustbin before making their move. Once the military drum roll of urine on metal had ceased, Travis slid the bolt on the large wooden gate, took Cheryl by the arm and crept inside the nightspot's cluttered backyard. A harsh fluorescent street light enhanced Cheryl's worried features as she pushed her face in close to Travis's.

"I still think it's crazy breaking in here when it's full of people," she whispered. "We're bound to get caught?"

"I suppose you'd rather we came back later when it's deathly quiet and all the alarms are turned on?"

Cheryl didn't answer.

"No, I thought not. Now just quit you're griping. All you gotta do is remember what I told you in the car; if anyone sees us, we just make out we're a couple of drunken tourists who took a wrong turn. Trust me honey, I know what I'm doin'."

Travis spotted the steel doors covering the delivery chute

leading down into the cellar. "Okay honey, I think I found a way in." He pressed his back into the whitewashed wall and gestured for Cheryl to do the same. Travis waited for the right moment before peeling back the doors; the sound of their groaning hinges masked by the whoops and wails of the partygoers inside singing along to the music. He peered down the hole and into the gloom. "Quick, hand me the flashlight honey."

"Flashlight? I thought you had it."

"Jesus Christ Cheryl, are you telling me you've left it in the car?"

"I didn't leave it there, you did!"

Travis panicked as her voice echoed around the yard. "Sshh, keep your voice down god damn it." He looked back down the chute. "Alright, we'll just have to make do without it. Come on."

Cheryl clung to the arm of her husband as he led her down a narrow set of steps which ran alongside the steep chute. Inside, the cellar was dimly lit and cool; its grubby bricked walls lined with crates, wine racks and beer barrels. He took the letter from his pocket. "Now it says somethin' here about Jac and another fella called Old King Cole. Who do you think that could be huh?"

Cheryl sighed. "It's Jabberwocky."

"The furry guy in Star Wars?"

"No; not *'the Wookie'* you dickhead. *'Jabberwocky'*. It's that jumbled up poetry I told you about in the hotel. Don't you ever listen?"

Travis slowly stalked the cellar's perimeter until he stumbled across the old coal bunker. "Jesus, take a look at this," he hissed, crouching down next to it.

"Yeah great," said Cheryl, unimpressed. "It's a coal bunker; so what?"

"Well don't you get it? Old King Cole ain't no person. Lennon was talkin' about this thing. Come on Cheryl, The Jac; Old King Cole; what the hell else could it mean huh?"

Good point. Cheryl knelt down beside her husband. "My God, I actually think you might be right."

"See, what did I tell you? Honey, I think we just hit pay dirt."

Travis poked his head inside. "Jesus, I can't see a damn thing." He removed his Stetson and handed it to Cheryl. "Here, hold onto this for me will you."

She put his hat on top of a beer barrel and watched as Travis lay flat on his stomach and pushed his head and shoulders into the depths of the coal bunker.

"Well? Can you see anything?"

Travis's voice was muffled. "What the hell do you think I am; a god damn bat?"

The sound of laughter and music gained a couple of decibels when the door from the bar upstairs was suddenly pushed open. Too shocked to speak, Cheryl thumped Travis's leg when she heard footsteps clunking down the cellar stairs. Quick as lightening she scurried behind a stack of empty beer crates and held her breath. Cheryl watched with a hand clamped over her mouth as a barman studied a wine rack. She prayed he would not set eyes on Travis's legs poking out of the bunker just a few feet away. The barman found his bottle and trudged back up to the bar closing the door behind him.

Cheryl rushed back over to Travis and tapped him on the back. "It's okay, he's gone. Now hurry up. I wanna get the hell out of here." She kept her eyes fixed on the door while her husband continued to grope around aimlessly.

"Wait a minute; I think I felt something there." Travis reached out further, the tips of his fingers brushing against something long and slim. "Yeah honey, there's definitely something in here. Come on baby," he coaxed, "come to Daddy, come on…Gotcha!" Travis's heart began to thump out the beat of victory. "I got it honey!" he shouted, throwing caution to the wind. "Pull me out of this hellhole will you."

Cheryl grabbed onto her husband's legs and yanked hard. He emerged choking for breath in a plume of black dust clutching his prize above his head.

His irate wife jumped to her feet and kicked him in the shin. "It's a god damn shovel you moron!"

"What?" He pulled himself up and knocked the dust from his clothes. He looked down at the shovel and angrily kicked it across the floor. "God damn it!"

"Wait a minute!" Cheryl ran over and picked it up. "What's this tied around the handle?"

Travis snatched it from her. "My God it looks like some kinda note?"

Cheryl gave him a pair of nail clippers and he frantically picked at the string holding it in place. He pulled it loose and spread the curling scrap of soot-streaked paper out on top of a beer crate. Cheryl watched her husband's eyes light up as his finger traced along the scrawled handwriting.

"Well, come on; what does it say?"

Travis picked up the shovel, grabbed Cheryl by the hand and dragged her towards the chute steps. "I'll tell you on the way to the graveyard honey."

* * *

The Albert Dock was buzzing as hundreds of diners spilled out of the many waterfront bars and restaurants in search of a place to party. Below the busy cobbled walkways inside The Beatles Story, two men were engrossed in a delicate operation.

Billy Sheridan applied just the right amount of pressure to prise open the alarm housing before darting a pair of cutters around the wires and disabling the system. "I think that's the last of them." He turned to hand the cutters to his young apprentice but he was nowhere to be seen. "Franny?" Billy hissed.

"Over here," he whispered, "behind the counter."

Cautiously, Billy crawled over to find him emptying the shelves of the souvenir shop into a canvas bag. "What the hell do you think you're doing?" he snapped.

A look of puzzlement crossed Franny's face. "Robbin' the place?" he blinked.

"Put it back," he ordered, fighting to control his anger. He held up a torch to illuminate a long and winding corridor. "What we're looking for is down there. Now come on." Franny vaulted over the counter and dutifully followed his master into the shadowy depths of the museum.

* * *

Cheryl offered the note up to the reading light inside the car and squinted at it. "Are you absolutely sure about this?"

"Honey, when Orville and Wilbur Wright sat in that homemade flying machine of theirs were they absolutely sure they weren't gonna plummet …"

"Travis if you start feedin' me any more of that bullshit so help me God I'll shove this note right down the back of your god damn throat." Cheryl pushed it back into Travis's hand and looked out across the road to the cemetery gates. "Now just do whatever you've got to do will you. This place gives me the god damn creeps."

Travis checked his flashlight. "What the hell are you worried about? It's me that's got to go in there?" he said, twisting around to grab the shovel from the back seat. He inched open the car door, took a quick look around to see no one was coming and hopped out.

Cheryl leaned over. "Just hurry up will you."

"Wish me luck." he said, clicking the door shut.

Woolton Cemetery rested serenely in the pale light of an early harvest moon befitting a scene from any vintage horror film. Right on cue, an owl hooted and swooped into the long grass which rustled softly in the cool breeze. Beyond the thin iron railings, sprawled out as far as the eye could see, lay a forest of twisted headstones. The task ahead was not going to be easy. Travis threw the shovel over the railings and scrambled over. Watching from the car, Cheryl heard the distant cry of a fox piercing the night air. She shivered inside.

Travis was methodical in his approach, trotting down the rows in a gridiron pattern, flashing his torch from stone to stone. It was over an hour later when he eventually found the grave he had been searching for. Tired and exhausted, he fell to his knees to catch his breath and gazed at the smooth grey tablet before him. The headstone of Eleanor Rigby was a plain affair and not at all what he had been expecting. He pulled the note from his pocket and swept the torch across the scrawl.

'Keep one step ahead of Eleanor'

With his back to the headstone he assumed the position and took one large step forward. He looked at the note again for the next instruction.

'Dig it!'

Travis took off his jacket and picked up the shovel. Taking a final look around, he raised it high above his head and plunged it hard into the ground.

* * *

Billy knelt in front of the glass display case housing the banjo replica and scrutinised the array of wires attached to its locking mechanism. He stretched an arm out behind his back and snapped his fingers impatiently. "Pliers."

Franny's shaking hands fumbled inside the tool kit until they found the desired instrument. Billy carefully separated the wires. "Cutters," he urged, his hand thrashing behind his back like an elephant's trunk as his tolerance began to evaporate. The cutters were deployed and Billy snipped the connections. The alarm was now rendered helpless and the lock succumbed to Sheridan's probing screwdriver with a splintering crack. He leaned inside the glass cabinet and took the banjo from its mounting, silently placing the instrument into its case.

* * *

Back at Woolton Cemetery, Cheryl awoke from a restless

doze and pulled her collar up around her stiffening neck. The distant trill of a finch and the pale palette of pink and powder blue just above the horizon told her that dawn would soon be upon them. She checked her watch. Travis had been gone over two hours. She looked across to the cemetery but he was nowhere in sight. The blue flashing light of a police car suddenly lit up her face as it coasted to a halt and Cheryl slid down into her seat.

Holy shit.

She heard the dull metallic thud of the police car doors and the sound of crackling walkie-talkie banter, then, something more worrying; the rattling of the cemetery gates being scraped open. She inched her head up and watched in horror as two police officers armed with powerful flashlights ventured inside.

Oh my God. Travis.

* * *

Billy gently closed the display case door and slung the banjo under his arm. "Okay Franny, we're all done here," he whispered. "Have you put all the tools back in the bag?"

No answer.

Billy's head spun around. "I said are all the tools back in the…?"

The faint sound of a piano reverberating through the museum cut him off in mid-flow. *You've gotta be bloody kidding.*

Flinging the tool bag over his shoulder, Billy broke into a sprint expertly negotiating the maze of winding corridors like a well-trained lab rat. He found Franny seated at

Lennon's famous white piano happily tinkling a childlike rendition of Chopsticks. Billy was incensed. He threw down the tool bag, clipped his foolish apprentice around the ear and waved the banjo in front of Franny's blinking eyes. "One more note out of you and I'll ram this thing so far up your arse . . ."

Terrified, Franny jumped up from the stool and reached for the piano lid.

"No!" Billy shouted, "don't close the ...."

As the lid fell down over the keyboard the ear splitting whirr of sirens sounded throughout the building.

* * *

Travis had been busy and was kneeling in a narrow pit three feet deep frantically clawing at the earth with his bare hands. "Come on you son of a bitch," he grunted, "I know you're down there." Then something caught his eye. A beam of light bounced off the surrounding headstones casting long-fingered shadows deep into the graveyard. He heard voices approaching. *Shit*.

Throwing himself into the shallow grave, he lay down on his back like a freshly laid out corpse. Overhead, he watched as the morning moon slid behind a patch of thick cloud plunging the graveyard into complete darkness.

He held his breath and waited.

"No sign of anyone in here Sarg," said one of the police officers into his walkie-talkie. "The light must have been coming from traffic on the other side of the cemetery; over."

The policeman turned to his colleague. "Come on; let's get back to the car."

Travis let out a long, slow breath as their footsteps receded. But the sound of Sweet Home Alabama jangling through the cemetery stopped the officers in their tracks and sent them creeping towards Eleanor Rigby's grave to investigate. With torches on full beam, they peered into the pit and found a man wedged inside trying to wrench a phone from his back pocket. Travis winced and threw a protective hand over his face as the twin beams hit him straight between the eyes. He smiled at the gawping officers through spread fingers. "Howdy."

Cheryl sat on the edge of the car seat with her phone pressed to her ear listening to her husband's voicemail message. Moments later, she heard the clanging of the cemetery gates and watched in despair as the two officers frogmarched Travis down the street and bundled him into the back of the police car.

Travis looked back at his wife and shot her a dirty look.

'I'm sorry,' she mouthed, as the police car whisked him off into the night.

CHAPTER SEVENTEEN

The following morning Barry took his usual early morning bus ride into the city centre, his head juddering against the cold rain-streaked window. It was the day of The Beatles Convention but for a guy who lived and breathed everything Fab he was in an unusually miserable mood. It was not Cheryl's untimely farewell the previous night that caused his spirits to go hurtling into the abyss, nor his spat with Sid the night before that. Upsetting Brenda, the only real friend he had, was definitely a contributing factor, but it was the fiasco at Gambia Terrace and overall lack of success with the search for the banjo that troubled him most.

He knew Joe and Steve's commitment was teetering on a knife edge and, unless he could come up with a substantial new lead, the quest which started off brimming with optimism and promise would end with his friends throwing in the towel.

To make matters even worse, there was no Magical Mystery Tour to help take his mind off things either; all the main roads had been closed off to make way for the many outdoor stages erected throughout the city. Instead, Barry had volunteered to lend Joe and Steve a hand in the store. But given their current misgivings, the idea of spending an entire day listening to snide remarks and recriminations was not something he was looking forward to.

The bus lurched to a stop and jolted Barry from his daydream. Sombrely, he watched a group of cheerful shoppers jump off and head into Liverpool One for a touch of retail therapy. As he waited for the bus to move off again, he took in a weary breath and read a fresh billboard poster inviting him to the launch of a new and exciting nightclub called 'Cloud 9'. It was wasted on Barry. Never the nightclub type, his idea of a good time was to settle down in his flat and absorb the contents of a Beatles encyclopaedia whilst being serenaded by the Fab Four.

A sudden loud thump on the side of the bus sent a surge of adrenaline through his body and he pressed his face up against the window to investigate. Outside on the road, a young boy dressed in a bright red Liverpool football strip was retrieving his ball from the gutter. Barry smiled for the first time that day as he watched the lad dribble the ball down the street. Then something caught his eye; the number 9 on the back of the boy's shirt. It reminded him of an early John Lennon drawing of a footballer wearing a number 9.

Number 9?

His eyes darted back to the Cloud 9 poster.

Number 9?

Barry's eureka moment hit him between the eyes like a speeding bullet.

"Number 9! That's it!"

* * *

Tired, dishevelled and caked in dried mud, Travis shuffled from his police cell and approached the desk. Merseyside Police had taken the matter most seriously and Travis was lucky to get off with a caution. Should he be foolish enough to return to the cemetery he would be arrested, charged with trespass and vandalism, and summoned to appear before the local magistrates' court. The desk sergeant pulled a sealed polythene bag from a drawer and emptied the contents onto the counter. He ticked each item off a list before handing them back to Travis. "One wristwatch, one leather wallet, one cell phone, one tie…"

"Still can't believe you thought I might hang myself," Travis said, as he slung it back around his neck. The policeman ignored his flippant remark and carried on ticking his boxes. "One scrap of paper," he looked up at Travis, "one shovel…"

Travis picked up his phone and noticed he had seven missed calls; all from Cheryl. Punching in her number he was greeted by three beeps as the battery gave up. *Great.*

Back at the hotel, Travis bore the critical glares of fellow patrons as he trudged across the hotel lobby and made for the lift. He swiped his key card and the hotel door clicked open. "Hi honey. Guess where I've just spent the night?"

Cheryl rushed over to greet him. "Sweetheart, you're back," she said, her face flushed. Her forced upbeat tone told him something was wrong.

"I was just explaining to *our guests* that you've been closing that deal for Mr DeVito."

Guests? Travis pushed open the door and felt his knees buckle.

Carl was reclining on the sofa watching an episode of Judge Judy while Wayne sat at the table cramming his mouth with peanuts. "Fellas! Great to see you," Travis gushed, rushing over to shake Carl's hand. "When did you get into . . . ?"

"About an hour ago," said Cheryl, anticipating the question, her eyes burning into Travis's.

Carl wiped his hand on the arms of the sofa and pushed back his hat. "Do you know how many times DeVito's tried calling you?"

"DeVito? Call me?" said Travis, feigning surprise. "Oh, wait a minute; I know what's happened here." Travis pulled the uncharged cell phone from his pocket and handed it to Carl. "Damn thing's broken, see."

Wayne flicked a peanut in Travis's general direction. "Hotel phone ain't."

"What? Are you telling me DeVito has been trying to call me here; at the hotel?" Travis turned to Cheryl and wagged his finger. "Remind me to speak to the manager about those monkeys on reception. Not passing on important messages; they need their butts kicking!"

Carl stood up and approached Travis. "DeVito's real pissed with you right now. Thought you'd taken off with his money."

"Taken off with his money," cackled Travis. "Honey did you hear . . ."

"Shut up, I ain't done yet."

"Sorry."

"Now he says, *if you ain't got the banjo*, we're to see to it that the money is returned to his account immediately."

Travis sidled over to the bedside table and picked up the

phone. "Listen, why don't I just give him a call huh? I'm sure we can sort this out without having to resort..."

Wayne jumped out of his chair and snatched the phone from Travis's hand. "I don't think the boss wants to talk to you right now," he said, replacing the receiver.

"Would you two guys like me to make you another coffee or something?" asked Cheryl, trying to ease the tension in the room.

Neither man replied. "So," said Carl, "has the deal been done or what?"

"Why yeah, 'course it has," Travis cackled through a nervous laugh.

Carl held out his hand. "Then hand it over."

Travis's mouth went into bullshit overdrive. "Now come on fellas, you don't expect me to have it *here* do you?"

Carl folded his arms across his chequered chest. "What d'you mean?" he grunted, suspiciously.

Travis rolled his eyes and laughed. "Come on Carl, you're joking with me right? Only a real dumb ass would leave Mr DeVito's banjo; worth *millions of dollars*, lying around in some shitty hotel room?" Travis looked over at Wayne. "Ain't that right big fella?"

Wayne chortled in response and pointed a ridiculing finger at his buddy. "Yeah Carl, only a real *dumb ass* would do that!"

Travis relaxed a little and clasped his hands together. "Listen fellas, you must be real tired after that long flight so why don't you get yourselves something to eat and grab a couple o' hours shut eye." He checked his watch. "If you call back here at, say, two o'clock, I'll have the banjo all ready and waiting for you to collect. How's that sound?"

"Come on Carl, what's a couple of hours?" said Wayne, riding to Travis's rescue. "I'm starved; let's go get some food."

Travis struggled to maintain the forced smile etched into his deadbeat face.

"Alright," Carl conceded, "two o'clock. But be warned," he said, poking Travis in the chest, "if that banjo ain't here when we get back we're gonna bust you up so bad your pretty wife here will have to mop you up with a sponge."

"Enjoy your breakfast fellas," Travis said, opening the door for his guests. As soon as he saw them disappear into the lift, Travis slammed the door shut and ran to the bedside phone.

"Pick up Billy; please pick up the god damn phone." Billy's voicemail droned out and Travis cast the phone down onto the bed. "Shit!"

Cheryl grabbed Travis by the arm. "You don't honestly think DeVito's gonna be fooled by some cheap fake do you?" she shouted.

"Nope, but it ain't DeVito I've gotta fool right now; it's Dumb and Dumber out there filling their fat faces. I can easily smooth things over with DeVito later."

"How?"

"The way I figure it; by the time they get back to Texas, I'll have found the real thing. Once that's done I can tell fatso that sending Carl and Wayne over here was jeopardising the deal and I had to think of somethin' to get rid of them. He'll buy it."

Cheryl let go of her husband's arm. "But that means…Jesus; you ain't seriously thinking of going back to that graveyard are you?"

Travis was adamant. "'Course I am. The banjo's in there; buried behind that headstone." He checked his watch again. "Look, I can't stand here arguing with you all morning, I'm supposed to be meeting Billy at noon to collect the replica."

"But what if he don't have it?"

Travis thought hard. "Good point. Tell you what, let's pack all our stuff away and dump it in the car. That way, if Billy don't come up with the goods we can just hightail it out of town without having to come back here."

Fetching her suitcase from the wardrobe, Cheryl threw it on the bed and began cramming it with clothes as her husband hit the shower. "That's the best idea you've had all week."

* * *

Barry eased into a slow jog as he rounded the corner of Mathew Street willing his aching legs to carry him that little bit further. Inside The Beatles Store, Joe and Steve were preparing for what they hoped would be a very profitable day.

Every year, The Beatles Convention concluded with The Mathew Street Festival, an event which attracted hundreds of thousands of people from across the globe to celebrate the music of Liverpool's most famous sons. It was started in 1993 by the owners of The Cavern Club and at that time was confined to Mathew Street alone. But year on year it grew, spilling out into the surrounding streets until it eventually engulfed the entire city. For retailers like Joe and Steve, this was the day they could offload some of their dead stock and, more importantly, it would keep the bank manager off their backs for at least a few more months.

Joe arranged the counter top display to make the most of all the small, cheaper items which would serve to entice the impulsive Beatle browser. As Steve turned up the radio to catch the latest football results, Barry staggered into the store just in time to hear the tail end of the local news:

'Well, it's that time of year again and it seems that some people will do almost anything to get their hands on a piece of Beatles memorabilia. In the early hours of the morning, an American businessman was arrested in the grounds of Woolton Cemetery . . .'

"Sshh listen!" Joe turned up the radio and gestured for everyone to keep quiet:

'...His motive for attempting to dig up the grave of 'Eleanor Rigby', the namesake of one of The Beatles most famous songs still remains unclear. More news coming up after the break . . .'

For the first time in months, The Beatles Store rang out to the sound of laughter.

"I told you they'd fall for it didn't I?" said Steve, struggling to take a breath. He turned to Barry. "Well done mate, we played a blinder there didn't we eh? That'll keep 'em busy for a while."

Joe gave his brother a playful nudge. "Who played a blinder? It was *me* that wrote the fake letter; all that stuff about The Jac and Old King Cole; that was all my idea!"

"Yeah, but I wrote the note?" Steve argued. "*And* I had to

sneak into The Jacaranda and tie it to the handle of that bloody shovel!"

Joe wiped a tear from his eye. "I still can't believe they fell for all that shit about Eleanor Rigby though."

"Why not?" laughed Steve, "they're Americans aren't they? But come on Joe, the star of the show has got to be Barry here." Steve acknowledged his approval with a firm slap on the tour guide's back. "How the hell did you manage to keep a straight face while she was round at your place eh?"

Barry's answer was subdued. "It wasn't easy I can promise you that. I suppose a part of me was hoping you might have been wrong about her."

Joe put a consoling hand on Barry's shoulder. "Sorry mate, but as soon I saw that cowboy hat on the stool next to Cheryl in the Philharmonic pub I remembered the guy with her was the one skulking behind the shelves over there; when you first told us about the banjo."

"Hmm." Suddenly, Barry's mood lightened. "Hey, never mind about that now. I think I've got us a new lead!"

The smile dropped from Joe's face. "Not interested Barry, not today."

"Just hear me out will you, you'll love this," Barry insisted. "The number 9 played a big part in Lennon's life didn't it?" Barry's revelation was met with vacant expressions.

"Come on lads; John lived at 9 Newcastle Road, Brian Epstein discovered The Beatles on November 9th, The Beatles played their first gig at The Cavern on February 9th."

"Yeah, so?" said Steve.

"So… I think the number 9 is a clue to where John hid the banjo."

Joe was laughing again. "What a load of bollocks."

"No it isn't," Barry insisted, "John was convinced he had a fateful connection with the number 9; that's why he wrote Revolution 9 and #9 Dream."

"Maybe he just liked the number," replied Joe, dismissively. "Have you ever considered that?"

Barry would not be silenced. "Look, I said we had to get inside the mind of Lennon if we're to have any chance of finding Julia's banjo didn't I? Well that's exactly what I've done. John was obsessed with the number nine, and with good reason. He met Yoko Ono on the 9th, his son Sean was born on the 9th, The Beatles signed their contract with EMI on the 9th, they did their first Ed Sullivan Show on the 9th. Come on Joe, this means something?"

Joe shook his head. "It's a coincidence Barry, that's all."

"He was born on the 9th and he died on the 9th!"

"Got ya!" said Joe, pointing an accusing finger, "because that's where you're wrong. John Lennon died on the 8th. Isn't that right Steve?"

"Sorry Barry, but Joe's right. He died on the 8th December 1980."

Barry leaned across the counter. "Yes, in America he did. But in England, *the place of his birth,* John Lennon died on the 9th." Joe and Steve exchanged glances.

"Alright smart arse," said Steve, "if this number *is* so important, why isn't it mentioned in the letter?"

"Oh, but it is." Barry took the letter from his pocket, walked back a few paces and held it up. "Tell me what you see?"

"From here? Bugger all," said Steve.

"Try again. Look at the cartoon face."

Joe and Steve examined Lennon's drawing; the profile of a grotesque face with bulging forehead, huge eye and long upturned chin.

Steve spotted it first. "Christ Joe, Barry's right."

Joe rushed around the counter for a closer look. There was no doubt about it; Lennon's cartoon doodle was a number 9.

Barry reached for a shelf and began thumbing through the books. "There's a book in here that lists all The Beatles early gigs. If I'm right, one of those gigs will have something to do with the number 9. It could be the old haunt we've been looking for." Barry soon found it and his fingers flicked through the pages.

"What did I tell you!" he said excitedly, peeling the book open on the counter. "Right, listen to this. On the 9th September 1961, *remember,* that's the *9th of the 9th,* The Beatles played a gig at the Aintree Institute."

Joe shook his head. "I'm still not convinced."

"Aren't you?" Barry moved in close. "Tell Joe what district of Liverpool the Aintree Institute is in Steve?"

Steve did not need to open his mouth; the expression on his face said it all.

"That's right," said Barry smugly, "Liverpool 9."

Barry was ready to burst. "I'm going to get over there right away and see if I can arrange for us to have a look around. I'll be back in about an hour."

* * *

Travis's car screeched to a halt outside the hotel and he jumped out. While he struggled to load the luggage piled up outside the main entrance, Cheryl sat on a suitcase, lit up a cigarette and watched the hordes of people making their way towards The Cavern Quarter. In the distance, echoing off the walls of the tall surrounding buildings, Beatles songs pumped from outdoor stages, merging together to form a soundscape so surreal Lennon himself would have been proud of it. Liverpool was about to explode with a feverish intensity.

"Dammit Cheryl, can you quit daydreaming and give me a hand back here?"

Cheryl flicked her cigarette into the gutter and dragged her suitcase over to the car.

"Shit! Now look what's happened," snapped Travis, as a bus filled with tourists pulled to a stop directly in front. "That son of a bitch has blocked us in!"

But Cheryl's attention was not on the bus, it was on Carl and Wayne, sitting in a car on the opposite side of the road outside a burger bar.

She shook Travis's shoulder. "Oh my God, they're here."

Carl wiped his mouth and belched his satisfaction into the air. He looked out across the road and elbowed his buddy in the ribs. Wayne's burger missed his mouth and it fell into his lap. "Hey, what the hell are you doin'? I was eatin' that!"

"Look over there, dick for brains. That asshole is trying to run out on us!"

Cheryl threw the last of her belongings into the trunk and Travis slammed it shut. She looked across the road and saw Carl and Wayne glaring back at her from behind a stream of traffic. "Oh God I think they've seen us."

Travis ran over to the bus in search of the driver but he was nowhere to be seen. Grabbing Cheryl by the arm, he gently ushered her in the direction of the revolving door of the hotel.

"Just keep calm, act natural, and whatever you do, don't look back."

"But what about the car?" she bleated.

"Never mind that now. I gotta get that banjo from Billy before those two find out what I'm up to."

Carl watched them disappear inside. "Hey! Come back here you double-crossing son of a bitch!"

Once in the hotel, Travis and Cheryl made a run for it. "Quick, out of the fire exit," he said, manhandling his wife down a service corridor.

"Get off me," she protested, shrugging him away. "I ain't taking another step until I know what you're plannin' on doing!"

"I'm gonna do the only thing I can; collect the banjo from Billy, bring it back here and hand it over to Carl and Wayne at two o'clock as agreed."

"Are you crazy! We can't come back here, they'll kill us!"

Travis grabbed Cheryl by the shoulders. "Not if I've got the banjo they won't. Trust me honey, I know what I'm doin'."

Carl and Wayne danced through the busy traffic to the sound of horns and expletives and ran to the revolving door of the hotel. Carl pushed past an elderly lady struggling with her suitcase. "Sorry lady, but we're in kind of a hurry?" He flung himself against the door but it jammed in mid-revolve, crumpling the brim of his Stetson as his forehead buffeted against the glass. On the other side of the door the old lady was most apologetic. "I'm so sorry," she said, pulling on the protruding handle of her suitcase, "but it appears to have got stuck."

Wayne doffed his Stetson. "Allow me mam." He drew back his foot and launched the bag into the air with a ferocious penalty kick.

"Thank you," she said in a cut-glass voice before scurrying off to retrieve it from the other side of the street.

* * *

Standing in a car park on Longmoor Lane, Barry's déja vu moment brought tears to his eyes. Just like the other two Beatle haunts he and his friends had hoped to search, the Aintree Institute was gone; flattened in the name of progress to make way for a brand new shopping complex aptly named, 'Aintree One'.

The Beatles had played at the Institute over thirty times between 1961 and 1962 but over the decades the ornate building had been allowed to fall into a state of disrepair and neglect. With the prospect of hundreds of new jobs being created and much needed parking spaces, musical heritage was not high on the agenda when the local authority granted the planning application.

Barry rushed into one of the shops and confronted the first person he saw wearing a name badge. "Excuse me, but what happened to the Institute?"

The young female trainee swung her feet idly from the swivel chair behind the till and looked up from her copy of

'Hello' magazine. She stretched a ribbon of pink chewing gum across her tongue before blowing it into a tight bubble. It popped with a high-pitched crack. "Ask Eddie over there," she said, turning her orange face back to the magazine. "I think he used to work there or something."

On hearing his name being mentioned, an old man sweeping the floor stopped what he was doing and leant on his brush. Barry thanked the girl and wandered over to him. "Hi Eddie, the girl behind the counter said you used to work at the Institute. Is that right?"

The old man glared at him with suspicion. "Who wants to know?"

"Sorry, I'm Barry," he said, shaking Eddie by the hand. "I work as a Beatles tour guide in the city."

The old man relaxed. "Eddie James," he replied, "I was a bartender there for over forty years."

"Then maybe you can help me? When they demolished the place, do you know what happened to all the fixtures and fittings?"

"They took it all down to the tip as far as I can remember."

Barry's heart sank like a lead weight. "The tip?"

"Yeah, except for the brass and the roof lead; that went to the scrap yard."

The tour guide's eyes dimmed and he walked to the door. "Cheers mate; thanks."

"Hey!" Eddie called after him. "You haven't told me why you want to know."

Barry smiled back at him. "Oh, I just thought they might have saved a few things for posterity, you know, seeing as The Beatles used to play there."

"What? Like old speakers systems and amplifiers do you mean?"

Barry's head spun around. "Yes."

"And musical instruments; that sort of thing?"

He ran back inside the shop. "Yes."

"They found a load of stuff under the old stage when they were ripping it out. Christ, some of it must have been down there since before the war judging by the look of it."

Barry was ecstatic. "Do you know where it is now?"

"As far as I know it was put into storage. Said they couldn't throw it out in case it still belonged to someone; frightened of getting sued or something."

Barry's ears pricked up. *Storage?* He pulled a twenty pound note from his pocket and squashed it into Eddie's hand.

"I don't suppose you could tell me *where* it was stored could you?"

* * *

The carnival atmosphere of the town was in full swing as Travis and Cheryl fought their way through the claustrophobic crowd on Whitechapel towards the relative calm of Stanley Street. Cheryl spotted a bench seat and flopped down. "Travis stop," she gasped, "I need to rest up for a while."

Travis sat down beside her and checked his watch. "You got two minutes."

Sitting at the far end of the seat was a bronze figurine of a woman. Cheryl pointed at the plaque above the statue's head and began to laugh.

'Eleanor Rigby. Dedicated to All The Lonely People…'

"Alright, knock it off," said Travis, failing to see the funny side of this further encounter with the lonely old woman. He stood up and surveyed the swarm of people moving through the town. His stomach lurched. Floating on a sea of heads were two Stetson hats; and they were getting closer.

"Holy shit," he said, pulling Cheryl up from the seat. "Come on, over there. We need to lose ourselves in the crowd." They ran across the road to The Cavern Quarter situated at the far end of Mathew Street where they were quickly enveloped and buffeted down the narrow street.

Barry arrived back at The Beatles Store and brought Joe and Steve up to scratch with the latest developments. "So what do you reckon then lads?" said Barry, in the most persuasive voice he could muster. "It's got to be worth a look?"

Steve scratched his head. "Huskisson Dock's a massive place you know. It'll be like looking for a needle in a bloody haystack."

"No it won't," Barry argued, pulling a piece of paper from his pocket and slapping it down on the counter. "I've already found out everything we need to know; bay number, container number; it's all written down here."

"And just when were you thinking of taking us on this little excursion of yours eh?" Joe asked, suspiciously.

"Tonight, after you've locked up?" said Barry.

Steve crossed his arms. "And how are we supposed to get in?"

Barry smiled back at him. "Come on Steve; you and Joe worked on the docks for long enough. You must know that place like the back of your hand."

Outside in the mayhem, Travis and Cheryl were not making much headway. For every step they took forward, the crowd coming at them in the opposite direction sent them spinning off into a whirlpool of heaving bodies. Travis panicked when he took another look over his shoulder. The Stetsons were moving in on them. "Have those bastards got radar or somethin'?" Travis shouted in Cheryl's ear. "Why the hell can't we shake 'em off?"

Cheryl looked up at Travis's hat and snatched it from his head.

"It's your god damn hat you asshole! If we can see theirs, they can see yours!"

Wayne craned his thick neck and shaded his eyes from the glare of the afternoon sun. "Hey! Where did that asshole go?" he shouted.

"Just keep movin'" urged Carl, ignoring the insults from fellow pedestrians as he bulldozed past.

With the gap closing fast, Travis pulled his wife into a shop doorway and ducked down. Keeping his eyes fixed on the approaching Stetsons; he reached behind his back and grappled with the door handle. With a final hard twist, the door succumbed and he dragged Cheryl inside. She turned around and her heart missed a beat.

"Barry?"

"Cheryl?"

Joe and Steve were nonplussed. Travis ran over to them and got down to business. "Have you guys got a back door?"

"Yes thanks," said Joe, folding his arms defiantly.

Steve leant on the counter and looked the couple up and down with a critical glare. "You've got a bloody nerve coming in here after what you did."

"Looks like we're not the only ones they've pissed off," said Joe, looking out of the window. "There are a couple of mean looking cowboys heading this way."

"Friends of yours are they?" Steve asked, through a sarcastic smile. Cheryl glanced over her shoulder and saw Carl and Wayne hovering outside the store. "Please Barry, I know what I did was wrong and I'm truly sorry, honest I am, but if you don't let us through those guys out there are gonna kill us!"

"And why should Barry help you after what you did to him?" Joe demanded.

Travis marched over to Joe and looked him in the eye. "'Cause your friend here don't strike me as the kind of guy who could live with accessory to murder on his conscience!"

"Please help us," Cheryl pleaded. "I promise I'll explain everything to you later?"

Joe looked at Barry. "It's your call mate, but if I were you I'd tell 'em to go take a hike."

Barry glanced out of the window, then back at Cheryl. "Come with me," he said, running to the counter and lifting up the hatch. Travis and Cheryl followed him down a dilapidated corridor strewn with empty cardboard boxes; through a disgusting kitchen until they reached the back door. Barry pushed it open and ushered them out into a cobbled alleyway. "Follow this alley right the way along and it will bring you out on the main road."

"They're at the door!" yelled Steve.

Travis turned to Barry. "Listen; take care of my wife for me will you. I wouldn't want her to be around if those two catch up with me."

"Wife!" gasped Barry, casting Cheryl a stare of sheer disbelief.

Cheryl ignored Barry's outburst and grabbed her husband's arm. "No Travis! Where you go, I go."

Travis kissed Cheryl on the forehead and looked deep into her eyes. "Honey, I can make much better time if I do this alone. Now quit worrying, I know Barry here will look after you. As soon as I've met up with Billy I'll be right back to pick you up." Without giving her a backward glance, Travis slipped out of the door and ran off down the alley.

Barry scanned around for a place to hide. The crumbling outside toilet seemed as good a place as any. "Stay in there 'til the coast's clear," he said, ushering Cheryl inside.

Carl and Wayne rushed into the store and without a word of explanation began searching behind the racks and bookshelves scattering merchandise to the floor as they went.

Joe ran around the counter. "Hey, what the hell do you think you're doin'?"

"Those folks that were in here?" snarled Carl, "where'd they go?"

"Hey mate!" Steve shouted, joining his brother, "we get hundreds of people in here; you know, this being a shop like."

"No sign of 'em back there Carl," said Wayne, wafting his hat to fan cool air into his ruddy face.

Carl looked over Joe's shoulder. "The back door; where

is it?"

Steve squared up to him. "And why would we tell you?"

Carl reached for the hatch but Joe grabbed his hand and pushed it away. "That's private."

Before the situation had a chance to escalate, the bell above the door rang out heralding the arrival of Beatles tribute band, The Fab Four.

Dressed in their colourful Sergeant Pepper uniforms, John, Paul, George and Ringo had dropped in on their friends for a welcome break. "Get the beers out of the fridge," John Lennon shouted, patting Steve on the back. "We've got about ten minutes before we have to go back on."

Steve kept his eyes fixed on Carl. "Not now mate; it's not a good time."

"Ah, come on Ste'," he moaned. "It's ten deep in every pub in town."

Carl poked John in the chest. "Butt out Beatle boy. Can't you see we're talkin' here?"

The Fab Four formed a line of solidarity behind their friends. George turned to Ringo. "He's not very nice is he Ringo?" he said, mimicking Harrison's Liverpudlian drawl.

"Not very nice at all," replied Ringo; with a characteristic dulcet tone.

"I don't think they're very nice either," squeaked a high-pitched Paul, his eyes dancing around in their sockets.

"So why don't you just piss off back to America eh?" rasped John, through his drooping moustache.

"Yeah," added Paul, with a limp-wristed wag of a finger, "Get Back… to where you once belonged!"

Carl pushed up his hat. "See Wayne," he said shaking his

head, "it's that kinda loud-mouth disrespectful attitude that made my Aunt May burn all her Beatles records back in the sixties."

Wayne cracked his knuckles and marched over to Joe. "I'm tired of this shit. Now are you gonna let us through or am I gonna have to…"

With perfect timing, Joe and Steve threw identical right hooks which landed squarely on the unsuspecting chins of the Texan duo. They hardly flinched.

Joe and Steve nursed their bruised hands and stared at each other in disbelief.

"That could have gone better," groaned Steve.

Wayne rolled up his sleeves. "Are you done?" he sneered, winding back his fist, "'cause now it's our turn."

John nodded to his fellow band members and held up a two-fingered salute. "Peace!" he yelled, before launching his Cuban heeled boot into Wayne's groin. The rest of The Fab Four jumped in behind him, wrestling Carl and Wayne to the ground in a multi-coloured, psychedelic mayhem.

Outside in the street, Aguri and Sachiya pressed their faces against the window in search of a souvenir to take back home to Japan; something to remind them of their pilgrimage to the city of peace and love. John Lennon was the first person they saw when they entered the store; flying past them in a lime green blur having just received an uppercut from a cowboy in a ten-gallon hat.

"Did you see that?" cried Aguri, "that big guy just hit John Lennon!"

He and Sachiya let out a bloodcurdling war cry, jumped into a fighting stance, and launched themselves into the affray.

Aguri's foot connected with Carl's jaw and he followed it up with a blurred flurry of chops and kicks sending the Texan sprawling into a rack of CDs. Joe and Steve seized their opportunity and wrestled Carl to the ground. "Back of the net!" Steve shouted, when Aguri delivered another flying kick to the cowboy's skull.

Wayne released his grip on Ringo's throat and rushed over to assist his buddy. He grabbed Aguri by the hair and threw him across the room like a rag doll. Barry entered the fracas just as Wayne was moving in for the kill. Fearing for the young Aguri's life, Barry grabbed his weapon of choice and sneaked up behind Wayne as he wound back his fist. Raising the heaviest book in the shop high above his head, the gentle tour guide smashed The Beatles Anthology down on the cowboy's head with all the strength he could muster. *Goodnight.*

CHAPTER EIGHTEEN

Situated on Hardman Street near St Luke's Church, the Sound Bite Café offered internet access and an eclectic menu of cheap food and booze for its predominantly student clientele. It was the preferred meeting place for Billy Sheridan, giving the weasely bachelor a chance to study the pretty female students while he concluded his shady deals.

Taking a slurp from his cappuccino, Billy slid down in his chair and tried to sneak another look up the skirt of a young woman seated opposite as she crossed and uncrossed her legs.

"More my type I think mate," said Lee, a tall muscular guy in a black leather jacket and designer sunglasses. He sat down beside Billy and reached under the chrome topped table to hand him a package. Billy rested it on his lap and checked the contents.

Lee let out an exasperated sigh. "No need to check it," he said quietly, "everything's in there."

"I'll check it all the same if it's alright with you," said Billy, not bothering to look up. "You don't know the nutters I'm dealing with."

"Satisfied are we?" asked Lee, when Billy finally put the package on the table and reached into his pocket. He handed

Lee an envelope bulging with banknotes which he immediately ripped open and began to count.

"No need to check it," Billy sneered, "everything's in there."

Billy looked up and the smirk drained from his face. He kicked Lee in the shin. "Police."

"Where?"

"Outside the window."

Lee slid the money into his jacket and turned to take a look.

"No, don't look 'round you bloody idiot," scolded Billy, "you'll only raise his suspicions."

Billy watched the policeman chatting to a passer-by and saw him pointing down the street. "It's alright; I think he's just giving someone directions."

Lee stood up. "Sod this for a game of soldiers, I'm out of here." He looked at the package lying on the table and whispered in Billy's ear. "I'd hide that somewhere if I were you mate," he said, glancing over his shoulder at the policeman. "You're looking at ten years if you're caught with that shit. See ya."

* * *

Travis ran to the top of Bold Street and took a right into Hardman Street. With the Sound Bite Café now in sight, he darted out into the busy road with eyes fixed solely on the door. The sudden blaring of a car horn caused him to leap onto the pavement. Lee screeched his flashy car to a halt and angrily wound down the window. Although his expletives were drowned out by the techno beat thumping from the stereo system, Travis was able to lip read most of them and he thrust up a middle finger in defiance. "And you asshole!" he shouted, as Lee sped off down the street in a haze of burning rubber.

Inside the Sound Bite Café, Billy heard the door open and peeped out from behind a newspaper.

"Psst, Travis. Over here."

Travis rushed over and shook his hand firmly. "Christ Billy boy, am I glad to see you." He sat down at the table. "Did you get it?"

"Does a bear shit in the woods?" Billy replied, smarmily.

"Great. Hand it over."

"Money first," Billy demanded, thrusting out a hand. Discreetly, Travis passed him a roll of banknotes tightly bound together with an elastic band. "Here. Three thousand sterling as agreed."

Billy dropped the wad into his pocket and stood up. Travis grabbed him by the arm. "Where are you goin'?"

"To count it."

Travis raised his voice. "Hell Billy, I ain't got time for…"

"Two minutes Travis," Billy interrupted, forcefully. He patted him on the head. "Now be a good cowboy and just wait there."

Reluctantly, Travis settled back and checked his watch before stretching his aching legs under the table. He felt something firm buffeting against his foot and ducked down to investigate. Lying at his feet was a black banjo case. Taking a quick look around, he slipped on a pair of leather driving gloves and slid the case up onto his knees. He flicked opened the lid and peeked inside. *Perfect.*

After counting his money in the privacy of a toilet

cubicle, Billy stuffed it into the inside pocket of his denim jacket and washed his clammy hands. He wiped them dry on the back of his jeans and smiled to himself as he swung open the toilet door to conclude his business with Travis. But the corners of his mouth soon dropped when he strolled back into the café to find Travis gone.

Clutching the banjo case to his chest, Travis dashed back down Bold Street and into the maze of Victorian alleyways which would lead him back to The Beatles Store and Cheryl. In the sweltering heat of the August bank holiday afternoon, he spat the taste of the backstreets into the gutter as the overpowering stench of urine and unemptied garbage cans clung to the back of his throat. As he was about to turn another corner, Travis saw the elongated shadow of a Stetson looming from the adjacent alley and he ducked for cover behind a row of bright purple wheelie bins.

"We're just burnin' daylight here," breathed Carl. "That son of a bitch could be anywhere by now."

Wayne scratched his head. "Say Carl; Travis was packin' his car outside the hotel before he ran off weren't he?"

"Yeah, so what?"

"Then ain't that where he'll be headin'?"

"Hell Wayne," said Carl, patting his buddy firmly on the back, "that thump on the head must have upped your IQ. Come on!"

Travis waited until they had disappeared back around the corner before emerging from his hiding place. But when he got to his feet, the banjo slipped from his grasp sending a muffled twang echoing down the alley as it hit the ground.

As he knelt down to pick it up, Wayne pounced, snatching the banjo from Travis's grip. Carl moved in behind him and threw Travis up against a wall, pushing the breath painfully from his lungs.

"What did I tell you Wayne?" said Carl, tightening his grip around Travis's throat. "If you wanna catch a rat all you got to do is look in the trash."

"Look, I know what you guys must be thinking," Travis squealed, "but I was just on my way to the hotel to hand that thing over to you. I swear to God I was."

Wayne buried his fist into Travis's stomach.

"That's bullshit! We saw you packin' your car ready to skip town, didn't we Carl?"

"I wasn't trying to skip town," Travis coughed, staggering to his feet.

Carl helped him up and then proceeded to land a left hook on Travis's unshaven jaw.

"You're a damn liar!" Wayne shouted, as Travis hit the ground again. "DeVito was right not to trust a snake like you. Hell, I'm glad he set you up!"

Carl shot Wayne a killer glare. "Shut up Wayne."

Holding his jaw in one hand and nursing his guts with the other, Travis squatted against the wall and stared up at them. "Set me up? What the hell are you talking about?"

Wayne leaned over and grabbed the lapels of Travis's jacket. He pulled his face in close. "You were just gettin' too big for your boots boy and you needed bringin' down."

"I said shut up Wayne!" Carl shouted, nudging him with the toe of his boot.

Wayne jumped up and squared up to his partner. "Hell, what's it matter now anyway Carl!" he said, thrusting the banjo into his face. "We got what we came for."

"Would one of you two gentlemen please tell me what's goin' on?" Travis groaned.

"Ah, what the hell," Carl relented, "I suppose you're gonna find out soon enough anyway." He crouched down and looked Travis in the eye. "That paintin' you bought at the auction back in Coopersville?"

"What about it?"

"It was a plant. DeVito put it there."

"Uh huh, that's impossible," said Travis, sniffing a trickle of blood back up his nose. "I found out about that from a *very* reliable source."

"Oh, you mean that informant of yours?" scoffed Carl. "Hell Travis, DeVito's had that guy feedin' you bullshit for months."

Travis struggled to his feet and pointed a brave finger at him. "You're wrong. Three of those tip-offs he gave me came good remember?"

"Only 'cause the boss wanted it that way," said Wayne smugly. "See, those deals were just ground bait to get you all primed up, ready to reel you in for the big one at the auction."

Travis shook his head and smiled. "Good try fellas. But this little story of yours has got one major flaw. See, you seem to have overlooked the fact that there was another dealer bidding for that painting too, not to mention DeVito himself!"

"DeVito knows how you tick Travis," Carl gloated. "He knew that if he goaded you enough you'd just keep on goin' rather than let him get the better of you. And as for the guy in the black hat…?"

Travis began to look worried.

"He's just a friend of DeVito's. The boss brought him in to make everythin' look more authentic."

"And to help drive up the price," cackled Wayne.

"I still don't buy it," Travis argued. "If DeVito wanted to ruin me; why in God's name would he give me a job?"

"So's he could keep an eye on you and stop you rebuilding your business of course. Come on Travis, you know how much DeVito hates any kind of competition. Remember what he did to old Jack Wilson?"

"Keep your friends close and your enemies even closer," Wayne chipped in. "That's what the boss always says ain't it Carl?"

"Why the conniving son of a bitch," Travis muttered under his breath.

"Yep," laughed Carl. "And it gets worse, for you anyway. See, DeVito told us that, once we'd collected this here banjo, we were to tell you that you don't work for him no more."

Wayne patted the banjo case. "That's right; and guess what? He's promised to give us *your* twenty percent cut as soon as we deliver this to him and it's been sold."

Travis began to laugh. "What? You don't honestly believe DeVito will cut you in for a slice of the money do you? Hell, you guys must be dumber than I thought."

Wayne shot Carl a nervous glance.

"Don't listen to him Wayne. DeVito wouldn't cheat us."

Travis hobbled over to them. "Wouldn't he? I wouldn't bank on that. Look what he did to me; look what he did to old Jack! Forgive me for pointing this out fellas but…" Travis hesitated.

"But what?" Carl prompted him with a firm shove.

"Well, not to put too fine a point on it, but how long do you reckon it's gonna be before DeVito finds someone younger and fitter to replace you guys huh? A couple of years maybe? And what are you gonna do when your services are no longer required; flip burgers? Pump gas? Come on fellas, you're livin' in a dream world if you believe that asshole's gonna give a shit what happens to you? Money, money, money; that's all people like him care about."

"What's he gettin' at Carl?"

Travis pointed at the banjo. "Do you know how much that thing your holding is worth? Now, a smart guy would say to himself: Hey, I'm sick of my boss treatin' me like shit; I've done enough of his dirty work. I think it's high time I looked after number one for a change!"

"Are you sayin' what I think you're sayin'?" asked Carl.

A look of confusion crossed Wayne's close set eyes. *"What is he sayin' Carl?"*

"That maybe we should keep that thing for ourselves?" Carl answered.

"Hell, that's not such a bad idea?" said Wayne; still clutching the banjo to his chest like a newborn baby. "We don't owe DeVito anythin'. Remember when Stacy got his leg all busted up trying to repossess that car for him? DeVito refused to pay a dime towards his medical expenses; had to sell his home to cover all the hospital bills; ended up in a god damn wheelchair; no job, no money, no nuthin'!"

Travis threw up his hands. "There you go, what did I tell you?"

Wayne glanced over at Travis. "I reckon he's right Carl; we should keep this for ourselves and enjoy some of the good life for a change."

Feigning panic, Travis began waving his arms in the air. "Whoa, now just hold your horses for a minute there fellas. See, I wouldn't want you to do anythin' foolhardy. I mean, just 'cause a *smart guy* would catch the next flight to Dubai and sell that banjo to one of those oil rich A - rabs with more money than sense don't mean *you* should?"

"Why not?" Wayne growled, angrily. "We're smart too. We can do whatever we damn well like now we got this; ain't that right Carl?"

"That's right," Carl nodded, shoving Travis out of the way. "Come on Wayne, we got a plane to catch. So long loser, we'll send you a postcard when we get to Dubai."

Travis did not feel Wayne's farewell kick in the shin; his brain was far too busy working out his next move.

Bending down to pick up the contents of his jacket pockets strewn across the ground, he froze when he heard the sound of footsteps running along the alley towards him. Travis coughed a sigh of relief when it was Billy Sheridan he saw sprinting around the corner. "Where the hell did you run off to?" said Billy, gasping for air.

"Billy? What the hell are you doing here?"

"Never mind that. Where's the banjo."

"The banjo?"

Billy's face contorted in anger and he grabbed Travis by the shirt. "Just give me the bloody thing will you!" he said, shaking him violently.

Travis gripped Billy by the wrists and pushed the wiry figure away. "Just what in God's name has gotten you?" Travis demanded. "You got your three grand."

"In the café, before you arrived," he panted, "I hid a stash of drugs and a handgun inside the banjo case."

"A gun? My God Billy, that's real serious shit."

"Yeah, tell me about it. And if I don't deliver that stuff this afternoon, I'm a dead man."

Travis seized his opportunity. "Gee, I'd like to help you out my friend," he said, trying his best to look traumatised, "but just before you turned up, a bunch of guys kicked the shit outta me and ran off with it." Travis patted his bleeding nose with a handkerchief to add credibility to his argument.

Billy was inconsolable. "Oh Christ. Which way did they go?"

"That way," said Travis, deliberately pointing him in the wrong direction. "They ran down there." As Billy sprinted off to meet with destiny, Travis took off his hat and held it respectfully to his chest. "Good luck Billy boy," he muttered under his breath. "It's been real nice knowin' you."

Despite his bruised jaw and aching groin, Travis walked back to The Beatles Store with a spring in his step; even stopping momentarily to watch a Beatles tribute band performing on one of the outdoor stages. *Strange,* he thought, *John Lennon looks like he's got a black eye?*

Further inspection revealed Travis's eyes were not playing tricks. Indeed, the rest of the band were also carrying a selection of cuts and bruises, as were the two Japanese fans singing along on the front row.

* * *

By the time Travis was back inside The Beatles Store most of the wreckage had been cleared up. Cheryl, who had felt obliged to lend a helping hand, threw down her mop and ran to him with outstretched arms.

"Travis, thank God. Are you alright?" she asked, examining the bruises on his face. "What happened?"

Travis took Cheryl's hand and walked her to the door. "I'll tell you on the way back to the hotel."

"Wait a minute," she said, retrieving her hand from his grasp. "Ain't you even gonna say thanks to these guys for helping us out?"

Travis turned to Barry, Joe and Steve who were gathering up the books and CDs that had been displaced during the punch up. "Thanks guys," he said, walking towards the door.

Steve looked up. "*Thanks guys?* Is that all you've got to say to us after what we did for you. Take a look around knobhead; those two cowboy mates of yours have wrecked our store!"

Joe threw down the books he was holding and marched up to the Texan. "Yeah, not to mention the money we've lost? We've had to close the place on our busiest day of the year because of you!"

"Alright, alright," said Travis, reaching inside his jacket pocket. He pulled out a cheque book. "Someone give me a god damn pen."

"Over there by the till," said Steve.

While they continued tidying up the mess, Travis wandered over to the counter and cleared a space to write out his cheque.

"Here," he said, wafting the ink dry before handing it to

Joe. "That ought to cover the damage and any money you've lost. Come on honey; let's get the hell out of here."

Cheryl folded her arms and cast her husband a disapproving glare. "Ain't you forgetting somethin' else?"

Travis looked at her and shrugged his shoulders.

"Barry's letter?"

Travis quickly pulled her to one side. "Are you out of your tiny mind?" he spat through grating teeth.

Cheryl stamped down hard on his foot. "Give it back to him god damn it! Can't you see it's already got us into enough trouble as it is?"

"It's alright love," said Steve, trying to mask a smile. "He can keep it."

Travis could not believe his ears. "What?"

"The letter mate; you can keep it," said Joe, biting his lip. "Oh, that reminds me; have you seen anything of Eleanor Rigby recently?"

"Yeah; and how's Old King Cole getting on?" jibed Steve.

Joe and Steve could not help themselves and they burst out laughing.

Travis raised his eyes to the air. "I get it. It's a fake ain't it?"

The laughter stopped. "'Course it's a bloody fake," Steve replied, sternly. "Just like you two."

Travis pushed his wife towards the door. She turned to Barry. "Guess we had it coming huh?"

"I guess you did," Barry replied, sheepishly.

"Bye fellas," Travis shouted, ushering Cheryl up the steps. "Have a nice day!"

Travis walked Cheryl back to the hotel and filled her in

with the details of his encounter with Carl and Wayne. She thought he would be livid having been duped by the fake letter but, to her amazement, he did not even mention it. As far as Travis was concerned, lady luck was finally beginning to return to their lives. "It's perfect Cheryl. Now that Carl and Wayne have taken off with the banjo, DeVito won't get to know it's only a replica, *which means*, I don't have to worry about returning his money!"

Cheryl stopped walking and looked up at her husband's bruised face with fear in her eyes. "Travis, once those guys find out that banjo is worthless, which they will as soon as they try to sell it, they're gonna catch the next flight home and tear you to pieces."

Travis winked at her mischievously. "Then I guess I'd better make sure that don't happen then huh?"

"How?"

Travis strolled on. "All in good time honey, all in good time."

Cheryl was first into the hotel room and froze in her tracks when she saw a Stetson lying on the bed. "Travis," she said, pointing at the hat. "Please tell me that thing belongs to you." Before Travis had chance to reply, Tony DeVito strode out of the hotel bathroom. "Coffee over here makes you piss like a steer don't it?" he said, buttoning up his trousers.

For the first time in his life, Travis was lost for words.

DeVito flopped down on the sofa and made himself comfortable. "I take it from the look on your faces the boys didn't tell you I was in town then huh? I guess they wanted to surprise you."

Travis tried to remain calm and poured himself a drink.

"If you're here to collect the banjo," he said casually, "Carl and Wayne already have it."

"Great, that's what I wanted to hear. You were right Travis. I found a buyer prepared to pay six million for that little thing."

Cheryl ran over to DeVito and jabbed an accusing finger in his face. "And what about us? Those apes of yours told Travis how you screwed us over you son of a bitch!"

DeVito waved his stubby hands in defence. "Now just hold on a minute lady; Travis forfeited his twenty percent commission when he failed to return any of my calls and I had to send my boys over here to do his job!"

Travis felt his blood boil, his green eyes flashing with rage. "She's not talking about my commission you dumb son of a bitch! She's talking about the painting in Coopersville; you know, the one I paid hundreds of thousands of dollars for which turned out to be a god damn fake! The one *you* planted there in order to put me out of business!"

DeVito seemed shocked by Travis's revelation and was hesitant in his reply. "Oh that," he muttered.

"Yeah, that!" said Travis, spitting venom. "Your *boys* told me everything."

DeVito's bravado returned and he stood up. "C'mon Travis, you're a businessman; you know how these things work. I mean, I didn't hold your hand up in that auction did I? If you were dumb enough to fall for the oldest trick in the book then that's your problem!"

Cheryl had a question of her own. "You took one hell of a chance just to get one over on my husband didn't you? What if Travis had dropped out of the bidding? You'd have been stuck with that fake."

DeVito smiled. "Oh I had that covered sweetheart. You see, if that had happened, all the money I'd have paid for it would have gone to Old Ma Dillon's grandson."

Travis looked confused. "The guy who lives in Europe? That don't explain nothin'."

DeVito smiled sweetly. "Oh but it does Travis. See, Old Ma Dillon's grandson don't live in Europe…*he lives in Dallas."*

The penny dropped.

"It's you isn't it?" Cheryl gasped. "*You're the grandson*!"

"That's right," winked DeVito, smugly. "Old Ma Dillon was my dear old granny. And thanks to your husband here, I ended up with the biggest pay cheque of my life! Sweetest deal I ever pulled."

Cheryl let fly. "Enjoy it while you can fat man 'cause as soon as we explain to the Law Society how you planted that painting and rigged the auction they'll shut you down and throw you behind bars!"

DeVito eyeballed her. "Lady, you breathe a word to anyone and I'll have my boys shut *you* down… permanently!"

"Oh I don't think that's gonna happen Tony," said Travis, taking a sip from his glass. "See, there's somethin' I forgot to mention." He sidled up to DeVito and whispered in his ear. "Your boys have run out on you big fella; they're on the way to the airport as we speak. And they've taken your old-age pension with them."

"Bullshit," DeVito huffed, punching Carl's number into his phone. He paced the floor and waited for a reply.

"A thousand bucks says they don't pick up," Travis

goaded.

No answer.

DeVito moved to the window. "Just a bad signal that's all."

"Maybe?" said Travis, with a sly glint in his eye. "It *is* difficult getting a decent signal in an airport; ain't that right honey?"

"Sure is," Cheryl sneered, "especially if you're already on the plane."

DeVito cracked. Grabbing his hat and coat he bolted for the door. "Get the hell out of my way," he shouted, shoving Travis to one side.

Cheryl waited until the fat man was out of sight. "Are you sure it was a good idea to tell him they'd gone to the airport?" she asked, anxiously.

"Yep," said Travis grabbing her by the hand. "See, I know somethin' he don't. Come on, I gotta get to a public phone."

* * *

Huddled inside a telephone kiosk in Lime Street station, Travis looked up at the clock over the main concourse. Forty minutes had now passed since DeVito stormed out of the hotel and, if his calculations were correct, he would be arriving at Liverpool John Lennon Airport just about now. Travis put on his leather gloves and pulled his Stetson down over his eyes. Dialling a number, he covered the mouthpiece with a handkerchief and waited for a reply. "Hello," he said, in his best English accent. "Could you please put me through to someone in airport security?"

On the other side of the concourse, Cheryl studied her husband as he made his call. His brow was furrowed and his face flushed as he clawed the last of the loose change from his pockets and pumped it into the hungry payphone. With an urgent wave of the hand he beckoned for Cheryl to bring him more coins. Cheryl ran to the phone booth and swung open the door. Travis was in mid-flow; "How the hell should I know if they're terrorists?" he ranted; his fake English accent slipping back into Texan drawl. Cheryl handed him another coin and he fed it into the slot. "Listen buddy, I've told you everythin' I know. You're the security experts, you figure it out!" He slammed down the receiver and pushed Cheryl out of the booth. "Come on honey; let's get the hell out of here before the police trace that call."

* * *

DeVito barged through the doors of the airport terminal building like an angry bull and peeled his deep set eyes. Somewhere amongst the crowd were two double-crossing sons of bitches making off with his banjo worth millions of dollars.

Over at a ticket desk, Carl and Wayne thanked the pretty lady behind the counter and checked the board for the flight times. "Looks like we got over an hour to kill Carl; what say we get ourselves a drink."

"Sounds good to me," said Carl, patting Wayne on the back. "Lead the way."

They turned around to find their path blocked by their old boss.

"And just where the hell do you think you're goin' with my property?" snapped DeVito, lunging for the banjo. Carl pulled it high out of his reach and pushed him away. "We don't take orders from you no more DeVito," he grunted.

"That's right," said Wayne, with a smug grin. "See, we've resigned."

"Like hell you have," he replied venomously. "Give me that god damn banjo!" Wayne grabbed his ex-boss by the waist and hurled him into a nearby restaurant area sending cups and saucers flying as he slammed into a neat row of tables. Under the gaze of John Lennon's bronze statue, DeVito charged straight back at them and fought to relieve the instrument from Carl's clutches. The fracas came to an abrupt halt when a female airport official stepped in. "Excuse me gentlemen, but is there a problem here?"

DeVito punched out his crumpled hat. "You're damned right there's a problem lady. These two apes are tryin' to steal my property."

"It's ours!" shouted Wayne. "Ain't that right Carl?"

Carl nodded. "That's right mam," he said holding up the banjo. "This thing belongs to us."

DeVito was fuming with rage. "That's bullshit! I paid hundreds of thousands of dollars for that banjo and they stole it from me!"

The airport official looked concerned as a small crowd began to gather. "Look, let me find somewhere where you gentlemen can discuss this matter in private."

"Lead the way lady," said DeVito, brushing down his suit.

She whispered discreetly into her walkie-talkie as the

three men followed her down a corridor into a stark office containing only a selection of uncomfortable plastic chairs and a single desk. DeVito, Carl and Wayne looked shocked when their eyes fell upon the burly customs officer sitting behind it. He gestured for the Texans to sit down. "Thanks Jenny," he said to the airport official, "I can take it from here." He pointed at the banjo. "Do you mind?"

Reluctantly, Carl pushed the case over to him and sat back in his chair. The officer spun it around to face him and opened the lid. He smiled when his eyes fell upon the beautiful antique banjo nestling in the crimson crushed velvet. "So, who's the George Formby fan?" he asked, jokingly.

Wayne looked bemused and turned to Carl. "Ain't that the boxer guy with the griddle?"

"That's George Foreman you meathead," Carl replied, swiping Wayne with his hat. He turned to the officer. "Say mister, can you move things along here? We're in kind of a hurry."

"Yeah," said Wayne. "See we got to be at Heathrow by six to catch our connecting flight to Dubai."

"I see," said the officer, leaning forward in his chair eyeing them up suspiciously. "And why would you gentlemen be wanting to travel to the Middle East?"

DeVito was losing his patience. "Look, can't we just cut to the chase here fella. They stole that banjo from me and I want it back."

Suddenly the door opened and a colleague whispered something into the customs officer's ear. The officer removed the banjo from its case and placed it on the table. "Gentlemen," he said, authoritatively, "I want you to think very carefully before answering my next question. Who is the owner of this instrument?"

DeVito, Carl and Wayne sprang from their seats and shouted in unison, "I am!"

The officer stood up. "Then I have no choice but to place you all under arrest."

No sooner had he finished his sentence, the door burst open and a squad of armed guards rushed in brandishing firearms.

"You three!" shouted the commanding officer waving a semi-automatic in their faces. "Get down on the ground and put your hands above your heads where I can see them. Do it now!"

"What the hell is goin' on here?" squealed a terrified DeVito.

A second guard shoved the barrel of a gun between DeVito's shoulder blades. "Shut up and do what he says!"

The Texans dropped to the floor as instructed and lay face down. Once they had been thoroughly frisked, handcuffs were snapped around their wrists and they were hauled back onto their feet. The customs officer spun the open banjo case around to face them. Hidden in the compartment used to carry spare strings and accessories was a Beretta Tomcat 32 Auto handgun and several dozen wraps of white powder.

"Now wait just a god damn minute," DeVito protested. "You don't think…"

"You have the right to remain silent…" interrupted the officer, as he read them their rights.

Moments later a young male medical officer entered the room and slipped on a pair of surgical gloves. Unscrewing the top from a tube of lubricating jelly, he smeared it liberally over his fingers before turning to face the three Texans. "Who's first?"

DeVito, Carl and Wayne glared at one another and swallowed hard.

CHAPTER NINETEEN

The flat backed lorry hissed to a stop inside the gates of Huskisson Dock and three pairs of eyes peered out from under a billowing sheet of tarpaulin. Barry, Joe and Steve waited until the driver had disappeared into the security hut before clambering out and darting silently over to the vast warehouse.

Pressing his body in close to the damp red bricks, Joe slid a sports bag down from his shoulder and pulled out a length of rope. He looked up at Barry. "You wait here and keep an eye out for us," he whispered, slinging it over his shoulder.

Barry was gutted. "Aren't I coming with you?"

"After what happened at Gambia Terrace?" said Steve, "you must be bloody joking."

While Joe tested the strength of a wrought iron drainpipe running up the gable end of the building, Steve's mind flashed back to his time as a striking dock worker; huddled around a burning dustbin as he and his comrades picketed outside the main gate. It seemed ironic that the place he associated with so much heartache could, in fact, hold the key to his future happiness.

The brothers made short work of their ascent up the drainpipe and once safely on the roof took a moment to catch their breath. Below them, the River Mersey shimmered under a blanket of flickering stars as it ebbed along the coast before eventually succumbing to the dark foreboding waters of the Irish Sea.

Sightseeing over, Steve held open a skylight while Joe dropped down the rope. With torches gripped between their teeth they abseiled into the cavernous black hole and onto a gantry.

Outside, the bark of a dog shattered the silence and Barry sucked himself into the shadows. Chancing a look across to the security hut his worst fears were confirmed.

"What is it Otto?" said Vince, the security guard, following the eye line of his slavering companion. The dog's ears pricked up like cathedral spires and it turned its fibrillating black slug nose to the air. The lead jerked hard and Vince was dragged across the cobbled dockyard towards the warehouse. Barry quickly pulled his head back around the corner and with eyes wide like a bush baby, searched for a place to hide. To his left, his eyes were met by a brick wall; to his right, a teetering stack of wooden pallets. The only way was up.

Wiping the sweat from his hands on the back of his trousers, the spooked tour guide gripped the flaking paint of the drainpipe and its corroded bolts grated in the masonry as his feet left the ground. Moments later, Otto and Vince rounded the corner. Barry willed his weak, trembling arms to bear his weight as a torch beam swept the area below. Gnawing on the carcass of a dead seagull, a rodent the size of a small domestic cat reared up, its blood red eyes reflecting like LEDs in the dazzling white light. The dog went wild.

"Calm down Otto, it's only a rat," said Vince, patting him on the flank to reassure him. Defiantly, the rat snatched another ragged morsel before scurrying under a sheet of twisted corrugated metal.

Breathing again, Barry waited until Otto and Vince were out of sight before pulling himself up the final two metres. But as his white knuckled hands reached out for the gutter, the sound of twisting iron rang in his ears and with a sickening creak the drainpipe lurched away from the wall carrying Barry with it. Like King Kong swatting aeroplanes from the side of the Empire State building, his flailing arms desperately searched for something to grab hold of.

* * *

Joe and Steve looked down from the gantry at hundreds of metal containers spread out like matchboxes below them. "This isn't going to be easy," sighed Joe. "Give me Barry's notes."

Steve felt a sickening lurch in the pit of his stomach. "But I thought you had them?"

"Bloody hell Steve, are you telling me you've left them in the shop?"

"Since when was I put in charge of the notes?" Steve fired back angrily.

"Well can you remember anything he wrote down?" Joe asked in desperation.

"Er, I think bay number five rings a bell."

"You think? I'm warning you Stephen," Joe blasted, "if

this turns out to be another balls up I'll wring your bleedin' neck. Now come on."

Back outside, Barry was fighting for his life. With the drainpipe now pitched at a thirty degree angle, the sudden jolt of cramp running up his thigh was all he needed. Convinced he was about to die, he whispered a few Hail Marys and prepared to meet his maker. With eyes clenched tightly shut, he felt an unearthly feeling of weightlessness and a tightening around his chest. It was something he had not experienced before and it crossed his mind that, perhaps, he had already hit the ground and was dead.

"Well, don't just hang there like a sack of corn!"

Barry unscrewed his eyes and saw the silhouette of two figures standing on the roof.

"Grab the rope!" one of them shouted. The lasso around his waist pulled tighter and Barry gripped it as they hauled him in like a beef steer.

In bay number five, Joe and Steve had found the container belonging to the Aintree Institute and like desperate pirates, were too busy plundering its contents to notice they had company.

"Well you're in the right place; I guess it's just a case of going through all this stuff."

The warehouse rang out to the clang of a dropped crow bar. "You!" shouted Steve.

A look of smug satisfaction radiated from Travis's tanned face as he waved a crumpled piece of paper at the brothers. Steve snatched it from his hand. "You thieving bastard." He turned to Joe. "These are Barry's notes; he must have taken them when he was in the store writing that cheque!"

"Shouldn't leave things lying around," said Travis with a sardonic smile.

Joe pushed him hard against the container and drew back his fist. "I've had just about enough of you for one day!"

"Hey, you just cut that out," shouted Cheryl. She pointed at Barry. "Your friend over there would have fallen to his death if it hadn't been for my husband!"

"I knew it," said Steve. He jabbed an accusing finger in Barry's face. "What the hell were you doing on the roof?"

Joe released his grip on Travis's throat and craned his head in Barry's direction. "You were supposed to be keeping a look out for us you dickhead."

"Guys, guys, calm down," Travis urged, straightening his bolo tie. "Jeez, this is getting us nowhere. Alright, so Mr Tour Guide here might not be the sharpest tool in the box but whose bright idea was it to leave him out there in the first place with that crazy hound running wild?"

Silence.

"Thank you," said Barry, enjoying the guilty expressions on the brother's faces.

Travis patted him soundly on the back. "No problem big fella. Now the way I see it you owe me one so I'd be more than happy to hear any proposals you might have to help resolve this situation."

"We're not cutting you in if that's what you're getting at," Steve growled.

"Listen buddy, I'm trying to be reasonable here. Just because Beatle boy lucked out and found some letter don't mean you have a God-given right to stake a claim on that banjo. From where I'm standing, I got just as much right to a slice of the action as you have."

Barry was quick to react. "We're not doing this just for the money you know."

Travis snorted mockingly. "Bullshit. Like hell you ain't!"

"You don't get it do you? This is much more important than money. Without Julia's banjo... *there wouldn't have been a Beatles.*"

"Speaking as a Lynyrd Skynyrd fan myself," said Travis, with a lopsided grin, "I really couldn't give a shit."

Barry resisted the temptation to slap the smirk off the Texan's face. "Is that right? Then get this; without *The Beatles,* your life, my life; everything we know today would be different. Fashion, music, art, politics, you name it; The Beatles influenced all of it." Barry paused for breath. "I want to find the banjo for one reason; because it changed the world."

Travis clapped his hands. "Great. So I guess you won't have a problem handing over your share of the profit then will you?"

Barry looked up from the hole he had just dug himself into and said nothing.

"There, see," said Travis, pointing an accusing finger at the tour guide. "It is about the money; always has been, always will be. Cheryl's said some real nice things about you; telling me what a fair-minded, decent human being you are an' all, but now I'm beginning to have my doubts."

Cheryl squirmed. "Travis, don't."

"What's wrong honey? I'm just letting everybody know how honest and respectful you said he was." Travis rested a hand on Barry's shoulder. "Even had a tear in my eye when she told me what happened to your daddy; passing away like that when you were just a kid. See, we're not that different you and I."

Barry gave Travis a dubious look. "Eh?"

"I grew up without a daddy too; ran out on me and my momma the day after I was born."

"I'm not bloody surprised," Steve mocked.

"You think that's funny?" said Travis, earnestly. "Well how's this for a punch line; after that son of a bitch abandoned us, my momma ended up taking her own life and I was left all alone in the world to fend for myself. Laugh that up!"

"No reason to grow up into a smarmy conniving git though was it?" said Joe, dryly.

"You can put it that way if you like. I prefer to call it self-preservation." He turned his attention back to Barry. "The thing is my friend, when it all boils down to it; you're just like every other asshole out there; ready to shit on whoever gets in your way to make a fast buck."

"That's not true." Barry insisted.

"Aint it? I could have been in and out of here with a banjo under my arm if I hadn't wasted my time on that roof saving your hide. And what thanks do I get for my trouble huh? Why I reckon if your dear old ma could see you now she'd be turning in her grave like a spit roast."

Barry threw his arms up in surrender. "Alright, alright, you can have half of my share."

Travis's hand shot out like a striking rattler. "Deal!"

Steve rushed over and spun Barry around by the shoulder. "Are you bloody mad? You're not really gonna fall for all that crap are you?"

"I owe him," said Barry, shrugging him off.

"Tell him Joe!" Steve ranted.

"It's Barry's call mate. If he wants to reward this guy for somethin' any decent person would have done for free, that's up to him."

Outside, security guard Vince was enjoying an otherwise trouble free tour of duty. Strolling along the cobbles he stopped occasionally to allow Otto to snuffle a scent and mark his territory. The dock gates had been checked and rechecked on his meticulously planned circuit and he approached the security hut on the corner of the gargantuan brick warehouse tired and ready to hand over to his colleague. It was just coming up to midnight when a car screeched through the dock gates with drums and bass thumping from its speakers. Vince recoiled as the glare of the headlights hit him between the eyes and a spray of gravel peppered his shins. The driver's door swung open and a silhouette stepped out.

"So, what do you think then?" said Lee, stroking the bonnet of his car with pride.

Vince walked around the throbbing mass of shiny metal and scratched his thinning hair. "Yeah, it's nice?"

"No Vince. Fluffy bunny rabbits are *nice*. What you're looking at is a fifty grand pimped up, tricked out beast!"

"Fifty grand eh?" he said, casting a suspicious look at his colleague. "Surprised you could afford it on the wages they're paying us?" Vince stroked the paintwork appreciatively.

Lee grabbed his arm. "Touch it again and I'll rip your bloody hands off."

Otto cocked a hind leg and watered a white walled tyre. Luckily for Vince, this act of desecration had been screened by the open driver door.

"That cargo of aluminium ingots; has it been delivered yet?" Lee asked.

"Came this afternoon."

"Good. Now piss off while I make a phone call."

Lee waved his colleague away with a dismissive hand. Billy Sheridan's answer phone message was less than brief. '*I'm out; leave a message.*'

"It's on," said Lee, "bring the van 'round to the dock gate at one o'clock."

Now operating like a well-oiled machine, Barry and his unlikely companions worked their way through the effects salvaged from the Aintree Institute; tables, chairs, bingo machines, a selection of drums, cymbals and two 30 Watt VOX amplifiers were passed down the line and onto the floor of the warehouse.

Travis raised his hand in a halting manner. "The light; over here quick."

The beam from Joe's torch danced around the container before settling on a heap of gaudy tangerine curtains. Cheryl whisked them away like a magician's assistant and uncovered a stack of slim, black leatherette covered boxes.

"They're guitars!" said Barry excitedly. "We must be getting close."

With renewed enthusiasm the guitar cases were hastily unstacked to reveal another case, different from the others, much smaller and shaped to follow the contours of the instrument within.

"My God," gasped Travis, stooping to pick it up. "Hell, we got to get this thing open!"

Joe's hand clamped down on his wrist. "Don't you think you should let Barry do that?" he said, regarding him coldly.

With reverence, Barry carried the banjo case out of the confines of the dark container and into the half-light of the warehouse. Like a high priest under the spell of an ancient relic, he rested it on a tea chest altar and stood back in awe. The others formed a tight circle around him and waited expectantly. Barry gently traced his fingers around its stitched perimeter and brought them to rest on the tarnished silver lock. The moment he had waited for all his life had finally arrived and he turned his radiant face to the others. "Here goes then." He applied pressure to the lock and it sprang open with a hollow clunk.

Like a gathering of relatives eager to get a glimpse of a newborn baby for the first time, everyone leaned forward as Barry slowly lifted the lid. Inside lay a banjo; its rosewood veneer in need of a good polish and the skin torn in places, but finely crafted nevertheless. Barry's voice cracked with emotion. "Bloody hell, I think this is it."

"Listen, I don't want to piss on anyone's bonfire," said Joe in a low, ominous tone, "but how can you be sure that's the one?"

"Check the back," Travis hissed, "it should have a mother of pearl inlay."

Clearly impressed, Joe raised his eyebrows and shot him a side glance. "You've been doing your homework haven't you?"

Barry lifted the banjo from the case and flipped it over. The mother of pearl still shone like new as the torch light shimmered off its iridescent surface. Travis whooped and threw his hat in the air, grabbed Cheryl by the waist and spun her around before planting a kiss on her lips.

It took a few moments for this life-changing event to hit the Benson brothers. First came denial; no way could Barry, a guy who spent most of his time talking complete and utter bollocks, have guided them into pulling off such an impossible feat. Then came realisation; not only had they participated in the quest to find the holy grail of pop memorabilia, they had *actually succeeded* because there it was; real, tangible, just as Barry said it would be. The slow burning fuse of emotion finally hit the powder keg and exploded into euphoria.

"*We're in the money, we're in the money!*" Steve and Joe sang at the top of their voices, jumping up and down like cheerleaders on acid.

"Christ, just think about it Joe," said Steve, clearly overwhelmed. "No more getting up at the crack of dawn every morning; no more feeling down the back of the couch for beer money!"

"No more scrimping to buy new stock!" Joe volleyed back.

"New stock? In a few months time we'll have our own bar in Tenerife, soaking up the sun, surrounded by beautiful women!"

While Travis went to find his hat, Cheryl watched Barry cradling the banjo in his arms. "What was the name of the song John Lennon learned to play on that little thing?" she asked softly.

Barry dragged his eyes away from the instrument and smiled back at her. "That'll Be The Day by Buddy Holly. It was one of the first songs John and Paul played together too."

"Well, I guess this is *your day* now Barry," she said, warmly. "I'm really pleased for you."

Travis returned brushing the dirt from his Stetson. "Sorry to break up the party folks but don't you think we should get everything tidied up and back in that container before the security guard comes snoopin' around?"

While Steve and Joe hopped back inside and began putting things back in order, Barry placed the banjo back in its case and laid his coat around it for added protection. "Hey Barry, give me a hand with this will you," said Travis, struggling with a fully laden tea chest. Barry went to assist and together they dragged it over to Joe and Steve who stacked it against the wall.

"Here let me help you with that honey," Travis shouted to his wife, as he watched her attempt to lift up a heavy amplifier. He stepped out and slid it towards Barry's feet. "Pass this to the guys will you!"

Barry acknowledged him with a nod, trundled the amp to the back of the container and in doing so, played straight into the Texan's hands.

"Nice knowing you fellas!" he said, swinging the doors shut and sliding the bolt.

"What the hell do you think you're doing?" shrieked Cheryl.

Travis picked up the banjo and dangled it in her face. "Looking after number one? You don't seriously believe those assholes in there were gonna share the money with us do you? Now c'mon, let's get the hell out of here!"

He grabbed his reluctant wife by the arm and together they ran for the service ladder leading to the skylight.

Entombed in the metal sarcophagus, the three men used

the amplifier as a battering ram and eventually the bolt jigged itself loose. Like caged lions released into the Coliseum, Joe and Steve sprang out of the container and bounded after the thieves.

Barry climbed out and saw his coat cast down next to the empty banjo case and sank to his knees.

"This is your day now Barry..."

Once again he had allowed himself to be taken for a fool, lulled into a false sense of security by Cheryl and her Southern Belle charms. But his feelings of betrayal and disappointment were soon replaced by burning fury and he leapt to his feet.

Climbing steadfastly upwards, Barry followed Joe and Steve up the service ladder hell-bent on regaining his pride, dignity and...the banjo. Three floors up, the Bensons heard Travis and Cheryl's desperate feet pounding along the gantry directly above their heads.

"You take the other ladder. We can cut them off at the top," breathed Joe, heavily.

Labouring upwards, Joe caught sight of a snakeskin boot and grabbed Travis by the ankle. A bone-crunching stamp to the fingers swiftly followed by a kick in the head was his reward. Temporarily dazed, Joe slid back down the ladder and landed in a heap on the gantry below.

Cheryl stopped climbing and clung onto the rungs like a lizard. "Jesus Travis," she said, with genuine concern. "Will he be alright?"

"Don't just hang there gawking," Travis scolded, "keep moving!" He pushed his wife up the last couple of rungs and they scrambled onto the top gantry. The skylight was now in sight but to their horror, so was Steve Benson. He rushed at them from the far end of the walkway. "Here take this," said Travis, handing the banjo to Cheryl. "Get to the roof while I try and hold him off."

"Who the hell do you think I am? Lara freakin' Croft!"

Travis pushed her away. "Try god damn it! Try!"

But as Cheryl turned and ran, Barry and Joe emerged from the shadows cutting off her escape. She skidded to a halt. Joe wiped a trickle of blood from his nose. "Game's up love. Hand it over."

Steve barged past Travis to complete the pincer movement and slowly the three men moved menacingly towards her. Cheryl clutched the banjo close to her chest and her eyes welled up. "Travis?" she whimpered, as the hopelessness of the situation sank in.

"It's alright Cheryl, no one's going to hurt you," said Barry, holding up a reassuring palm. "All we want is the banjo."

Travis looked on helplessly as they took another deliberate step closer to his terrified wife. His mind flashed through the options. There was only one.

"Throw it to me!"

With all her remaining energy, Cheryl lifted the banjo above her head and let it fly.

Barry's paralysed brain saw everything in slow motion; the banjo's mother of pearl shimmering as it tumbled through the air; Travis's desperate leap to catch it; watching it brush past his fingers before slipping over the guard rail...

The accentuated sound of splintering rosewood and torturous dissonant twangs exploded in his ears as the holy grail of pop memorabilia bounced down the stairwell and smashed into the ground.

"No!" Barry screamed, running down the ladder with terrified, wide open eyes.

Ignoring Travis and Cheryl's escape, the Bensons rushed past the twitching rope leading to the skylight and ran after their inconsolable friend.

* * *

Travis took a peek over the edge of the roof. A security guard was strutting like a peacock around a customised car while another looked on with feigned admiration. Travis did a double-take when he recognised the car as the one that almost mowed him down outside the Sound Bite Café. The driver's guttural insults were still etched in his memory.

"How in God's name are we supposed to get off this roof with those two hangin' about down there?" Cheryl whispered.

"Quit squawkin'. All we need is a little decoy."

Travis looked down at Lee through narrowed eyes. *Payback time.*

Otto's ears swivelled like satellite dishes as his predatory eyes honed in on the warehouse roof. Suddenly, his heckles bristled like a yard brush and he let out a cascade of ferocious barks. "Shut that bleedin' dog up!" snarled Lee, pumping up the volume of the car's stereo, "I'm trying to listen to this!"

"Look out!" cried Vince, beating a hasty retreat. The heavy Victorian drainpipe, wrenched loose by Barry, groaned like a sinking ship as it crashed down onto the bonnet of Lee's beloved car. Travis retracted his boot and looked down with satisfaction at the chaos below.

Chew on that you asshole.

While Vince helped his shell-shocked workmate back to the security hut for a hot, sweet brew neither they, nor Otto, noticed Travis and Cheryl slipping out through the dock gates.

But Lee wasn't the only one in tears that night. Inside the warehouse, Barry was on his knees picking through the shattered remains of the banjo.

"Well that's the end of that then isn't it?" said Steve, kicking the splinters across the dusty concrete floor.

Through watery eyes, Barry looked down at the relic and stroked it lovingly like a dying pet. His fingers caressed the cold metal of the retailers name plate screwed to the back of the headstock. He blinked hard and pulled the object closer to his eyes. "Oh my God," he gasped.

"Calm down mate," said Joe, squeezing his friend's shoulder sympathetically. "It's not the end of the world."

Barry looked up at him and smiled. "I know it's not; because this isn't it!"

He stood and faced the brothers. "Look at this name plate; it says Frank Hessy."

Joe and Steve stared back at him blankly.

"Oh, come on lads," said Barry with irritation. "Frank Hessy's was the most famous music shop in Liverpool."

Steve sighed. "Your point being . . . ?"

"John's grandfather was a merchant seaman. He brought the banjo *we're looking for* back from one of his trips and left it to his daughter, *Julia*, when he died."

"He's bloody lost me," said Joe, scratching his head.

The tour guide's patience was beginning to wane. "Oh for God's sake lads, do I have to spell it out for you? If the banjo originated from overseas, *which I know for a fact it did*, there's no way it could have a Frank Hessy name plate screwed to it is there?"

Barry was joyous. "Julia's banjo is still out there!"

* * *

The Beetham Tower marked the end of the dock road and stood like a sentry on the northern approach into the city. In its shadow, Travis revved the engine of the hire car and waited for the traffic lights to change. He turned to Cheryl. "I don't suppose my apologising would do much good at this moment in time?"

She brought her fist down hard into his crotch; her face as cold and hard as granite. Travis let out a visceral groan. "No, I thought not."

Joe had parked his car just beyond the Stanley Dock Bascule lifting bridge and the long walk down Regent Road was thankfully coming to an end. Barry had not stopped wittering since they left the warehouse and it was now beginning to fray Joe's nerves.

"I'll have another look on the computer when I get back and try and find us some more places to look," Barry said enthusiastically.

Joe hit the key fob and the car's amber lights flashed in response. He flung open the rear passenger door and ushered Barry inside. "Sorry mate, I've had enough of all this shit. You're on your own."

Barry leapt back out of the car. "But you can't give up now? We're getting so close. I know we are."

"Close?" Joe snorted, dismissively. "The only thing I'm getting close to is a nervous breakdown. This idea of yours has been nothing more than a right royal, fur-lined, ocean-going balls up from start to finish. Now get back in the car. It's over, and that's final!"

Barry turned his attention to Steve. "But what about Tenerife; the bar?"

"Sorry Barry," Steve replied, looking into the anguished eyes of his brother. "It was a nice dream… but that's all it was. Now do you want a lift home or what?"

Barry slammed the car door and stormed off down the road. "Shove your lift!"

"Come on Barry, don't be like that!" Steve shouted after him.

"Let him go," said Joe. "He'll get over it."

Barry shuffled aimlessly through the streets of Liverpool and mingled with the last of the revellers as they staggered back to their hotels. The monotonal hum from portable generators was punctuated by the high-pitched whirr of power tools as men in fluorescent yellow overalls began the arduous task of dismantling the numerous outdoor stages. Leaning in a doorway at the bottom of Castle Street, Barry looked on as one of the workmen ripped down a Beatles poster, screwed it up into a ball and kicked it into the gutter. Lennon's crumpled image rolled like tumbleweed past the tour guide's feet before being caught up in the spinning brushes of a garbage van. A dagger pierced his heart. The dream was over.

CHAPTER TWENTY

Early the next morning, Barry awoke from a torturous night's sleep on a Pier Head bench and stretched the life back into his tingling arms. He coughed the damp air from his lungs and swung his numb feet to the floor. The Liver Bird's massive clock faces told him it was seven o'clock and as he gazed across the river to the rolling mound of the Wirral peninsula he pondered the events of the last few days. It seemed hard to believe that only forty-eight hours earlier he had walked past this very spot with a beautiful woman on his arm and a head full of dreams.

Flipping his cap onto his messy head, Barry cowered when a cascade of loose change rained down his face, chinking as it sifted through the wooden slats and onto the cobbles. He smiled. The thought of a charitable passer-by tossing coins into his hat on the assumption he was a tramp was heart-warming and it helped raise his dampened spirits. Barry soon found himself following the high stone walls of the docks northward past the great white Nordic ships, grain silos and the mangled heaps of scrap iron towards an old familiar sanctuary.

Brenda opened the door of the Atlantic pub in her

nightdress and peeped out before collecting the milk from the doorstep. Glancing down the street she noticed a solitary man leaning against a dock gate post, his shoulders hunched. "Barry?" she shouted. "Is that you?"

Barry snapped out of his daydream and turned his weary face to her. "Oh, hi Bren," he cracked in a hoarse voice.

"And where are you off to so early in the morning?" she quizzed, folding her arms like a scolding mother.

Doe-eyed, he looked up at his old friend from beneath the rim of his cap. "Just walking," he replied sheepishly.

She looked at his crumpled clothes and unshaven face. "You look bloody awful. Come in, I'll make you a cup of tea."

Barry basked in the delicious warmth of the bar and sipped his hot sweet tea while Brenda regarded him with a worried expression. "I don't know," she said softly, "staying out all night. You could have caught your death of cold."

Barry shrugged. "I'm alright," he said, crunching on a piece of toast.

But his words did little to allay her concern. "I've been worried about you, you know. Why haven't you been in?"

He looked at Brenda with an intensity that caught her off guard. "Didn't want to get in the way of you and Sid did I?" he said, with an edge to his voice.

Brenda laughed and reached for his hand across the table. "What; me and greasy Sid? You must be bloody joking!"

"But I saw you two together," Barry insisted, "when I came in the other night."

Brenda looked down, her face flushed with embarrassment. "Oh that was all Sid's idea. He said that if I made you jealous it might...well you know."

Barry's heart skipped a beat. "What?"

"Bloody hell Barry, do I have to spell it out for you. It's you I like, not Sid. I always have done; right from the minute I first saw you bounce through my door."

"Then why didn't you say somethin'?"

Brenda smiled at him sweetly. "I thought it might spoil our friendship. You know what some men are like; the slightest hint of a woman wanting more than just friendship and they run a bloody mile."

Barry took Brenda's hand and looked into her eyes. "And is that what you really want; for us to be more than just friends?"

"Well that depends. Look, I hope you don't mind me asking but..."

"She's gone," blurted Barry.

Brenda needed no further explanation. "Then the answer is yes."

Barry being Barry, completely misread her cue for him to lean over the table and plant a kiss on her lips and instead just grinned back at her like the Cheshire Cat. "Brilliant!"

Barry's cheerful smile was more than enough. "So I take it you'll be 'round for your dinner tonight then? Hey, I've just remembered," Brenda said, jumping out of her chair and walking behind the bar. "I was going to show you those old photographs I found in the cellar wasn't I?"

She returned and emptied the contents of a battered shoe box onto the table. Barry rubbed his hands and began to flick through the photos.

"These are great Bren. All of the family are they?"

"Most of them," she replied.

Suddenly, Barry did a double-take and held the picture he was holding up to the light.

"Bloody hell, have you seen this one?"

Brenda took it. "Let's have a look." The white-edged glossy card displayed a black and white image of a well-built middle-aged man holding a baby. Flanking him on either side were two leather-clad youths, one of them wearing black thick-framed spectacles.

"Guess who the baby is?" she challenged Barry playfully.

"It's not you is it?"

"Yeah, cute wasn't I? That's my dad holding me. It was taken at my christening party."

Barry took the photo back and pointed at the two youths. "You do know who those two lads are standing next to your dad don't you?"

"Customers," Brenda mused, "friends of the family maybe? I'm not sure really."

Barry hardly dared to believe his eyes and checked it again. Finally, he announced his verdict. "It's John Lennon and Stuart Sutcliffe!"

Brenda narrowed her eyes and looked closer. She was not convinced. "You what?"

Barry was insistent. "It is, look!"

Brenda looked again before bowing to the expert's judgment. "I wouldn't know Stuart... whatever his name is, if I fell over him but the other lad, the one with the glasses, I suppose he does look a bit like John Lennon."

Barry struggled with her scepticism and stood to make his point. "It doesn't just look like him, it is him! What year was this taken?"

"Well it'll be the year I was born won't it? 1960."

"Do you know where it was taken?" he pressed.

"Of course I do. It was in here."

Barry looked around the room and failed to see a comparison with the photograph. "Nah, it couldn't have been," he said, shaking his head dismissively.

"I do know my own bloody pub Barry," Brenda replied haughtily. "That picture was taken in the old function room upstairs."

"Function room?"

"Yeah, 'course it hasn't been used for years. Just before dad died the council told him it needed an external fire escape; something to do with new health and safety regulations. Poor dad; he was too ill to get the work done and died not long afterwards."

"I'm sorry," said Barry comfortingly.

"So am I. This place just isn't the same without him."

"And what's up there now?"

"I just use it as storage space. After dad died I stopped going in there; too many memories I suppose."

Barry's eyes darted back to the picture. "Bren," he said hesitantly, "would you mind if I had a quick look in there?"

Brenda smiled. "Now how did I know you were going to say that? Wait there, I'll get the key."

The lock on the function room door was stiff from lack of use and required some persuasion from Brenda's strong grip. Eventually it clunked open and the panelled door creaked ajar. "There you go," she said, "you have a look around while I get the bar ready for opening time."

"Thanks Bren," said Barry, as she disappeared back down the stairs.

Brenda shouted up a final instruction. "Oh and Barry,

make sure you lock the door before you come back down!"

Pushing the door fully open, Barry's bulky silhouette filled the frame. Tentatively, he moved into the musty gloom and felt his way along the flock covered wall, following a slim shaft of light which shone through the curtains until he reached the window. Pulling the heavy drapes apart, a thick cloud of powdery dust engulfed him. Barry rubbed his watery eyes and waited for it to settle before taking in the scene.

An upright piano stood on a small stage at the back of the room flanked by rows of pale ecru topped tables and metal framed chairs. In the far corner next to the bar, an ancient Wurlitzer jukebox lay dormant under a blanket of grey dust waiting for a shilling to spark it back into life. Next to it hung a dartboard; three darts embedded in its red and black face. Still legible, etched in chalk on the blackboard was the score. Apparently, 'Fred' needed a double twenty to win.

Barry strolled through the time capsule holding the photograph at arm's length until he eventually found the spot where it had been taken. His imagination now firing on all cylinders, he transported himself back to 1960 and the night of Brenda's christening party.

* * *

Up on the tiny stage, a skiffle band thrashed out a rough rendition of Lonnie Donegan's 'Rock Island Line', while, next to the jukebox, the darts match played on. Fred plugged three darts into the board but was dragged onto the dance floor by his tipsy wife leaving the game unfinished.

Seated at a table near the stage were two quiffed youths. Alternating between puffs on their Senior Service cigarettes and sips from their scotch and cokes, John and Stuart nodded at the band appreciatively, tapping their winklepicker boots in time to the music.

Barry pushed himself through the jiving crowd towards them, his heart pounding. In the midst of it all he saw Brenda's dad proudly cradling his baby daughter as he swayed to the rhythm. A few steps more saw Barry within touching distance of his idol. Reaching out to tap him on the shoulder, he pulled back when he heard Brenda's dad's voice booming across the dance floor. "John! Stuart! Come over here and have a photo taken with me and our little Brenda!"

Barry stood there and watched as John Lennon and Stuart Sutcliffe left the table and took up their positions next to Brenda's dad. Just before the flash of the camera bleached out his face, John turned slowly and looked Barry straight in the eyes. Lennon opened his mouth to speak.

"Barry! You'll have to hurry up," Brenda shouted up from the bottom of the stairs, "you're going to be late for work!"

Barry blinked and the precious moment was lost. He looked into the face of John staring back at him from the photograph and wondered. *What was it he was going to say to me?* Taking a final look around, Barry slipped the photograph into his pocket, closed the door behind him and turned the key in the lock.

Brenda let him keep the picture which he promised to treasure and keep safe.

It was almost ten o'clock by the time he had left the pub and, with his friendship with Brenda now firmly back on track, the day seemed to be turning out to be better than expected.

* * *

In the lobby of the hotel, Travis browsed the newspaper stand while Cheryl settled the astronomical mini-bar bill. They were checking out for good this time and planned to head straight for the airport and home. Picking up a copy of the Liverpool Echo, Travis's eyes were drawn to the lead story on page one.

"Honey," said Travis, tugging on Cheryl's sleeve, "you know you've been worrying all night about bumping into DeVito and his boys back home?"

"Thanks for reminding me," she replied. "What of it?"

"Well cast your pretty eyes over this."

Cheryl snatched the newspaper and scanned the headline:

'Texan Trio Arrested At Liverpool John Lennon Airport'.

"Oh my God, does this mean . . .?"

"You're damn right it does," said Travis gleefully. "A drugs bust would have been bad enough, but taking a loaded gun into an airport with all those terrorist guys runnin' around? Hell, Her Majesty's gonna throw away the key! DeVito and his two shit heads are history honey."

"Oh I don't know Trav," said Cheryl, fidgeting with her wedding ring. "It all sounds too easy. Those three ain't just gonna let you ride off into the sunset. They're gonna be squealing your name from the rooftops."

Travis folded up the newspaper and tucked it under his arm. "So what? I got nothing to worry about. The cops ain't got a shred of evidence to connect me to that banjo. Hell, they had me locked up in jail when it was stolen!"

"Fingerprints?" she said, wafting his coffee breath from her face.

"Gloves?" Travis replied, waving his hands in the air like Al Jolson. "Quit worrying sweetheart, we're home and dry. And get this; even after paying off Danny Bakula, we still got nearly two hundred grand sitting in the bank! See, didn't I tell you I knew what I was doin'?"

Travis and Cheryl left the hotel arm in arm. "Say honey, how do you fancy taking a small detour before heading back to Texas?"

"If it's got anything to do with a banjo you can forget it!"

Travis smiled down at his wife from under the shade of his Stetson. "It ain't," he said, pulling her in close. "I was thinking of Paris or Rome."

CHAPTER TWENTY-ONE

The Magical Mystery Tour bus rumbled to a stop outside the gates of Strawberry Fields and the tourists disembarked to pay homage. Sid took a drag on his cigarette and flicked the stump into the gutter as Barry sidled over to him. He hesitated before breaking the silence. "Look Sid, about the other night..."

"Oh, so you're talking to me again are you?" he said curtly.

"I saw Brenda this morning."

"Oh ey?" Sid waited with folded arms for him to continue.

His colleague came straight to the point. "She told me you were only trying to help."

Sid gave him a gentle nudge. "I thought you were gonna rip my bloody head off."

Barry giggled with embarrassment. "Yeah, sorry about that; I should have realised Brenda could never fall for a bloke like you."

Sid's dirty look went unnoticed as the tour guide fumbled in his jacket pocket and took out the photograph. He pushed it in front of Sid's face. "She gave me this. Look who's on it."

Sid's eyes widened and he snatched the picture from Barry's hands to study it in more detail. "Bloody hell mate, this is fantastic!"

"I know," he said, pleased at his reaction. "John Lennon and Stuart Sutcliffe. Who'd have believed it eh?"

"Sod them," he scoffed, "I'm talking about Colin McMahon."

Confusion crossed Barry's face. "Who?"

"Colin McMahon," Sid repeated, irritated by his ignorance. "Oh come on Barry, he was one of the best wrestlers this city ever produced. Built like a brick shithouse he was too. I used to go and watch him at the Liverpool Stadium back in the fifties."

Barry pointed at the man in the photo. "But that's Brenda's dad?"

"Never," Sid gasped.

"It is. That's Brenda there." He pointed at the baby.

Sid laughed. "Christ, who'd have guessed it eh? Colin 'The Bridge' McMahon is Brenda's dad."

Barry's ears twitched and he pushed his face into Sid's.

"What did you just call him?"

"Colin 'The Bridge' McMahon. That was his professional name. But we all knew him as 'The Bridge'. All the wrestlers had daft names like that; Mal 'King Kong' Kirk, Giant Haystacks, Big Daddy..."

Barry dashed for the bus. "What have I said now?" Sid shouted after him.

The tour guide jumped into the driver's cabin and fired up the engine. Gripping the steering wheel with one hand, he released the handbrake and hit the gas.

"Barry! Come back!" Sid shouted, running down the hill after him. "You can't drive!" Sid sank to his knees and watched helplessly as the colourful bus disappeared around the corner.

The unscheduled event had not escaped the notice of the tourists. "Excuse me; is there some kind of problem here?" asked a tanned American man in a baseball cap.

Sid's sweaty face looked up at him with contempt. "You wanted a Magical Mystery Tour didn't you mate? Well now you've bloody got one."

Unable to gain control of the clutch, Barry had to resort to using both hands to pull on the gear stick while his trembling knees continued to steer the bus. There was more to this driving lark than he'd imagined. Once on Speke Boulevard, he managed to maintain a steady speed and prayed that every set of lights would be on green. He glanced up at Sid's rosary beads swinging from the rear-view mirror and snatched them into his hand. If he was to survive this journey, he would need all the help he could get. Twenty minutes later, Barry heaved a huge sigh of relief as the bus lurched to a stop outside the Atlantic pub.

Behind the bar, Brenda jerked her head up from a newspaper as the door burst open. "What are you doing back here love? I thought you were working today."

Barry rushed over to her. "Your dad? Was his name Colin McMahon?"

Brenda was taken aback. "What's this all about?"

"Please Bren, this is really important," he said. "Was that his name?" Barry took her hand, squeezed it tightly and closed his eyes in anticipation of the answer.

"Yes, but how..."

"Sid recognised him in the photo," rushed Barry. "He was a wrestler wasn't he?"

"Until he injured his back he was. He ended up working the door at The Liverpool Stadium."

The Beatle nerd's brain went into overdrive as the pieces began to fall into place. "Of course; that's where your dad will have met John and Stuart! Allan Williams used to put groups on in there."

Brenda was beginning to show her frustration and she pulled her hand out of Barry's. "Are you gonna tell me what this is all about?" she demanded.

Barry ignored her and ran back outside.

He turned to face the mud spattered front door and traced his fingers over the screw holes where a number had once hung. Spitting on his fingers he rubbed the surrounding area and stood back. Although no longer there, the impression it had left on the paintwork was unmistakable. It was the number 9. He darted back inside. "Bren, I know you probably think I'm going mad but I promise I'll explain everything to you later. I need to see that function room again. Can I have the key?"

This time the door was flung open without ceremony and he rushed inside. Armed with all this new information, Barry took Lennon's letter from his pocket and spread it out on a table. The verse he had dismissed as Jabberwocky or perhaps an unfinished Lennon poem jumped from the page as he examined it again with fresh eyes:

'Talk to the bridge where the river meets the ocean. There, lying between Chaplin and Keaton, is Mother'.

Barry rubbed his chin. "Talk to the bridge?" he muttered under his breath. "It's Brenda's dad; it's got to be." He read the next six words. "Where the river meets the ocean?" He rushed over to the window overlooking the river Mersey and he thought hard. *Well I can see the river but where is the . . . Of course; the Atlantic pub. This is the ocean!*

Hanging on the wall behind the old bar he spotted framed posters and photographs of actors and musicians from a bygone age. He shivered uneasily as their eyes peered at him through the gloom. He looked at the next line of the verse:

'There, lying between Chaplin and Keaton, is Mother'.

In the top right-hand corner above a long shelf hung a portrait of the most famous comedian of them all. His heart thumped in his ears as he ran over to take a closer look. *Buster Keaton.* He scanned the wall eagerly searching for the next clue. *Come on Charlie where are you?* In the opposite corner, a cleaner patch of wallpaper marked the spot where a painting once hung and Barry moved to investigate. The sound of snapping glass underfoot drew his eyes to the floor. Lying face down at his feet was a broken picture frame. The palms of his hands tingled as he stooped to turn it over. Staring back at him was the face of Charlie Chaplin.

There, lying between Chaplin and Keaton is... He mouthed the final word. "Mother?" Like the number 9, Barry knew this word was significant in Lennon's life; significant enough for him to use, not just as a title for another song about his mum, but as a pet name for his wife,

Yoko Ono.

Mother? It meant something; something important.

He dragged a table across the room and positioned it underneath the shelf. Gingerly, he climbed on top and with outstretched arms began to feel his way along. Spluttering with disgust when he swept a mummified wasp into his open mouth, Barry jumped down and moved the table a few feet further along before clambering back up for a second attempt. His hands patted along the shelf until his eager fingers brushed against something smooth and curved. Teetering on tiptoes, he grabbed the object and jumped off the table.

In his grimy hands was a banjo, encrusted with dust, a dark film of nicotine and harbouring a musky odour which reeked of decades of neglect. Weak-kneed, he staggered over to a seat and lowered himself onto it hardly daring to cast his eyes upon the instrument. Despite his elation, one nagging doubt still remained. How could he be certain this was the most important piece of pop memorabilia in history? It was time to examine it in more detail.

The tour guide threw off his jacket and used the sleeve to wipe away the years of sticky grime. He noticed three letters; O, T and E had been scrawled into the side of the instrument. Another frantic wipe revealed three more. Suddenly, emerging like the winning line on a scratch card, the letters M, H and R completed the word. "MOTHER," he gasped.

Barry knew he had won the jackpot; but it would take more than a few scrawled letters to convince the sceptics.

He turned the instrument on its front to examine the mother of pearl inlay and as he did so a rattle from within caught his attention. He lifted the banjo to his ear; another gentle shake confirming his suspicions. There was something hidden inside.

Resting the banjo on a table top, Barry's sweaty face peered down at it from beneath his upturned cap. Stretching out his arms, he cracked his knuckles in preparation for the delicate task ahead. Very carefully, he unscrewed the bolts holding the fragile jaundiced skin to the body and slowly peeled it off.

Inside, hidden from the world for over half a century was Lennon's personal stash. A mouth organ; a packet of five Senior Service cigarettes; a condom and a hand-drawn comic called 'The Daily Howl'. Everything a teenage John Lennon would have wanted to hide from the prying eyes of his Aunt Mimi was in there.

No further authentication was necessary. Barry Seddon had found Julia's banjo.

THREE MONTHS LATER

Barry whistled happily as he put the finishing touches to The Beatle Store's Christmas window display. Brushing the glitter from his hands he took in the festive Mathew Street scene and smiled proudly. In the distance, two familiar figures approached and Barry rushed back to take his place behind the counter.

He greeted Joe and Steve with open arms. "Hi lads. Can't keep away from the place eh?" he joked.

Joe looked around with approval. "So, what's it like to be the new owner then Barry?"

"Brilliant! Me and Brenda have got some big plans for

this place."

Steve nodded as he checked out the décor. "Bet she was over the moon when you split the money with her."

"It was only fair. I did find the banjo in her place after all."

Steve clasped his hands together and got to the point. "We're leaving for Tenerife in the mornin' so we thought we'd better drop in to say goodbye."

Joe pushed a bag over the counter. "Here. We've got you a present."

Barry peeked inside. "Beatles Monthly magazines. How did you guess?"

"I found them in the back of a cupboard while I was packing," said Joe.

"Oh, if you find any letters in there," Steve interrupted, "keep it to yourself eh."

Joe stepped up to the counter. "Listen mate, me and Steve; well we really appreciate you giving us a share of the money even though we bailed out on you like that."

Barry smiled. "That's alright. You gave us a good price for the store and besides, we're mates aren't we?"

Brenda emerged carrying two cups of tea. "Hi lads; you're off then are you? I hope you'll be coming back for the wedding." She flashed the ring on her engagement finger and grinned up at Barry.

Steve winked at her. "Wouldn't miss it for the world Bren."

"Have you decided what you're going to do with the pub yet?" asked Joe.

"We're keeping it aren't we," she said, kissing her fiancé on the cheek. "It's part of the magical mystery tour now;

doing great business." She heard a ping from the microwave oven. "Gotta go lads, have a safe journey; see you at the wedding. Your lunch will be ready in a minute Barry so don't stand here chatting all day," she said, before disappearing around the back.

The brothers wanted to know more about the fate of the memorabilia which had allowed them to live their dream and escape to the sun. "What are you going to do with the stuff you found inside the banjo?" Joe asked.

"I've loaned it to The Beatles Story," Barry replied, slurping his tea from the saucer.

Joe raised an eyebrow. "And the banjo?" he quizzed. "Are you going to tell us who bought it or is it still a secret?"

Barry laughed. "I've told you, I can't. It was a strict condition of the sale. But I will tell you this; it couldn't have gone to a better home."

* * *

Outside a farmhouse in the twilight of an early December evening, a slim elderly man sat huddled over the orange glow of a crackling bonfire. Holding a banjo to his chest he quickly found the notes to Buddy Holly's classic song That'll Be The Day and began to hum along. After a couple of renditions he rested the instrument on his knee and ran his fingers along its rusty strings as the memories came flooding back. He turned his sparkling doleful eyes up at the heavens.

"Where are we going Johnny!" he shouted.

Even though a reply was not forthcoming, it did not

matter to him anymore; he already knew the answer.

To the toppermost of the poppermost!

That is what John had promised him all those years ago and that is where he had been ever since. Macca picked up the banjo and played on.

Printed in Great Britain
by Amazon